Better Choices

By
Rod Pennington
&
Jeffery A. Martin

Integration Press
Jackson, Wyoming

Better Choices

Copyright © 2020 by Rod Pennington

ISBN: 979-8-63007-277-1
ASIN: B086675G95

Integration Press
P.O. Box 8906
Jackson, Wyoming 83002

CHAPTER ONE

NEVER TEMPT FATE.

What began as a lovely late-spring morning got off to a rip-roaring start. First was the phone call from my twins' high school. They were requesting yet another personal appearance by one or more of their parents at our earliest convenience in the office of the humorless assistant principal in charge of discipline and decorum. With graduation on the horizon, hopefully this would be my last chat with the odious Ms. Taylor-Smith where we would discuss the latest mayhem my offspring had inflicted on the school facilities or the student body. I had to admit, I wasn't going to miss her cold glares that always said volumes about her opinion of my parenting skills. My takeaways from our four years of "counseling" were twofold. First, we could agree that my kids are a handful. And, second, never put much stock in the recommendations on childrearing from an unmarried woman who had read all the "right" books but never had kids of her own.

While changing for my appointment with the moral guardian of public education, the phone rang again. This time it was the young lady at my husband's office who handled travel arrangements. I had expected her to tell me that he had been delayed in Brussels because, as usual, the EU officials he was meeting with never knew when to shut up. Instead she tearfully informed me that Lindsey, the father of my children and "devoted" spouse for the past twenty-eight years, no longer loved me. Instead, he had found his true soulmate in her. "Her" being a former Pilates instructor who was born two years after I had walked down the aisle on my daddy's arm in a flowing white dress. Having met her once or twice at company functions, I vaguely remembered her, but the only lasting impression she had made on me was her tendency to proudly slip into conversations that she had graduated in the top half of her class at junior college secretarial school.

She was gobsmacked when I informed her that if she got the "I'm going back to my wife" story from Lindsey, it meant that, despite a tight butt, perky breasts and youthful enthusiasm, he had gotten tired of her and was moving on. Surprisingly, she didn't want to be added to the email list of the Lindsey Clark Former Bimbo Support Group.

She hung up before I could tell her if she wanted that hot mess of a man, she was welcome to him. While it wasn't common knowledge, Lindsey and I were already in the process of filing for divorce and planned to sign the papers shortly after the twins graduated from high school and headed off to college. That day was fast approaching, and Lindsey had already approved a more-than-fair division of assets. I suspect his agreeability came in part because my lawyer had presented his lawyer with a lengthy witness list of women he planned to call to the stand if we ever went to trial.

They say the opposite of love is not hate, it is indifference. Lindsey and I had been indifferent toward each other for some time now. We never argued because I knew he was never going to change, and he knew I didn't want the stigma of being a "single mom" or "divorcee" and all of the baggage that carried. In the intervening years, we had pretty much led separate lives. While we still lived in the same house, we had our own bedrooms and we hadn't had sex in years. Hell, I wouldn't even touch his laundry. With him on the road over one hundred days annually, and either on the phone or in meetings the other two hundred sixty-five, it wasn't going to be much of a marital adjustment on my part.

At this point in my life, with a sham marriage and the perpetual state of chaos surrounding my twins, the idea of Lindsey moving out and the kids going off to college, leaving me with an empty nest, was sounding better and better every day.

While so far this wasn't the worst day of my life, it was certainly in my top five bad mornings before a second cup of coffee.

Then I did something profoundly stupid.

I made the mistake of asking out loud, where the universe could hear me, *how could this day possibly get any worse?*

And God was listening.

She had a good laugh, then decided to show me.

While the Keurig was brewing my encore cup of French roast, the phone rang again.

CHAPTER TWO

"HORSE HOCKEY," MY mom, Edna O'Connor, barked as she adjusted the less than flattering gown and shifted uncomfortably in the emergency-room hospital bed. By any measure, Mom was an imposing woman; what she lacked in heft she more than made up for in height and grit. When standing, she was just under six feet tall and had the ramrod posture of a Marine drill sergeant. Incredibly active for a woman her age, she had never developed any of the sags and bulges that had reshaped the topography of so many of her friends. In fact, sixty-two years after saying "I do," she could still fit into her wedding dress.

Coming of age in the pre-sunscreen days and when houses had neither air-conditioning nor a television, a love of being outdoors had been ingrained in her since childhood. These days, with a ten-acre backyard with sprawling flower beds and a greenhouse that would rival anything you might see in the finest English country home, she was seldom indoors. Despite my constant nagging, she refused to wear either a hat or apply sunblock while working in her garden. The relentless lifetime pounding by the sun had given her face deep smile lines and a dark, coarse texture, like well-oiled leather. This made the contrast between her skin and her vivid blue eyes startling and more than a little intimidating. Currently, Edna's hawk-like eyes burned into the young cardiologist.

"All I'm saying," the doctor said as he noticed Mom's glare aimed in his direction and took a half-step back before turning to me for support, "is that your mother should not be living alone."

Thankfully, I had inherited my mother's height and metabolism which, other than a year of pregnancy and recovery, had kept me shopping in the size-eight rack since I had reached puberty. While similar in physical appearance and sharing the same cynical worldview, we were polar opposites in our temperament and personality. I was guarded and non-confrontational to the point of often being considered a pushover, while Mom tended to let 'er rip and let the pieces fall where they may.

I looked down at my mother, sighed and shook my head. "Mom. Let's listen to what Dr. Frazier has to say."

Edna folded her arms across her chest and snorted. "Why?" she demanded. "I've got socks older than him."

Studying the doctor, I had to admit Mom had a point. Dr. Norman Frazier looked more like a college student playing dress-up for a Halloween party by wearing surgical scrubs than the top heart specialist in the area. He had a round, rosy-cheeked baby face surrounded by unruly curly hair and looked to me more like a cherub in a Renaissance oil painting than a surgeon. The good doctor was hardly the poster boy for an active lifestyle. He was office soft with his waistline measurement exceeding his inseam by at least six inches.

Dr. Frazier dramatically checked his watch and glared at the plump, middle-aged nursing supervisor.

Nurse Blanche Johnson just shrugged. "Social Services said she was on her way."

Dr. Frazier made no effort to conceal his displeasure as he shook his head in disgust. I got the distinct impression there was a good chance the head of the Social Services Department would be getting a call later today.

"Mrs. O'Connor," Dr. Frazier said distinctly, enunciating each word slowly and carefully. "You were fortunate your episode occurred when you were around people who could call for an EMT."

"Don't speak to me like I'm an idiot or a child, Doctor," Edna snapped. "The problem is my heart, not my brain."

Dr. Frazier glanced in the direction of first my brother, Robert, then me, looking for support. We both just shrugged. Mom could be difficult on her best day. On a hospital bed with electrodes embedded in a slimy gel attached to her upper body and a variety of mechanical

5

devices beeping behind her, as far as we were concerned, the good doctor was on his own.

"Dr. Frazier is one of the best cardiologists in the area, Mother," Robert said weakly. "You need to listen to him."

Edna turned away and muttered something to herself that I didn't quite catch but was pretty certain was well beyond PG-13. Despite this unexpected bad turn in her health, she was still a tough old bird.

My brother had always favored our late father, Charlie. He had a ruddy complexion, winning smile and a full head of hair that was gradually moving from auburn to gray. He was an inch shorter than me and had been an impressive physical specimen in his younger days. Combined with being the heir apparent to take over O'Connor Industries when our father stepped down, he was considered quite the catch and never wanted for female companionship. He was a confirmed bachelor, at least until his first wife, Lilith, got pregnant. Married by a Justice of the Peace at twenty-eight and a father six months later, Robert had settled into a turbulent, drama-filled and loveless marriage. He had thrown himself into his work as second-in-command at the family business.

In the first thirty years after he graduated from college he had added about fifteen pounds a decade. Fortunately, his broad shoulders let him carry the added weight and he just looked big, not fat. In the past two years since our dad had moved on to the great real estate investment company in the sky, Robert had dropped over twenty-five pounds and had taken to running half marathons. He had also gotten a more serious interest in his personal appearance and now favored tailored over off-the-rack suits. Weight wasn't the only thing he had lost. Within a month of Dad's funeral, he dumped the odious Lilith and a year later had married his second wife, Gabrielle. The fact that she was barely half his age was probably the reason he had taken a newfound interest in his appearance.

Dr. Frazier shook his head, and his eyes locked on the only other man in room, Robert. "I would like to keep your mother for a few days...."

"I'm over here, Doogie Howser," Edna said. "Talk to me and not my son."

Frazier looked like he didn't want to talk to anyone and glared at the nurse who seemed to be enjoying herself. It looked to me like the grumpy Dr. Frazier was mentally adding another name to his call list, the head of nursing.

"I would like to get you stabilized, then run a series of tests and we will see if medication and lifestyle changes are sufficient or if we need to consider other options."

My hand shot to my mouth. "Are you talking heart surgery?"

"Possibly," Dr. Frazier answered. "But based on my preliminary examination, and considering your mother's advanced age…"

Edna blew a raspberry in Frazier's direction.

Dr. Frazier rolled his eyes and continued. "She may not be a good candidate for surgery."

"Not a good candidate?" I asked. "What exactly does that mean?"

"We'll know more after the tests, but from my preliminary evaluation I would suspect the risk of surgery would likely exceed any possible benefits."

"I don't understand," I said softly.

"He means," Edna barked. "If he cuts me open, and I'm in half as bad of shape as he suspects, I'd be more likely to die on the table than see another Christmas." Mom turned her eyes to Dr. Frazier. "Does that sum it up, Doc?"

Dr. Frazier shrugged. "Let's not get ahead of ourselves. We'll know more tomorrow."

A heavy silence settled over the hospital room. "So, what are we going to do?" I asked Dr. Frazier with a slight hint of panic in my voice.

"If she wishes to continue living at home, she should not be left alone. If that is not viable, I would recommend an assisted living facility where she can be monitored at all times."

"Not happening," Edna said firmly.

"Mother! Please!" I snapped. "Let the man talk."

Edna grunted and folded her arms, dislodging one of the electrodes attached to her chest. Immediately, one of the machines behind her began to beep in protest. The nurse maneuvered around Dr. Frazier and reconnected Edna to the device.

"Aren't nursing homes pretty pricey?" Robert asked.

"First off, I'm not going into a nursing home. Period. End of discussion," Edna said with a dismissive tone and a wave of her hand. "Secondly, what the hell do you care what it would cost? The expense would come out of Allison's inheritance, not yours."

"We need to talk about that some more, Mom," Robert said.

I pulled back and my eyes danced back and forth between my mother and my brother. "What's there to talk about?"

Before Robert could answer, his cellphone started ringing. He fished it out of his pocket and looked at the screen. "I have to take this." Robert rose to his feet and headed toward the door.

"Really?" I said in disbelief.

Without apology or even a whiff of embarrassment, Robert left the room to take his call in the hallway.

"What's Robert up to now?" I asked.

Mom nodded in the direction of Dr. Frazier, then shook her head.

Now was not the time.

Dr. Frazier glanced at his watch again. "We'll get you admitted and we should have all of your test results back by tomorrow morning, Mrs. O'Connor. Then we can develop a plan of action for you."

"Be still my heart," Edna muttered.

"Never say that to a cardiologist, Mrs. O'Connor," Dr. Frazier said with a weak smile as he turned to leave. He nearly bumped into Robert as they arrived at the door at the same moment. They both held their position for a few awkward seconds as each waited for the other to yield, but neither man budged. Finally, since this was Dr. Frazier's home turf, Robert took a step back, nodded and allowed the doctor to continue his rounds. Frazier snorted and shook his head. At least the next patient he would have to deal with today would be less annoying. Full anesthesia limits awkward chit-chat.

"I have to go," Robert said, without even the slightest hint of remorse.

"You can't be serious," I said harshly.

"There is an emergency at work."

I started to protest and ask what could be so damn important at a real estate development company that it couldn't wait, but Mom patted my hand. "It's okay, Allie," Mom said softly. Robert took that as Edna's approval to leave and turned and left.

"I don't believe it," I said as I shook my head.

"I'm fine now and I'm sure…" Edna squinted and read the name tag of the nurse. "Nurse Johnson here will take good care of me."

Hearing her cue, Nurse Johnson said, "Can I get you anything?"

"Four fingers of Blackjack," Edna answered as she licked her lips.

"Sorry," Nurse Johnson said with a chuckle. "Coumadin and Jack Daniel's are a bad combination. Your selection is limited to juices, soft drinks or ice chips."

"Do you have Diet Dr. Pepper?" Edna asked.

"I doubt it, but I'll check," Nurse Johnson answered. "Do you have a second choice?"

"Water. No slice, no ice," Edna answered.

"That I can do," Nurse Johnson answered as she headed toward the door.

Alone for the first time in the hospital room, I turned to Mom. "What's going on with Robert? What does he need to discuss?"

Edna sighed and shook her head. "The division of my estate."

"What?" I said, a bit taken aback that this would even be a topic for discussion. What kind of jerk would want to discuss someone's estate while they're on a hospital gurney less than an hour after a major cardiac event? Sadly, that was a fairly typical move by my self-centered and manipulative brother. I shook my head in disgust. "We have a deal. Robert got control of the business when Daddy died, and I got everything else."

"Your brother thinks it only fair that since you and I got to keep 40 percent of the company, he thinks he should get 40 percent of my estate."

"That wasn't the deal," I hissed. "My 10 percent hasn't paid a penny in dividends since Robert took over after Daddy died."

"I know, I know," Edna said softly. "Robert doesn't have your daddy's head for business. But he is doing his best."

"Robert is a full-grown man, Mother," I replied with a snort. "He doesn't need you to keep defending him."

Before the conversation could go any further, there was a light tap on the door. Mom and I both looked up and saw a harried and mousey young woman in her late twenties with a clipboard clutched to her chest.

"I am so sorry that I was late," the woman said as she scurried into the room. "I'm Donna, Donna Pierson. I'm your personal care representative."

"Well, Donna, Donna Pierson. Why are you here?" Edna asked.

"I'm here," she answered, in the same measured tone that Dr. Frazier had used, "if you need help filling out any of your paperwork and to discuss your post-discharge options."

Edna looked at me in disbelief. "Does everyone in this place think I'm senile?" Edna turned her attention back to Donna, Donna Pierson and wagged a finger in her direction. "I'm perfectly capable of handling your paperwork without any help. And my discharge option is: I go home."

Pierson panicked and started flipping through the papers on her clipboard. "I thought you were a candidate for assisted living?"

"Well," Edna barked. "You thought wrong, Missy Miss. I'm going to one of two places when I leave here. Either my house or the funeral home."

CHAPTER THREE

"WE ONLY GOT one shade of green, lady!" a masculine voice shouted at me as he laid on his horn. Lost in my thoughts, I hadn't noticed the traffic light had changed. I waved meekly and rolled through the intersection.

In my life I've made three very bad choices.

First was marrying Lindsey. I knew he had a reputation, but I had convinced myself I could rein him in. For the first nine years of our marriage we were incredibly happy. We were your classic DINKs -- Dual Income, No Kids. I was busy building my own company and Lindsey was steadily working his way up the corporate ladder. We took amazing vacations, ate in the finest restaurants and couldn't get enough of each other. When I hit thirty, I started hearing the ticking of my biological clock. Lindsey reluctantly agreed it was time we started a family. When I was pregnant with the twins, I lost interest in sex, but apparently, Lindsey didn't.

That was when he had his first affair.

It has pretty much been downhill since then.

With my due date approaching, I received the first of a very long list of calls similar to the one I had earlier today. They all fit the same pattern. At first, Lindsey denied everything, and, like an idiot, I put part of the blame on my weight gain and lack of libido, so I took him back. I convinced myself this was just a one-off, and things would return to normal as soon as I got my figure back. After the twins were born, things settled down for a while. The next call came when the twins were three, and the one after that around the time they started kindergarten. Lindsey again denied everything, but copies of text messages and X-rated photographs, with my husband in the starring role, said otherwise.

This was when I made my second bad choice. I didn't want my kids raised without a father figure in their lives, so instead of kicking my philandering husband to the curb, I decided to look the other way. Unfortunately, Lindsey took my tolerance of his extracurricular activities as a green light to do whatever he wanted and immediately started to push the envelope. The calls began to increase in their frequency, and for the past few years, Lindsey hadn't even bothered to hide what he was doing.

With twins on the way, and still shaken by Lindsey's first affair, I made my third horrible choice. This one still haunts me. I stepped off the fast track at the public relations firm I helped create and focused exclusively on motherhood. Now, after eighteen years out of the job market, I was starting over. And worse, despite having a marketing degree from an Ivy League college, I found myself competing for positions with perky twenty-somethings who had graduated in the top half of their junior college and looked amazing in a sports bra and yoga pants on casual Friday. Fortunately, my old business partner and former high school sweetheart, Bernie Williamson, had taken pity on me. He had given me a part-time position doing background support for several key clients.

The job Bernie gave me was perfect, a fresh toehold, since so much had changed in the nearly two decades since I was in the business world. With computers, metadata, teleconferencing, keywords, etc., I had a lot of catching up to do. Bernie also knew about my pending divorce and kept dropping less-than-subtle hints he would love to have me back full time in any capacity I wanted. Now that over two years had passed since his wife had died in a car accident, and with his kids grown and out of the house, he had also made it abundantly clear he was willing to take up again where we had left off before Lindsey had muscled him aside. Whatever his motives, it was fine by me. After my divorce was final and the twins were someone else's problem at college, I'd probably take him up on at least the offer of full-time employment, more for the challenge than for the money.

With zero personal debt, after Lindsey and I divide up our assets and what I'll be getting from Mom's estate, I'd have plenty of "Screw You Money" and really wouldn't need income-producing employment. I had everything I wanted.

Well, almost everything I wanted.

What I wanted to do was go back in time and marry someone, hell, anyone, other than Lindsey. Then let this man of my dreams be a stay-at-home dad while I had the corner office and the big career.

Unfortunately, no one has been able to convert H. G. Wells' time machine to reality, so I'm stuck.

One thing Lindsey and I did right was having our seventeen-year-old twins, Charles and Angela. While they've had their moments, they were basically good kids who were going to be co-valedictorians at their high school graduation next week. Obviously, they're smart. They had figured out early on what was happening between their parents and avoided getting caught in the crossfire. While the twins had always been closer to me than their absentee father, recently they had become secretive and would stop talking whenever I entered the room. Worse, they would inexplicably vanish for hours without explanation. Even more disturbing, they had quit asking me for money. That didn't mean they had trimmed their spending habits; quite the opposite. In the past year they had both upgraded their phones and computers, and Angela's closet was overflowing with new clothes.

Whenever I challenged them on their source of income, the twins were evasive, but I had my suspicions their father was bankrolling their newly affluent lifestyle. That made perfect sense; Lindsey had always used money to compensate for his absence from their lives. He, always the consummate businessman, had taken the attitude that their love was for sale and he was in the market. And, with us about to drop the divorce bomb on them, I suspected he was trying to purchase some additional goodwill.

Now, add to the mix Mom. I knew that my brother wasn't going to be much help and that his new, much younger wife was going to be totally worthless. Every decision would fall into my lap.

I heard the horn again and glanced in my rearview mirror and saw the frustrated guy behind me with his hands in the air, mouthing "WTF." Looking down, I realized I was driving five miles below the posted speed limit, so I sped up. After a few blocks, with the impatient driver only inches from my rear bumper, I slowed down to make the right turn into my neighborhood. As soon as my turn signal went on, the guy behind me jerked his car into the left lane and roared past me while lying on his horn again.

"Learn how to drive!" he shouted through the open passenger window in passing.

"Learn how to quit being an asshole," I shouted back.

The jerk tapped his brakes and glared at me in his rearview mirror. I thought being bludgeoned as a victim of road rage would be a perfect capper for the day and possibly even a step up. Instead of turning around or backing up, he floored the gas of his shiny new Audi and left a trail of blue smoke from his tires in his wake. He was so focused on me, he didn't see the pothole just ahead and hit it full force. The undercarriage of his expensive car scraped on the pavement.

My day was finally starting to look up.

I weaved my way through the streets of the subdivision I knew so well. One of my father's companies had built every one of the 841 homes in the neighborhood. Years earlier, when old man Sullivan had died without an heir, my dad had bought his 6,700-acre farm for back taxes. As usual, everyone thought Daddy was nuts. Why would anyone want played-out land, zoned exclusively as agricultural, in the middle of nowhere? The only thing with any possible value was the old farm house, but it was over 100 years old with a leaky roof and a questionable foundation. As usual, my dad was a visionary with a nose for an opportunity.

He knew the area was growing and would be needing affordable housing.

In exchange for changing the zoning to residential, Dad made the township an offer they couldn't refuse. He pitched them that the new homes would increase their tax base. Plus, he offered to set aside land for a nice park, and then, once a certain number of units were sold, build a new elementary school and fire station and deed all of them to the township. Since it cost the township absolutely nothing, they quickly agreed.

The first phase, Charlestown Village, were snug, well-built, three-bedroom, bath-and-a-half ranch-style starter homes. Daddy's biggest asset was his ability to foresee a coming market and make whiplash-inducing adjustments. As he had predicted, the area grew and prospered. Seeing a changing demographic, where blue-collar workers were being replaced by dual-income white-collar professionals, he started phase two, Charlestown Acres. Instead of cookie-cutter homes on postage-stamp lots, he began building two-story, four-bedroom, two-and-a-half-bath homes with finished full basements on an acre-plus. His masterstroke, early on, was to set aside nearly 1,500 acres of arguably the best potential land and, instead of building homes, plant trees.

Again, everyone thought he was nuts.

Fast forward thirty years, with the township booming, Charlie opened Charlestown Reserve. He started building sprawling McMansions on beautiful multi-acre lots. The lots now had mature trees – all perfectly located to complement the homes he had envisioned decades earlier. And what homes they were. Six-bedrooms, seven-baths, world-class kitchens, media rooms, salt-water heated swimming pools and walk-in closets bigger than the master bedrooms in his phase one homes.

As I drove deeper into the subdivision, the row of phase one houses on the right-hand side of the street ended and gave way to an impressive eight-foot-high stone wall that ran for a few hundred feet. I slowed down and turned into the wide driveway, came to a stop and hit the button that rolled down my window to enter the four-digit code on the touchpad. I was startled when a dapper male senior citizen approached my car.

"Are you new?" he asked politely with a bit of a British accent and a mischievous twinkle in his jade green eyes. He was diminutive with fiery red hair with flecks of gray. Instead of salt-and-pepper, I would have called it salt-and-paprika. He had a shopping bag in his left hand.

"Excuse me?" I asked. "Do I know you?"

"Montgomery Wilson," he said with a smile as he extended his empty right hand. Reluctantly I accepted the offered hand; instead of the handshake I had expected, Monty gave my hand a kiss. Startled, I quickly pulled my hand back and resisted the urge to wipe it on my shirt. "My friends call me Monty."

"It was nice meeting you, Monty," I said as I entered the password on the keypad and the heavy gate creaked open. I pulled a few yards inside the gate and, using my rearview mirror, made sure my new friend didn't follow me in. When the gate clanked closed and I was sure Monty was still on the other side, I continued to the house.

"That was weird," I muttered to myself. It is not every day you get hit on by a horny, geriatric leprechaun.

Daddy had kept the front facade of the original building, and from the street it still looked like an old two-story farmhouse. Appearances can be deceptive. That was all of the original structure still remaining. Behind the false front he had more than tripled the size of the house by adding to the rear.

I pulled around to the back, passing the doublewide trailer our family had lived in off and on while the house was undergoing a seemingly endless string of renovations and expansions. The work had gone on for years. Dad used the remodeling to keep his best-skilled help busy during slow times. This kept his key people on the payroll and not out looking for other work and maybe never coming back. Dad had guys who had worked only for him for over thirty years, which was something pretty much unheard of in the local building trades.

This caused a problem for the family, as it meant the work on the house was always at the bottom of the priority list. After the new kitchen and laundry room were framed in, the crews got busy on income-producing projects and instead of installing the modern appliances and custom cabinets, they were shoved in a corner and stayed in their boxes collecting dust.

In all of my years living under the same roof with my parents, the battle over the kitchen was the only time I ever remembered my parents raising their voices at each other. After two years of sleeping in the house but eating in the doublewide and doing the wash at the local laundromat, Mom had reached her limit and issued an ultimatum: Either finish her damn kitchen and laundry room or she was going to take the kids and leave. Plus, Edna said, on her way out the door, she would burn both the doublewide and the farmhouse to the ground. Apparently, the half-dozen full five-gallon gasoline cans on the patio were enough to convince my dad that Mom was serious. Three weeks later, not only were the kitchen and massive great room finished, so was the rest of the house, and we never spent another night in the trailer again.

Briefly, the old trailer served as a satellite office for Dad while he had an eight-bay garage built a few hundred yards behind the farm house. Once finished, the garage served as both an office and a place for Daddy to store his classic car collection. After that, the trailer was seldom used. When Robert was in high school, Mom discovered my brother had filled the trailer's refrigerator with beer and nearly had a stroke when she found a box of condoms in one of the trailer's bedrooms. Furious, she cut off both the water and the electric to the trailer. When I left for college, the utilities were restored. After that Dad occasionally let one of his crew borrow it for the night or, in one case, for three months when one of his foremen and his wife hit a rough patch. My dad passed two years ago, and as far as I knew, no one had set foot in the trailer since.

Still, the old trailer was full of fond memories for me.

Because my brother, Robert, was two grades ahead of me, and a boy, he had little time for his bratty kid sister. Fortunately for me, a girl almost exactly my age moved into one of the first completed homes, which was right next door to the farmhouse. At first out of necessity, since we were the only kids in all of Charlestown, we started playing together, and over time, we became lifelong friends. Beth Longway, now Beth Woodrow, had a tough start. Her father died in an accident on an oil rig somewhere in the Gulf of Mexico before she was even born. Her mother, who worked for my dad at the time of the accident, used some of the impressive insurance settlement she had received and got a "friends and family" deal on the model house adjoining ours.

In the early days, the roads were paved before the houses were built so people could see the lots that were for sale. Starting when we were in grade school, Beth and I would roam the nearly empty subdivision on our bikes like it was our personal kingdom and the trailer was our castle. We would explore the partially constructed homes and play on the heavy equipment. Since everybody loved my dad, Beth and I were treated like royalty by the construction crews and new homebuyers alike.

Glancing at the old trailer again, I was glad Mom's yard service had kept it well-maintained and had not let it get overgrown.

I pulled around to the back side of the house. Daddy loved to entertain, and the long delayed combination kitchen and great room were amazing. It even included a solarium with a spectacular view. The combination great room, kitchen and dining room had a vaulted twenty foot-plus ceiling. The fourteen-foot-high windows overlooked a sprawling patio and swimming pool. There were a half-dozen parking spots near the kitchen door and additional overflow parking down by Daddy's garage/office. I pulled into the spot closest to the door leading to the mud room. The lock was keyless and had a touchpad instead. I entered the access code and, once inside, disarmed the security system.

The house, usually so full of life when Mom was around, and even more so when Daddy was still alive, was still and quiet. I found it a bit unnerving, so I hurried to Mom's bedroom to grab some clothes and toiletries, then started to retrace my steps. I stopped short when I heard the familiar rumble of a powerful V-8 engine. I pulled aside the curtain of Mom's bedroom window and I was surprised to see my son Charles's 1971 GTO pulling into a spot in front of the doublewide. Together, he and his grandfather had meticulously restored the vintage muscle car, and it was my son's pride and joy. In the front passenger seat was my daughter, Angela.

In the back was Charles's girlfriend, Paige. Surprisingly, sitting next to Paige was my new suitor, Monty Wilson. They all got out of the GTO, and Charles, Angela and Paige headed inside the trailer while Monty cooled his heels on the front porch.

"Why aren't you in school?" I muttered to myself and thought back to the call from the twins' high school. Less than two weeks from graduation and they're ditching class? "I'm going to kill both of you," I said softly. I started to turn toward the door but stopped when I saw, of all things, one of those oversized Enterprise Rent-A-Car shuttles, the kind you only see at airports, pull up and park. As soon as it rolled to a stop, more senior citizens started slowly piling out. All of them were carrying shopping bags identical to the one the odd little leprechaun had been carrying.

"What the hell?" I muttered.

I hurried back downstairs and sprinted across the patch of grass separating the old farmhouse and the trailer.

Around twenty seniors had formed a queue near the main door to the trailer.

Meanwhile, a massive man, well over three hundred pounds, was pulling camping equipment and folding chairs out of the rear of the oversized Enterprise van. From there, a slightly smaller but equally intimidating guy was carrying the supplies to the side door of the trailer that led to the old master bedroom and was taking the stuff inside. I maneuvered around the queue and headed for the front door of the trailer.

"There's a line here, young stuff," Monty Wilson said. "Wait your turn."

Suddenly, I had twenty senior citizens, some armed with walking sticks, glaring at me.

"You tell her, Monty," barked a silver-haired old biddy.

"That's right," others chimed in as they slowly began to surround me.

The commotion outside caused my son's girlfriend, Paige Thompson, to appear at the door.

Paige was a pretty, take-no-prisoners brunette known for speaking her mind. For senior superlatives she won the vote in two categories, "Best Legs" and "Most Outspoken." When told she needed to pick one or the other, she recommended they simply combine the two categories and give her "Biggest Bitch," but the yearbook advisor vetoed it. She and Charles had been dating off and on for the past six months or so, which was some kind of record for my immensely popular son.

Paige's eyes grew large when she saw me. "Ah, man," she muttered, then stuck her head back in the trailer. "Charles. Angela. Your mother is here."

"Let her in," came Angela's voice from inside the trailer.

Paige pointed a warning finger in the direction of the senior citizens. "Back off," she snapped, and they slowly retreated, leaving the path to the door unobstructed.

Stepping inside, I blinked a few times to let my eyes adjust to the lower light level, then stopped dead in my tracks. The twins were sitting behind my father's old desk. In the middle of the desk was a large pile of cash.

CHAPTER FOUR

"ARE YOU TWO dealing drugs?" I demanded.

"No, Mom." Angela laughed. "We're dealing shoes."

"Shoes?"

"Yeah, Mom. Shoes."

I blinked a few times, then shook my head. "Shoes?"

"Here," Angela said. "I'll show you."

Angela gently took my arm and guided me back outside and motioned to the people in line, and they opened their bags. I could see they all had four bright red Nike boxes inside their shopping bags.

"Today was release day for a new tennis shoe, and we paid these people to wait in line and purchase them for us."

My mouth started to move, but I discovered I had lost the ability to form words.

"What the hell, Angie?" barked the rough-looking piece of business who had been stowing the camping equipment. "I need to get the van back to my cousin."

Angela, all five feet, two inches of her, wheeled on the guy who was a foot taller and at least twice her weight. She pointed a warning finger in his direction. "Watch your mouth, Timmy," Angela said with fire in eyes as she nodded toward me. "This is my mom."

"Sorry, sorry," Timmy answered as he instantly dropped his attitude and took a step back.

A gray-haired woman next to me gave my arm a gentle squeeze. "You have such lovely children. You must be very proud."

At the moment, "proud" was not the word that immediately leaped to mind.

"You realize your grandmother is in the hospital?" I said to Angela.

"Of course," Angela answered with an expression indicating she was surprised the question needed to be asked. "I've talked to her a couple of times. She knew today was a release day and she insisted…"

"Wait? What?" I said. "You mean your grandmother knows about your little enterprise?"

Angela giggled. "Do you really think we could use this trailer for all of this time without Grammy noticing?"

"All of this time?" I shook my head. "How long has this been going on?"

Angela shrugged. "A couple of years."

"Years!"

"Look, Mom," Angela glanced nervously over her shoulder at the pile of money on the desktop. "I really don't like having that much cash outside of the safe. We only need about ten minutes to wrap this part up, then we'll explain everything."

Before I could protest, my phone rang. I checked the caller ID and sighed. "It's your Uncle Robert, and I need to talk to him."

"Lucky you," Angela said with a snort.

I pushed a button on my phone. "Hold on one second." I put my hand over the phone and pointed in the direction of the house. "I expect to see the both of you in the kitchen in ten minutes."

"Yes, ma'am." Angela gave me a quick, wrong-handed salute, then turned on her heels and went back inside the trailer. I started back toward the farmhouse but didn't get far before I felt a firm pat on my butt.

"Hey!" I shouted, as I wheeled around and saw Monty Wilson winking at me. He made his hand in the shape of a phone and held it up to his ear. "Give me a call sometime, sweet cheeks."

"We've talked about this before, Mr. Wilson," Angela said over her shoulder without even bothering to slow down. "Keep your hands to yourself."

I shook my head and turned my attention back to my phone as I continued walking back to the old house. "What do you want?" I said with a harsh edge in my voice.

"We need to talk," Robert answered.

"Talk about what?"

"Well, first off, where is Mom going to live?" Robert answered. "I spoke to Gabrielle, and she doesn't think she would be up to it."

"Surprise, surprise. Besides, I think Mom would rather go to a nursing home or put a gun in her mouth than be under the same roof as your new trophy wife."

"Can we be civil for just a few minutes?" Robert asked.

An icy silence settled over our conversation. For my entire life, Robert had exploited my passive nature and reluctance to make a scene to get what he wanted. He had figured out at a young age that his persistence could beat my resistance every time. He didn't exactly bully me; he would just wear me down. I knew it as well, but more often than not, I would get tired of the conflict, and it was easier to just let him have his way.

This time I needed to be strong. And civil. After all, this was our mother we're talking about. And my inheritance.

"What's on your mind?" I said in a somewhat softer tone.

"Will you meet us for a drink to discuss this in person?" Robert asked.

"Us?"

"Gabrielle and me."

The family business had not exactly thrived under Robert's management. Plus, Robert's new, much younger wife, Gabrielle, was high maintenance. Combine that with an ugly and probably expensive divorce and Robert's son, Bobby, having recently graduated from an expensive private college, I was pretty sure my brother was hurting financially.

"Look, Robert," I said tersely. "I'm not going to let you two double-team me."

"This is an important family matter, and Gabrielle needs to be there."

"If Gabrielle is going to be there, I'm bringing Beth," I answered.

"Why not Lindsey?"

"He's in Brussels," I answered.

"Why do you need to bring Beth?"

He knew exactly why I wanted to bring Beth. She was ten times tougher than me.

"Why do you really feel the need to bring Gabrielle?"

"Gabrielle is my wife, and we need to make some family decisions."

"To me, Beth is family. No Beth, no me. Take it or leave it."

There was a long pause as Robert was calculating his options.

"You know, you're right. Beth should be a part of this. Gino's at eight," Robert said.

"Fine." I ended the call wishing my cellphone had an app that would make the sound of the receiver being slammed down on the cradle of an old-style phone. The soft click just seemed lame.

I knew why he wanted to meet in person. He figured he would stand a better chance of intimidating me face-to-face than over the phone, which was exactly why I wanted Beth there as my wingman.

Wing woman?

Wing person?

Whatever.

She wouldn't let my brother and his child bride push me around.

I sighed and shook my head. For the moment, at least, my manipulative brother was only fourth on my priority list. Currently, dealing with my failing mother, my failing marriage and my rebellious teenagers all ranked higher.

I went back into the kitchen and jerked the oversized refrigerator open with enough force it rattled the items on the shelves in the door. I grabbed a can of sparkling water and pulled the tab. In the continuation of a hellish day, the liquid sprayed on my hands and face. "Son of a…" I reached for a dishtowel with my free hand as I held the still-spewing can at arm's length in my other hand and dropped it in the sink.

"Smooth one, Mom," Charles said as he strolled into the kitchen with a shoebox under his arm and Angela a half-step behind him.

I glared at my children. "If I were you two, I wouldn't be going for cute or cocky at the moment."

Seeing Charles and Angela standing side by side, it was hard to believe they were related, much less twins. A late growth spurt had sent Charles well over six feet tall, and he didn't seem finished yet. He was skinny as a rail, with a ruddy complexion and rosy cheeks that complemented his easy smile. He was topped off with a thick head of auburn, bordering on red, hair that was impervious to a comb or brush. Angela, on the other hand, was petite and curvy and looked much older than her seventeen years. She had my alabaster skin and her father's natural jet-black hair. Combined with her grandmother's blue eyes, by any measure, she was a stunning beauty. It was a combination that would make the average Goth envious.

"What are you two up to?" I demanded.

Charles glanced in the direction of his sister. When the two of them were together, she usually did all of the talking. This time was no different.

"We saw a business opportunity," Angela answered, "and we took advantage of it."

At that moment I saw the ghost of my daddy in my daughter. Angela looked and sounded exactly like him, right down to the inflection in her voice and the confident expression on her face.

I felt the anger seeping out of me. My twins had their moments, but neither had an evil bone in their bodies. "What kind of opportunity?" I asked softly.

"Two things," Angela continued. "In our neighborhood, we have people with lots of money but limited time."

"Okay," I said cautiously.

"We found people with lots of time but limited money, and we put them together."

Angela continued to sound more and more like her grandfather with every word she spoke. I forced myself not to smile and motioned for her to continue.

"There are items people with money would like to have, such as the latest sneakers...."

"Or the hot new phone or computer," Charles added. Then with a big grin, when he saw the look on his sister's face, pretended to zip his lips closed, lock them shut and throw the key away over his shoulder.

Angela glared at her brother as she continued. "We hire the people you just saw to stand in line for the people who don't have the time to do it themselves."

"And you can make money doing this?" I asked in disbelief.

Charles started to answer, but, seeing the look on his sister's face, thought better of it and stayed quiet.

Angela snatched the shoebox out of her brother's hand and flipped it open. "After sales tax, these cost $291.60 a pair with a four-pair limit per buyer. We give our people a gift card loaded with $1,166.40 on it to buy the maximum number of shoes. When they deliver them to us, we give them $400 for their time. We bill our customers $700 a pair...."

"Wait a minute, wait a minute," I said in disbelief. "People are willing to pay $700 for a pair of gym shoes?"

"We had to turn people away," Charles added before he realized his mistake and playfully cupped his hand over his groin as if he were afraid his sister might give him a knee.

Angela sighed. "Law of supply and demand," she said. "Our customers are happy to pay our rates."

I closed my eyes and did the math. "Wait a minute, wait a minute. You're telling me you two are making over $300 on each pair of sneakers you sell just for being the middleman?"

"At full resale, there is $308.40 in gross profit per pair," Charles answered. This time Angela didn't object to his input. Despite his "aw, shucks" appearance, he was the numbers guy for the twins.

"I must have seen over fifty boxes," I said in disbelief.

"116," Angela stated.

I closed my eyes again and did the rough math. "That's over $30,000!"

"If we got full resale on each pair, it would be $35,774.40," Charles corrected.

Angela nodded in her brother's direction. "What he said." While not exactly a math savant like her brother, she had also gotten a perfect score on the math portion of both her SAT and ACT exams. Plus, the duo had also scored a perfect 5 on their Advanced Placement calculus exams.

I rubbed my forehead. "So, you're telling me my two seventeen-year-old kids made over $35,000 today?"

"We're only going to net $30,694 after we cover all of our expenses and discounts," Charles said.

"Expenses?"

"Catering, transportation, security," Angela added.

"Security?"

"We're not going to leave a bunch of senior citizens out on the sidewalk all night, cold and hungry, and without someone watching out for them," Angela answered. "Big Tony can be pretty intimidating."

I remembered the big guy unloading the van and could see Angela's point. "How much money have you two made?"

"This is our best single day ever, and the balance in our account after today will be at around..." Angela's eyes unfocused as she started running the numbers, but her brother beat her to the total.

"$274,697," Charles answered with a matter-of-fact tone in his voice.

I put my hand on my chest and thought for a moment I might soon be in the bed next to my mother at the hospital.

"So, you're telling me my two children have over a quarter of a million dollars in the bank before they've even graduated from high school, and did it without me finding out?"

"Pretty much," Charles answered with a chuckle.

I took a moment to try to get my head around all of this, but it was too large for me to grasp. I was so stupefied I had completely missed seeing another car pull up. All eyes turned when the back door opened and my lifelong friend, Beth Woodrow, walked in.

"What are you doing here?" Beth asked when she saw me.

"I could ask you the same question," I answered.

"I was in court all day, so no phones, and I just got your text about Edna," Beth said. "Is she okay?"

"According to her doctor, she's circling the drain and needs 24-7 looking after. According to Mom, there is nothing wrong with her a bottle of whiskey couldn't fix."

"That sounds like Edna."

"Why are you here?"

Beth reached into her purse and pulled out a handful of cash as Charles handed her a shoebox.

"You knew about this?"

"Of course," Beth answered as she started putting $100 bills on the counter. "$400, right?"

"Why $400 and not $700?" I demanded. "Why does she get a discount?"

"Professional courtesy," Angela answered. "Aunt Beth is our attorney."

CHAPTER FIVE

"SO, LET ME get this straight," I said as I folded my arms across my chest and glared at Angela, Beth and Charles. "For the past two years, my two minor children, with the help of my supposed best friend, have been busy trying to corner the local black market?"

"Oh, please," Beth said with a dismissive wave of her hand. "Your dad set up the corporate structure...."

"My dad!" I exclaimed. "He knew about this, too?"

"Grandpa provided the seed money," Angela answered.

"What!"

"Will you relax?" Beth asked. "The kids pay their taxes, they have a business license and aren't doing anything remotely illegal."

I always hated it when she morphed into lawyer mode. I glared at Elizabeth Woodrow, Esquire, a.k.a. Beth to friends and family. She was the prototype of the modern alpha woman. Woodrow was one of three names on the door at the largest law firm in the area. She was in charge of the civil litigation division with a huge staff reporting to her. Outside the office she was supermom to her two kids and had a solid and frisky relationship with her polar-opposite, stay-at-home novelist-wannabe husband. While only an inch shorter and a few pounds heavier than me, we looked enough alike that we were often mistaken for sisters.

"If this was all on the up and up, then why did you keep it such a big secret?"

Beth, Charles and Angela all laughed.

"Oh, honey," Beth said. "Imagine if Angela had pitched this concept to you instead of your father." Beth turned to Charles and

Angela. "Who here thinks their mother would have thrown a fit and forbidden them from doing this?"

Both twins' hands immediately shot up.

"Shut up," I answered meekly, partly because of my no-drama temperament, but mostly because I knew they were right.

I turned when I heard the crunch of tires on gravel. Out the window, I saw a car pulling up by the doublewide.

Charles and Angela saw the car as well. Concerned expressions covered their faces.

"We really need to get back to the office to take care of fulfillment before there's a fatality," Charles said with a hint of panic in his voice.

"Fatality?" I said with a startled tone. "Is Big Tony dangerous?"

Angela snorted. "Tony's a pussycat."

"It's Paige we're worried about," Charles added.

"Hold on," Beth said, as her eyes grew large. "Paige Thompson is over there, by herself, dealing with the public?" Charles nodded. "Good Lord."

"What's the problem?" I asked. "I've met Paige, and she seems perfectly delightful."

"Around you, sure," Charles said. "Around some of our buyers, not so much."

Angela nodded her agreement. "She is amazing with logistics and organization, but customer service is not a big part of her skillset."

"Especially since the kind of kids who can afford $700 gym shoes are usually self-absorbed, entitled jerks," Charles said.

"She considers trust-fund babies to be her primary source of fiber," Angela added.

"Are we done here?" Charles asked nervously as he glanced out the solarium window and saw another car approaching.

"For the moment, but..." Before I could finish my sentence, the twins were out the door. Beth and I watched them as they sprinted across the yard. "We'll discuss this more later," I said to no one in particular.

"That's quite a pair you've got there," Beth said admiringly. "I can't believe you never told me about the twins' little enterprise."

"Have you ever heard of attorney-client privilege?" Beth protested. "They specifically asked that you not be told."

"They're minors! How can they even legally sign anything?"

"At least on paper, first your dad, then when he passed, your mom now has control of the business."

"My mom!" I shouted. "She's in on this too?"

"Only on paper." Beth gave me a dismissive wave. "But, as you would expect, Charles and Angela have always called the shots."

Then an ugly thought occurred to me. "What if something happens to my mom?"

"Relax," Beth answered. "I'm both the executor of your mom's estate and counsel of record for Charles and Angela, LLC. Besides, the way it is structured, all of that will be moot when the twins turn eighteen in a few weeks. At that point, your kids will have total control of their company." Beth paused, then continued, "And their lives."

"What does that mean?"

Beth hesitated, sighed then reluctantly continued. "You may not like this."

I had seen that look on my old friend's face before. It was always a prelude to bad news and it was not in Beth's nature to sugar-coat or spin anything.

I drew in a cleansing breath and released it. "Tell me," I insisted.

"Once they turn eighteen, if they decided they want to emancipate themselves from you and go their own way, there is absolutely nothing you can do to stop them, and they certainly have the resources if they want to go in that direction."

That gave me jolt of reality as Beth's words sank in. Here I had been worried about how the twins would take Lindsey and my divorce. It had never crossed my mind they may blow out their birthday candles then say "see ya" and walk out the door and never look back. That was a scenario I had never considered, and suddenly that quiet empty nest didn't seem so appealing anymore.

Beth noticed my reaction and gave me a friendly hug.

"You got your kids through high school and accepted into top colleges on full scholarships with no cavities, no pregnancies and no felony arrests. Every parent with a lick of sense would take that as a win."

That didn't make me feel any better and, apparently, it showed on my face.

"Look," Beth said. "I was in the delivery room with you the day they were born. You've done your job with them. You've got two world-class kids that are the envy of all of your friends and neighbors and they love the daylights out of you. They're not going to kick you to the curb, but," Beth let her thought hang.

"But what?" I demanded.

Beth made a face and rubbed her neck. "I meant for us to have this talk sooner."

"What talk?" I demanded.

"Your days of telling them what they can and can't do are about over."

Damnit! As usual, Beth was right.

"Your twins are not kids anymore, they're young adults," Beth continued. "You'll still have some input in their lives, but they're old enough and smart enough to make their own choices. You need to come to grips that you have zero leverage over them and that your opinions no longer carry the force of law. All parents have to face the reality that someday the entire balance in your relationship will change. For you, that day has arrived." Beth gave me another hug. "And you need to be strong."

I chuckled, "Says the lady who ran Costco out of Kleenex when her boys went off to college."

Beth shrugged but didn't argue.

I knew Beth was absolutely right and I had, on some level, known this day was coming. But, like so many things in life, it had arrived sooner than expected. My twins weren't children anymore, and, as their little shoe enterprise had proven, were very capable of finding their own way in the world.

"You're still close to your boys," I said softly.

"Of course I am!" Beth said with a laugh. "And you'll still be close to your twins." She gave me another hug. "It'll just be different. You'll be coming at each other as parent and grown child. You'll be equals." Beth got a wistful look on her face. "In some ways it is actually easier."

"How so?" I asked.

"You don't get bogged down in the details of their life and you let them make their own choices. Basically, you move to just being a trusted advisor who they know will have their back." Beth laughed. "It is kind of liberating for both sides."

"Okay," I said with a sigh. "The twins are growing up and there is not a damn thing I can do about it." Then I glared at my best friend. "I'm still mad at you for not telling me about this shoe thing."

"Boo. Friggin'. Hoo. Let's all take a moment and get past that, shall we?" Beth said with a laugh. "Your kids have Charlie O'Connor's entrepreneurial genes, and I have a sneaky suspicion, if your daddy had lived a few more years, it would be Angela and Charles sharing the corner office of O'Connor Industries instead of your brother."

"Speaking of Robert," I said. "We're meeting him and his child bride for drinks at Gino's at eight."

"We are?"

"Yup."

"I assume we'll be discussing what to do with Edna."

"The subject will probably come up, but, knowing my brother, I doubt that's what's on his mind."

"There is always something with Robert." Beth leaned back and folded her arms across her chest. "Tell me more."

"He's been pestering Mom to change her will."

CHAPTER SIX

"**O**H, FOR CHRIST'S sake," Beth said, "I wrote that agreement, which I thought was more than fair to him. Way more than fair, actually."

"I know, I know," I said with a sigh. "He seems to think since Mom kept thirty percent and I kept ten percent of the company stock he should be entitled to forty percent of mom's estate."

"Good luck with that argument," Beth replied. "We had independent appraisals of both the business and your mother's assets, and based on the valuation at the time, Robert came out way ahead of you."

"So you don't see a problem?" I asked.

"I didn't say that," Beth answered guardedly. "Our local probate judges aren't exactly on the shortlist for the next open seat on the U.S. Supreme Court. Most of them are hacks who will do the absolute minimum to keep collecting their paychecks. I've never seen any of them turn down a continuance request, so he could tie up your mother's estate for years."

"Robert can do that?"

"Uncle Robert can do what?" Angela asked as she and Charles unexpectedly returned to the kitchen. Both Beth and I fell silent. Angela pulled a pair of flavored seltzer waters from the refrigerator and, having watched my earlier effort, opened them over the sink.

"Uncle Robert can do what?" Angela repeated.

I looked at Beth and shrugged. "Like you said, they no longer eat at the kids' table, and this could potentially affect them as much as me."

Beth nodded, then turned to the twins. "Your Uncle Robert may contest your grandmother's will."

"Can't he even wait until she dies?" Charles said with a snort as he accepted his drink from his sister.

Angela leaned against the kitchen counter and eyed Beth. "We read the agreement you drew up when Grandpa died. I'm no lawyer, but it looked pretty airtight to me."

"How did you read the agreement?" I demanded.

"It didn't take a mad, genius hacker to figure out your password was 'Charles&Angela1!'" Angela said with a dismissive wave.

"Plus, taping a copy of your password under your desk lamp isn't going to win any security awards," Charles added as he took a sip of his drink.

"You little sneaks," I said with mock indignation.

"We prefer crafty," Angela answered with a laugh. "Can Robert tie up the estate in probate?"

"Absolutely," Beth answered.

"What would be his endgame?" Charles asked softly.

"Knowing Robert," Beth answered, then nodded in my direction, "he'll try to wear your mother down and get some sort of settlement."

"I'm not going to cave this time," I said with more confidence than I actually felt.

"Let's see how you feel when the proceedings have dragged out for four or five years with no end in sight," Beth replied.

"Why do you think he's doing this?" Charles asked with an unnerving and detached calmness in his voice.

Beth looked in my direction and I shrugged, which she took as permission to bring the twins fully up to speed.

"As you know, Robert's ex-wife really took him to the cleaners," Beth answered. "There is a rumor on the street that Robert is in financial trouble."

"Man, I guess that should be expected," Angela said. "Aunt Lilith was seriously pissed off. I guess it has to really bruise the ego to lose your husband to a younger woman."

I fell silent as Beth shot Angela a withering glare.

Angela was nobody's fool. She and her brother knew there was trouble in paradise at the Clark household. She instantly realized her mistake and her hand shot to her mouth. "I'm so sorry. I didn't mean…"

I gave Angela's arm a squeeze. "Forget it. Relationships can be complicated." I took in a cleansing breath to compose myself before turning back to Beth. "Back to Robert."

"Fortunately for him, like you, the house was his and not community property. This is just a rumor and I haven't seen anything concrete to confirm it. But I've heard from several people, after the divorce he started borrowing against his house, and now that the market has softened he is underwater." Beth saw the blank look on my face. I had never lived in a house with a mortgage on it in my entire adult life. I had no idea what she was talking about.

"It means he owes more than the house is worth, Mom," Charles added.

"That can't be good," I said.

"No, it's not, and it gets worse." Beth continued. "I understand that Robert still needed money, and since he had no equity left in his house, he used a large chunk of his shares of O'Connor Industries as collateral for a loan to stay personally afloat." Beth had a deep frown on her face. "Even worse, he had to renegotiate some of the long-term debt of O'Connor Industries, and he used outside counsel instead of me."

"Why?" I asked.

"I believe the company has had some cash-flow issues and, considering my personal relationship, I think he didn't want me to know how bad things actually were." Beth shook her head. "I also understand he has fallen behind on both the personal and corporate notes."

"Do you mean the family could lose control of the business?" I asked with a startled expression on my face.

"It depends on how much of the sixty percent of his stake in the company Robert has put at risk. Banks tend to ask for everything they can get, so I wouldn't be surprised if the bank didn't demand every share as collateral. If it is all of it, then, yes, your family could lose control of the company."

"Walk me through this," Charles said without even a hint of emotion or drama in his voice. His tone and body language were chillingly clinical and completely detached. "How serious is this?"

Beth sighed. "If Robert defaults on his loan or the bank calls the note for non-performance and he can't come up with the cash, the bank could take his shares and start looking for a buyer."

"Damn," I muttered. It was obvious now why Robert was in such a panic. He was on the verge of losing everything and taking the company down with him.

"It may not be as bad as it sounds," Beth continued. "At work, I deal with this kind of stuff every day. Unless someone wanted to buy the note, the bank would probably continue to carry it for a year or two and hope Robert can turn things around."

"What do you mean, buy the note?" Charles asked with new, sudden interest.

"Banks often sell non-performing loans to investors at a deep discount just to get them off their books."

"That makes sense," Charles muttered as a small smile formed on his face as he glanced at Angela, who smiled back at him.

"It might have made sense to you," I said as I nodded in my son's direction. "But I'd like a few more details." I glared at Beth. "In easy to understand layman's terms, please."

"I'll try," Beth said with a laugh. "Foreclosures with pictures on social media of the sheriff putting crying people's furniture out on the curb make for bad press for a bank. They sell the note on a secondary market, often for pennies on the dollar, then let the other guys be the heavy."

"Half the stuff Grandpa bought were distressed assets," Charles said.

"He used to always say," Angela added. "Cash was always the loudest voice in the room."

"Exactly," Beth said with a shrug. "But if I were you guys, I wouldn't be too worried. At least not yet."

"Why not?" I asked.

"In the current market, people aren't exactly lining up to buy shares in real estate development companies."

I motioned for her to continue.

"The law of supply and demand," Beth said. "If no one wants to buy the shares, then the bank will have to hold them until someone offers to take them off of their hands."

"At what point does O'Connor Industries become a hostile takeover candidate?" Charles asked in a cold, business-like tone.

"Hostile takeover? What the hell does that mean?" I demanded.

"It is when the value of the stock becomes low enough you can buy a controlling interest and then sell off all of the assets and make a profit," Charles answered calmly.

"How do you know this stuff?" I demanded.

Charles just shrugged. "Angie and I spent a lot of time with Grandpa and I learned how to read when I was six."

"Let's not get ahead of ourselves here," Beth said. "The bank hasn't come even close to reaching that point yet."

"Are you sure?" I asked.

"I'm chief outside counsel for O'Connor Industries. The bank wouldn't make an aggressive move like putting the shares on the open market without giving me at least a courtesy call."

"But," Charles asked softly. "If someone approached the bank with an offer for the loan, would they listen?"

"At this point, if Robert is in as deep of a hole as I suspect," Beth sighed and shook her head. "They would have to be crazy not to."

I gave the twins an odd look. It was unusual for Charles to be the one asking questions and even more unusual that Angela wasn't objecting. My eyes danced back and forth between my children. This was a new dynamic I had never noticed before.

I leaned into Beth and whispered. "Does Charles usually do this much talking?"

"When we're doing strategy sessions or discussing legal matters, he's usually the one with most of the questions and I hardly ever hear a peep out of Angela."

Then it hit me. They had been playing me for years. Every time the twins approached me, or anyone other than their womb mate, they had already worked out the details of what they wanted to say. Since Charles hated being the center of attention while Angela thrived on it, she was the perfect choice to be the spokesperson for the pair. I was also getting the impression, after hearing the way Charles could rattle off the numbers on the shoes and their account balance, that if you were in a business negotiation with the twins, it would be like a Vegas magic act. Angela, the attractive assistant, would get all of the attention while Charles would be the one you should be keeping your eyes on.

Listening to Charles hitting Beth with questions that never would have occurred to me in a thousand years, I heard the echo of Beth's words about the twins being young adults now. At the moment, they certainly weren't doing anything to disprove Beth's argument. She was right. They didn't need me making rules and checking up on them any longer.

Much of the cold angst and dread I had been feeling toward this new and rapidly evolving relationship with my children was starting to melt away.

CHAPTER SEVEN

B ACK IN MY car, I headed deeper into the subdivision to the five-bedroom home my father had given me the day before my wedding. It was one of the last and easily the biggest home built in the "Phase 2" period and was a bit of a dry run for the even bigger homes that were to follow. While larger and more expensive than any of the other homes on the cul-de-sac, it wasn't distinctive enough to generate much interest. It had been on the market for over a year when Daddy deeded it to me. Thankfully, my father had insisted it be in my name only, which meant it wasn't community property. This also meant that when Lindsey and I went our separate ways, one of my biggest assets would not be a part of the settlement negotiations and I would get to keep it after the divorce.

My father was not a clever or particularly well-educated man. He wasn't going to impress anyone with his knowledge of arts and letters or his take on geopolitical events. But he was a shrewd businessman and a master at reading people. Honest and straightforward, he was the kind of man people immediately liked and trusted.

Though he never said it, I always had the distinct impression my dad didn't care much for Lindsey. First there was the pre-nuptial deal with the house and then the cold glares the usually gregarious Charlie gave Lindsey, which started even before I realized Lindsey was a serial philanderer. At first I thought Dad resented Lindsey taking his princess away from him. But recently I had settled on a different reason. Charlie was rough-hewed and worked with his hands as well as his brain. Lindsey was wicked smart and a corporate climber, and the only blister he had ever had in his life was due to an ill-fitting golf glove. With the current situation, I suspected

Daddy thought Lindsey was the kind of guy who would cheat on me and that was why he put the house in my name only. As he had done the same for Robert before his shotgun wedding, it seemed like something Daddy would do.

I heard the rumble of the GTO followed by the sound of the garage door closing. The twins entered the kitchen through the laundry room and didn't immediately notice me. They had serious expressions on their faces.

"Do you think we can do it?" Angela asked Charles.

"Too many variables at the moment, but I will run some numbers...." Charles stopped mid-sentence when he saw me.

"Do what?" I asked sternly.

Charles and Angela exchanged glances, and Charles shook his head maybe a quarter of an inch in either direction, while Angela stayed silent.

I was right. Charles is the alpha dog and Angela is the front woman. How could I have missed that all of these years?

"We're just considering another business opportunity," Charles answered.

"Do I want to know about it?"

"Not really," Charles said. "It's still in the early stage and a longshot with minimal chance of success."

I knew they were holding something back, but right now I wanted to get something off my chest.

"I can't believe you two kept your little enterprise from me," I said as I shook my head disappointedly.

"Look, Mom," Angela started to say but I raised a finger which stopped her in mid-sentence.

"We will come back to this," I said. "Right now we need to discuss the situation with your grandmother."

The twins exchanged glances but, wisely, didn't speak.

"Your grandmother is insisting she will return to the Farm, and the doctor says she should not be left alone." My eyes bounced back and forth between my two children. "I'm proposing the three of us move in with Edna."

41

"Outstanding!" Charles said enthusiastically.

That was hardly the response I was expecting from my son. "Why is that outstanding?"

Charles shrugged. "We'll be right by our office and I'll be able to spend more time with Grandpa's cars."

My eyes moved to my daughter, who shrugged.

"I'm in," Angela said. "When are we making the move?"

"There is a chance they'll be releasing your grandmother tomorrow. If not then, the next day for sure."

Angela glanced at Charles. "We'll go pack."

Chapter Eight

I HAD DECIDED to pop in on my mother before meeting with my brother and drop off the items I had picked up from her house. They had moved her from the emergency room to the sixth floor. As I got off the elevator, I didn't need to ask the nurse at the station for directions. I recognized a laugh coming from a nearby room. For the first time all day, a smile broke across my face and I picked up my pace and headed down the hall.

In the room sitting on the bed was a plump, white-haired woman with leathery, sunbaked skin to rival my mom's. It was Aunt Tillie, my father's only sibling.

The table that rolled over the bed for Edna to take her meals was stacked high with photo albums and loose pictures. Tillie had one of the photographs in her hand and was leaning in to share it with Edna.

"God!" Tillie said a bit too loudly for a hospital setting. "You and my brother were so fall-down drunk that night...."

Aunt Tillie stopped when Edna nodded toward the door. Tillie turned, saw me and bounded off the bed and gave me a bone-crushing hug. "Well if it isn't Allison Clark, my favorite niece," she said in a rather odd cadence; enunciating each word slowly and carefully the same way the surgeon and the social worker had done with Mom.

"I'm your only niece," I replied as I tried to pry myself free of the hug. Finally, Tillie released me and returned to her spot at the end of the bed.

Sitting quietly in the corner, knitting, was Tillie's lifelong companion, Jolene Marshall. Although no blood relation, she had always been Aunt Jolene for as long as I could remember. Jolene looked up at me with a slightly confused expression as she studied me and processed the clues she had been given by Tillie. "Niece," she muttered. Then, after a few seconds, a light clicked on. "Allison Clark. Tillie's only niece." Aunt Jolene's face lit up like stadium lights as she motioned me over for a hug.

She felt frail and smaller than I remembered, and I was really glad Tillie had warned me about her failing condition. For me, the biggest difference was her hair. I always remembered her with shoulder-length or longer hair that was always well-styled and colored to hide the gray. Now her hair, what little there was of it, was snow-white and cut extremely short, military boot camp style, and didn't complement her oval face.

Tillie and Jolene were about as different as two people could be. Aunt Tillie was loud and bawdy while Aunt Jolene was soft-spoken and ladylike. Tillie could spend hours watching "SportsCenter" and arguing the case that the designated hitter had ruined major league baseball. Jolene, since her retirement from her tenured position in academia, preferred the company of a good book, and her conversations tended to focus around gourmet food and fine wines. For nearly 60 years, the two of them had been quite the pair.

"What are you doing here?" I asked.

"I figured this stubborn old biddy would put up a fight if they tried to farm her out to a nursing home, so we thought we'd move in for the duration."

"I don't need a babysitter," Edna said with a snort as she folded her arms across her chest.

We all ignored Mom's protests. "Great!" I said. "I was thinking about moving in with my kids...."

"Perfect!" Aunt Tillie said enthusiastically. "The more the merrier."

"Do I have any say in this?" Edna asked.

"No!" Tillie and I answered simultaneously.

"Is there enough space at the Farm for all of us?" Tillie asked.

"There are only four bedrooms," I answered. "I think we can convince Charles to stay in the doublewide or back at our house."

Aunt Tillie winked at me. "I'm sure he wouldn't be lonely. If you get my drift."

I got it and wasn't amused.

This grown child thing has its limits.

While I was sure Charles was sexually active and thought Angela probably was as well, I preferred the sweet bliss of ignorance.

Aunt Tillie saw the look on my face and shook her head. "The twins will be eighteen in two weeks and off to college in three months. They aren't babies anymore."

"You got that right," came Angela's voice from behind us.

All heads turned and we saw Charles and Angela in the doorway; close behind them was Paige, who, for once, wasn't reeking of self-confidence. Her eyes darted around the room and locked in on Jolene.

Charles had a Nike box under his arm.

"Oh, hell, yes," Tillie shouted as she bounded off the bed and headed toward her grandniece and grandnephew.

Angela was waiting for her hug with open arms, but Tillie blew right past her and snatched the Nike box out of Charles's hand. "Come to mama," Tillie said as she lifted the lid on the box and admired her new shoes. She sprinted past Angela again and returned to the edge of Edna's bed. She kicked off her work boots and put the sneakers on. "That's what I'm talking about."

"Nice to see you, too, Aunt Tillie," Angela said as she walked over and gave Aunt Jolene a peck on the cheek.

"Angela Clark," Jolene muttered to herself then her gaze moved to Charles. "Charles Clark." Finally, her eyes moved to Paige and she was stuck. Angela, seeing the problem, motioned Paige over.

"Aunt Jolene," Angela said gently. "This is my friend, Paige Thompson. You've never met her before."

A relieved expression covered Aunt Jolene's face as she put her knitting down. "It is nice to meet you, Paige."

45

"This is such an honor," Paige gushed and spoke much more quickly than her normal cadence. "I've read all of your books." Paige sheepishly pulled five heavily worn books out of her bag. "If it would not be too much trouble, would you sign these for me?"

"Of course, dear," Aunt Jolene said sweetly as she pulled a pen out of her bag and put the stack of books on her lap.

"I'm one of your biggest fans," Paige gushed. "I can't tell you the impact your writing has had on my life."

Aunt Tillie rolled her eyes. "Oh crap," she muttered. "Here we go again."

"What?" I asked.

"Because of her silly books, her starry-eyed fans put Jolene somewhere between Gandhi and God." Tillie shook her head. "I've seen her get the rock star treatment enough times over the years that it gets really, really old."

I, of course, knew that Aunt Jolene was a prolific and successful writer of self-help books and that a couple – "Forgive & Forget" and "The Choice" – had spent some time at the top of *The New York Times* bestsellers list. I had no idea she had such a rabid fan base. Then to discover that Paige Thompson, of all people, was an Aunt Jolene groupie was a real shocker.

"What's your name, dear?" Jolene asked sweetly.

Paige had a puzzled expression on her face, but Angela took over. "Her name is Paige," Angela said as she picked up the ringed binder with notes to help Jolene remember. Angela wrote "Paige" in bold letters and held it where Jolene could see it.

"Of course," Jolene muttered. "I just met Paige. She is Angela's friend."

Paige was speechless. Obviously her much-anticipated meeting with her hero had not gone anywhere close to what she had expected.

After signing the books, Jolene stood up and gave Angela a proper hug then did the same to Charles. Next, she turned her attention to Tillie, who had just finished lacing up her new sneaker. "Mathilda, you're being rude," Jolene snapped at my aunt.

Tillie ignored Jolene as she admired her new footwear in the mirror on the hospital room's bathroom door before sizing up Paige.

"Well, you're quite the looker," Tillie said with a mischievous gleam in her eyes. "When Angela said you were her 'friend'…"

Paige looked like a deer caught in the headlights. Subtle is a word seldom used to describe Aunt Tillie, and everyone in the room knew exactly what she was asking. Combined with her first meeting with a world-famous self-help author not being what she had envisioned, Paige was completely off balance.

Angela burst into a fit of giggles; Aunt Tillie frequently had that effect on her. "Paige and Charles are dating."

"Ah!" Tillie said as she looked at Paige again and nodded her approval before turning her attention back to her new footwear. "A perfect fit. Who won the pool?"

"Pool?" I demanded. "What pool?"

"Come here, you two," Tillie said as she hugged Charles and Angela. "We had a pool about when you would figure out what this pair was up to."

"Aunt Jolene bet you'd find out by accident on an event day," Charles said as he handed his aunt a handful of cash.

"You'd think by now I'd know better than to ever bet against this woman," Tillie said as she shook her head in disgust. "It's like she has some kind of sixth sense."

Jolene accepted the money, licked her thumb, and then started counting.

"What?" Charles protested. "You don't trust me?"

"Trust in God but tie your camel," Jolene said softly as she finished counting. She tucked the bills into her bra before returning to her knitting.

"I don't believe it," I said in disbelief as I felt my cheeks darken. "Exactly how dense do all of you think I am?"

An embarrassed silence settled over the hospital room.

Jolene smiled up at me. For the first time since I had entered the room she seemed to be back to her old self. "Ever since you were a little girl you have been one of the kindest and most trusting people in the world. You always see the best in everyone and assume they do the same. That makes it easy for you to be fooled." Jolene shook her head. "I know some would consider this a weakness." Jolene's eyes locked on my mom. "I consider it your greatest strength and I love you for it."

"No kidding," Tillie added as she kissed me on the forehead. "We're all kind of envious, actually."

"Thanks. I guess," I said as I read the expression my mom's face. Clearly Jolene's and Tillie's opinion of me was not shared by my mother. In her eyes I had always been a disappointment. A pushover. Too easily influenced by peer pressure. Afraid to take any chances. Always worried about what other people would think of me. Don't get me wrong, she has always loved me. But she had spent a lifetime trying to get me to stand up for myself, and I was always too timid and fearful of even trying.

I shook my head and turned to Charles. "With Tillie and Jolene here, would you mind staying alone in the trailer or at our house?"

"Sold," Charles said without a moment's hesitation as he glanced at Paige and smiled.

"The key word in that sentence was 'alone,'" I added with a stern glare.

"Define 'alone,'" Charles said with a mischievous grin.

"Don't make me park you on your grandmother's couch so I can keep an eye on you."

"I'm good with alone," Charles said innocently.

I shook my head and turned to the rest of the room. "Even if we relocate Charles, that would still leave five people and four bedrooms in chateau de O'Connor."

Everyone in the room laughed except me.

"What?" I demanded.

"Another perfect example of what makes Mom, Mom," Angela said with a chuckle.

"What does that mean?" I demanded.

"Oh, good lord, Allison," Edna muttered. "Tillie and Jolene have been sharing the same bed since before you were born."

I felt my cheeks darken again. Of course, I always had my suspicions, but the subject had always been taboo, especially around my father. It was one of those things that simply wasn't discussed.

CHAPTER NINE

GINO'S WAS A white tablecloth restaurant that had been in the same location for so long it had gone from prime real estate, to sketchy, to gentrified, to back to prime. It had survived in a changing demographic because it had always kept up with the times. In the early days it had catered to immigrants looking for great Italian food at a reasonable price. As the neighborhood changed, it added fire-baked pizzas. These days it thrived because it had the best wine cellar in town. A few years back, to cater to the new, young and affluent crowd that was showing up regularly, the third-generation owner, Marko Santino, had taken out some of the tables to increase the seating in the bar area. It had been a good call. When I entered, there were open tables on the restaurant side, but the "Wine Bar" was standing room only.

Robert and Gabrielle were sitting at a four-top table near the back and well away from any of the other diners. Neither noticed me at the hostess station. Robert was deeply engaged in an animated conversation with Marko Santino and a man in a white jacket whom I recognized as the head chef.

Marko had gone to high school with us and been a year behind Robert and a year ahead of me. With his olive complexion and a headful of jet black hair, dressed in his well-tailored suit, he looked like an Atlantic City pit boss.

Robert and the chef were leaning over and taking turns sampling food from an oversized platter in the center of the table then making their comments.

Gabrielle's eyes were focused on her husband.

Gabrielle was Robert's second wife and a stunningly beautiful woman exactly half my brother's age. I had never warmed to Gabrielle, but it was more an issue with my brother and me than with her. I would have preferred it if Robert had scratched his mid-life crisis itch by buying a sports car instead of tossing more than twenty years of marriage in the dumpster for a twenty-something trophy wife.

Personally, I'd never given her much of a chance. Every time I'm around her, all I could think about was that Gabrielle was like the steady stream of fluff that had passed through my husband's arms over the years. Jaw-dropping beautiful. A terror between the sheets and probably less reluctant than I to "try something new" when Lindsey suggested it.

I glanced around, looking for the always-prompt Beth Woodrow, who had never been late for anything in her entire life. Beth was clearly not in the half-empty dining room and I didn't see her in the crowded bar. I reached for my phone but dropped it back in my bag when I heard Beth's unmistakable cackle of a laugh. She could be cast as the witch in a Halloween haunted house. As I turned toward the wine bar I was intercepted by a young, dark-haired hostess who could have been the face on the cover of a Sicilian vacation package offer.

"Table for one?" the hostess asked hopefully.

"I'm going to go get my friend in the bar and then we will be joining them," I answered as I pointed at Robert and Gabrielle.

"Very good, ma'am," the hostess said politely.

Ma'am? Will this day ever end?

I weaved my way through the crowded bar. I found Beth sitting on a stool at a tiny high-top pub table, barely large enough to hold the empty wine glasses the overwhelmed server hadn't gotten to yet. Beth was bracketed by two handsome young men I instantly recognized.

David Woodrow, Beth's eldest, saw me coming and slid off of his stool to greet me. David was eight years older than the twins. Unlike Lindsey and me, Beth and her husband, Derek, immediately wanted to start a family. David had been born, tastefully, nine-and-a-half months after Beth's wedding day. David, like his mother, had become a lawyer and he looked the part. He was wearing a well-cut business suit, sported a professional haircut and had zero facial hair.

His brother Michael, also at the table with Beth, had followed along thirty-one months later. Michael had just graduated from Princeton and had shown no interest in law school. For the moment, he was planning to take a year off and see the world. Michael was scruffier and more casual than his older brother, but both aptly fit the description of tall, dark and handsome. Every woman in the room, attached or otherwise, was giving the Woodrow brothers the eye. David gave me a squeeze and a peck on the cheek as Beth located her bag.

"Nice to see you, Aunt Allison," David said as he turned me over to his brother for another hug and kiss.

Since I saw David fairly regularly, I patted him on the cheek, then turned my focus to his younger brother. It had been months since the last time I had seen Michael, and I held him at arm's length and examined him from head to toe. "You've grown up nicely. When are you starting your walkabout?"

"I'm flying to Amsterdam in three days," Michael said brightly.

I squeezed Michael's arms and gave him a shake. "Call your mother early and often."

"Okay," Michael answered with a wide grin on his face.

"I'm serious," I added. "I have no intention of listening to her weeping and wailing the entire time you're gone."

"I'll have you know," Beth said defensively as she pulled her purse over her shoulder, "I neither weep nor wail."

"Please," I said with a laugh. "You were inconsolable for two weeks every time one of these heart-breakers went off to college."

"I was not." Beth sniffed and started to tear up as she turned to Michael and poked him in the chest. "You had better call me at least three times a week."

"Relax, Mom," David said. "I've set up the GPS in little brother's phone so we can track him anywhere in the world in real time."

"I still want to hear your voice," Beth said as she straightened her shoulders and tried to regain a bit of dignity.

"Mom said you were meeting someone," David said mostly to change the subject.

"Yes," I answered. "My brother and his new wife." I nodded in the direction of Robert and Gabrielle.

Michael leaned around for a better look. "Isn't that Gabby McIntosh?"

"You know her?" I asked.

"Not nearly as well as Dave," Michael said with a laugh.

"Oh, no," Beth and David muttered in unison as they both closed their eyes and rubbed their foreheads.

"What does that mean?" I demanded.

"Didn't you take her to the prom your senior…" Michael stopped cold when he saw the look on his mother's and brother's faces.

"You didn't tell him?" David said as he shook his head in disbelief.

"He was away at college when they got married and the subject never came up."

"Hold on, hold on," I said with a stunned expression on my face as I wheeled on Beth. "Your son used to date my new sister-in-law and you didn't tell me!"

I spoke loudly enough, even over the din of voices and clanking of glassware in the crowded bar, that a few heads turned in my direction.

Beth leaned in and lowered her voice. "Well, I would say, judging by your reaction, it was the right call."

"She's actually very nice," David added.

Beth patted her eldest son on the cheek. "Don't help, sweetie." Beth tuned back to me. "But David is right. I found her to be perfectly delightful."

I glared at Beth. "Charles took Paige Thompson to the prom. If you and Derek ever break up, I'm sure Derek would find her delightful as well."

Beth sighed. "Fair point."

"Let's go see what's on Robert's mind," I said with a deep sigh.

Beth and I said our goodbyes to David and Michael, then weaved our way out of the wine bar and back to the hostess station. From there, we were escorted to Robert's table. As we approached, Robert had his eyes closed and appeared to be deep in thought. He licked his lips then shook his head. "I'm stumped."

"Tarragon," Gabrielle said softly. "Marko cut back on the thyme and replaced it with fresh tarragon in the white sauce."

Marko raised an eyebrow as he turned to Gabrielle. "And?"

Gabrielle took another small taste. "The wine is a bit drier." She nodded her approval. "You changed from your usual Pinot Bianco to maybe a Sauvignon Blanc?" she asked quizzically.

"You have an amazing palate." Marko clinked Gabrielle's wine glass with his own. "Do you approve?"

The question clearly made Gabrielle uncomfortable as her eyes danced back and forth between Marko and Robert. "It makes an interesting statement," Gabrielle finally answered diplomatically.

"But do you like it?" Marko demanded.

Gabrielle glanced at Robert for support. She obviously did not want to hurt Marko's feelings but she also wanted to give him an honest answer to his direct question.

"We both like it," Robert answered for the pair. "But, my old friend, what I think Gabrielle is too polite to say is your established clientele would howl if you made such a major change to one of the mainstays of your menu."

Marko was crestfallen. "Damn my grandfather and his Old World recipes."

"However, if this were my restaurant, Marko," Gabrielle said softly, "I would add it to the wine bar tapas menu. I think the younger crowd would really go for it."

Marko Santino shook a finger in Gabrielle's direction. "Brilliant, as usual."

"I'll get right on it," the chef said as he wheeled and returned to the kitchen.

Robert was beaming with pride.

Beth leaned in to me. "That's a bit unnerving."

"What do you mean?" I asked.

"Normally your brother looks like the Grim Reaper. If I'm not mistaken, he's actually smiling."

Beth had a point. His entire adult life, Robert had been a button-down bean-counter who took his work and his life seriously. The only time he ever seemed to relax and enjoy himself was when he was surrounded by good food and wine. Or, maybe, lately, Gabrielle.

At the sight of Beth and me, my brother immediately morphed back into his default demeanor. His smile vanished and was replaced with a scowl.

"I see you brought your reinforcements," Robert said as he glared at Beth.

I nodded in the direction of Gabrielle. "As did you."

Beth forced a thoroughly unconvincing fake smile. "Robert."

Beth Woodrow had the perfect temperament for a trial lawyer: smart, aggressive and relentless. She also didn't suffer fools gladly and hated bullies, and considered Robert both. In the nearly five decades that Beth and I had been best friends, she had often served as a buffer between Robert and me. She wouldn't let my brother walk over me and he hated her for it.

Marko gave me a friendly smile. "We have the lamb chops you like so much on the menu tonight."

"Thanks, Marko," I said as I looked past him and in the direction of my brother. "But with my mother in the hospital and all, I really can't stay."

Robert flinched.

"Give Edna my best and tell her she'll be in all our prayers," Marko said.

"I'll do that," I said as I took a seat directly across from my brother.

Before leaving, Marko poured Beth and me a glass of wine. He moved past Gabrielle, whose glass was untouched, then topped off Robert's.

I took a sip of wine and nodded my approval. I'm hardly a connoisseur but I knew that if Marko had brought it out to impress Robert and Gabrielle it was the good stuff.

After Marko was out of earshot, I turned to my brother. "You called this meeting," I said coldly.

"I thought we should discuss what we're going to do with Mother," Robert answered.

"It is all taken care of," I said flatly. "Aunt Tillie and Aunt Jolene are here and the twins and I are all moving into Mom's house. Between the five of us, she will never be alone." I picked up my napkin, dabbed my lips and started to get up. "Unless there is something else."

"Don't be coy, Allison," Robert snapped. "It's not in your nature."

I threw my napkin down on the tabletop. "We have a deal, Robert. You got control of the family business and I get Mom's estate. Get over it."

"The business turned out to be an empty box."

"Oh, gee," I said sarcastically as I scratched my head. "Who was the chief financial officer of O'Connor Industries before Daddy died?" I got a faraway look in my eyes. "Wait, wait. It's coming to me. That's right, it was you."

"Okay," Beth said calmly. "This has been a tough day for everyone. Let's all just take a step back and calm down."

Robert's eyes narrowed and he pointed a finger at Beth. "Says the shyster from the law firm that has been stealing from *our* family for decades." Robert put extra emphasis on the "our" as his eyes moved to me.

"What?" Beth demanded.

"You heard me," Robert said with a menacing tone.

Beth tried to maintain her composure, but it took all of her willpower to keep from reaching across the table and scratching Robert's eyes out. Instead she smiled sweetly. "So, the guy who was able to take a company that had been successful and profitable for half a century and run it into the ground in less than two years is looking for someone to blame."

Beth's comment drew blood, and Robert's face darkened. "I have a smoking gun," Robert said through gritted teeth as he reached for his phone.

Gabrielle put her hand on my brother's arm and gently said, "Don't do this, Robert."

"Do what?" I demanded.

Robert held up a finger to silence me then started talking into the phone. "Bobby?"

Beth and I exchanged befuddled glances. The only "Bobby" we knew was my nephew, Robert, Jr. After a less-than-stellar college career, where the rumor was he had spent more time high than in the classroom, it had taken him over four months to land a job after graduation. He had first tried to get on with a Big Four accounting firm in New York, but that had crashed and burned. Next he tried any major city, but none of them was interested in a mediocre student half a step away from rehab. Fortunately for Bobby, the O'Connor name still carried weight in this town, and he had taken the only job he was offered. An entry-level position at a local accounting firm.

We were only able to hear one side of the conversation, but Robert's tone was dead serious.

"I'm at Gino's Restaurant with your Aunt Allison. I need you to bring the documents."

There was something about Robert's tone that was somehow familiar, but I couldn't put my finger on it.

"Yes, now."

Robert was getting angrier and angrier as he listened to the other side of the conversation.

"Your objections are noted," Robert snarled. "Get your ass over here. Now."

Then it hit me. Robert was talking to Bobby in exactly the same dismissive manner our father used to talk to him.

"No," Robert said bluntly into his phone. "It would be awkward for Gabrielle."

What could possibly be more awkward for Gabrielle than being center stage for something like this? Glancing at her, she was white as a sheet and didn't look well.

Robert was seething, and his face was turning beet-red.

"Just do what you have to do." He ended the call and tossed his cellphone on the tabletop.

Before another word was spoken, Gabrielle leapt to her feet and bolted to the bathroom.

"Gabrielle!" I shouted. "Are you all right?"

"She's fine," Robert said coldly. "She's just had a bit of an upset stomach for the past few weeks."

Beth looked at Gabrielle's full wine glass and muttered, "Oh, my." Beth picked up Gabrielle's purse and a full water glass then turned to follow Gabrielle to the bathroom. "I'm going to check on her."

"I'm not finished with you yet," Robert barked.

"Oh, sweetie," Beth said as she batted her eyes in my brother's direction. "I've wanted to take you down a peg ever since I caught you spying on Allison and me in elementary school. Out of respect for your father and your sister, I've resisted the urge to eviscerate you many times."

"How dare you speak to me like that!" Robert shouted loudly enough that heads turned in not only the restaurant but in the wine bar as well.

"After Charlie passed, because I knew you didn't have the starch or brains of your father, I recommended we drop O'Connor Industries as a client, but I was outvoted." Beth leaned in and smiled. "If you think you can declare war on me and my law firm, you go right ahead and put on your big-boy pants and give it your best shot."

Whoa.

I knew Beth had never liked Robert very much, but I had no idea she had recommended dropping the family business as a client when the reins had passed to my brother. Then it hit me. The original agreement Beth had drafted had appeared to be very one-sided at the time, but it wasn't. She figured Robert wasn't up to running

O'Connor Industries. She put some distance between my mom and me by giving Robert complete control and thereby shielding our assets.

Brilliant.

"I'll go with you," I said as I tossed my napkin on the table in front of me and glared at my brother.

We arrived in the ladies' room and could hear Gabrielle retching in one of the stalls. After a few awkward moments, Beth and I heard the toilet flush and the stall door opened. Gabrielle emerged with her face blotchy and her eyes tearing. Beth handed the younger woman the glass of water. "Here, rinse your mouth out."

Gabrielle followed Beth's instructions, then surveyed the damage in the mirror. She looked awful.

"Does Robert know?" Beth asked gently as she handed Gabrielle a paper towel.

Gabrielle burst into tears.

CHAPTER TEN

"**D**OES HE KNOW?" Beth repeated.

Gabrielle shook her head.

"You have to tell him," Beth said as she leaned next to Gabrielle with her back against the sink.

"Tell him what?" I demanded.

"I can't," Gabrielle sobbed. "You saw him. He's under so much pressure it might break him."

Beth laughed. "I've known Robert for longer than you've been breathing. He's tougher than he looks." Beth handed Gabrielle another paper towel. "Have you two discussed the possibility?"

Gabrielle shrugged. "In general terms."

"And?" Beth motioned for Gabrielle to continue.

"At his age, he obviously had some concerns."

"But?"

"But," Gabrielle said, "he was open to the idea."

"Oh! My! God!" I shouted as I finally caught up. I gave Gabrielle a gentle hug. "Congratulations."

"Thanks," Gabrielle answered weakly. "With Edna and all, when do you think I should tell him?"

"No time like the present," I said as I gently put my hand in the small of Gabrielle's back and guided her toward the bathroom door.

Gabrielle hesitated. "I'm not sure this is the right time."

"Believe me, Gabby," I said gently. "This family could use some good news today."

Gabrielle puffed out her cheeks, then released a big sigh. "Okay."

Gabrielle opened her purse and pulled out a hair brush and lipstick then turned back to the mirror and tried some damage control. It was a losing battle.

"Was that Bobby he was talking to?" I asked.

"Yes," she answered. Having her secret out seemed to release some of the internal pressure on her, and she was rapidly returning to her normal youthful self.

"What's Robert up to?" Beth asked.

Gabrielle thought for a moment and was conflicted as to whether she should say any more.

"That's okay," I said gently as I found some tissues in my purse and handed them to her. "It looks like we'll find out soon enough."

"Robert hired Bobby's accounting firm to audit the company's books," Gabrielle blurted.

"What did Bobby find?" Beth asked with a concerned expression on her face.

"He didn't tell me." Gabrielle shook her head and her eyes locked on mine. "But he was furious."

"At me?" I asked.

"No, no, no," she answered quickly. "He was angry at your father."

"My father? Why?"

"I have no idea," Gabrielle answered. "But he said it might be the answer to all of our financial problems."

"How?" I asked.

Gabrielle glanced at Beth then back at me. "He said he was going to get money from Beth's law firm."

"Really?" Beth said in disbelief. "How?"

Gabrielle shook her head again.

Beth started to say something but stopped when I put my hand on her arm. She looked at me and I shook my head. She understood. If Robert wanted to pick a fight with her, that was one thing. But, Gabrielle didn't need to get caught in the crossfire. All things considered, she had more than enough on her plate at the moment.

"We can deal with Bobby later," I said as I straightened Gabrielle's blouse, then gave her another hug. "Right now you need to break the good news to your husband."

Gabrielle nodded weakly then headed toward the door.

We returned to the table where Robert was waiting. Beth motioned for Marko to join us. Robert had braced himself for a battle, but the body language he was picking up from us was all wrong. Instead of asking any questions, he sat quietly and let the events unfold.

When Marko arrived, Beth said, "Gabrielle has an announcement."

Tears filled her eyes and her lip quivered. "I'm pregnant."

Robert was a combination of thunderstruck and paralyzed. Finally, he regained his composure, jumped to his feet and gave Gabrielle a hug. "Oh my God! That is wonderful news."

Marko pulled a Montecristo Classic from his coat pocket and handed it to Robert. "You old dog, you!" Marko's deep baritone caused heads to turn in the dining room and the wine bar. When Marko saw he had an audience, he put his arm around Gabrielle and did a flawless impersonation of a broadcaster calling a goal in a soccer match. "Bambino-o-o-o-o-o-o!"

A round of applause went up, and David and Michael rushed over to join the celebration.

CHAPTER ELEVEN

AT LEAST FOR the moment, my brother and I declared a truce. Angela, Charles and Paige had joined the festivities and were on the other side of the room sharing a laugh with Gabrielle and Beth's two sons. Marko had broken out a bottle of his best bubbly and had also given Gabby, Paige and the twins flutes of sparkling water so they could join in. Everyone agreed there was no reason to spoil this happy moment. Plus, it gave everyone the chance to lower the temperature and let their blood pressure return to normal.

I wandered over to my brother and clinked his champagne flute with mine. "Congratulations."

Robert was still a bit off balance. He drew in a breath and shook his head. "I had no idea."

Finally, I asked. "What's going on?"

Robert finished his champagne in single gulp and shook his head again. "It's bad, Allie, really bad."

"What is?"

"Our father was stealing from the company."

I felt my eyes go large and my mouth fell open. I pulled my brother farther away from the others and lowered my voice. "What do you mean, Daddy was stealing from the company?"

"Apparently he had been skimming money into a secret account for decades."

"How much money are we talking here?"

"Millions, Allie, millions," Robert answered.

"You were CFO for over thirty years. How is it possible that he could have done it without you noticing?"

"You know Dad," Robert said with a laugh. "He conducted business with a handshake and he kept most of the details in his head and never wrote anything down. I spent my first ten years just trying to sort out the tangled web of deals he was committed to and trying to get them on paper." Robert shook his head. "You remember when he bought the Outland Mall?"

"That was all he talked about for over a year," I answered.

"The entire initial contract was on a cocktail napkin, which he handed to me and then ordered me to cut an eight-figure check." Robert shook his head. "He left it up to me to figure out the details without giving me the specifics of what he had actually agreed to. I felt like a mushroom."

"Mushroom?"

"Yeah," Robert answered. "To grow mushrooms you keep them in the dark, feed them manure, then when they grow up you cut them off at the root."

It had been obvious for years that my father and my brother were often at odds over the direction of the family business. But I had always thought it was just a difference in their style. Daddy was a larger-than-life wheeler-dealer who loved to have the spotlight shining on him. Robert was the detail guy, the numbers guy, the guy who preferred to avoid the limelight. I had always thought they had made a great team with their personal strengths counterbalancing the weaknesses of the other. Being detached from the day-to-day operations of O'Connor Industries and never that close to Robert because I couldn't stand to be around his odious first wife, Lilith, I had missed the pain he was in.

Between being trapped in a job he hated and his shotgun marriage to a gold-digger.... Then it hit me. It was no accident Robert had filed his divorce papers within a week of Daddy's funeral.

"Daddy made you stay married to Lilith, didn't he?" I asked softly.

"Yeah," Robert answered. "I can still hear his lectures on how a man has to take care of his children." Robert shook his head.

"That's what makes you a man," I added.

"I guess you've heard that lecture as well."

"Many times," I answered. "Why didn't you just quit?"

"He had me in golden handcuffs, Allie," Robert said with a shrug. "He paid me double what I could have gotten anywhere else and he dangled future control of the company in front of me."

"Still, Robert, if you were so miserable…"

"Plus, he threatened me."

"Excuse me?"

"He said if I ever left the company or divorced Lilith, he would cut me out of his will and leave everything to you."

"Me?!"

"That's what he said."

"I had no idea, Robert."

My brother just shrugged.

A heavy silence settled over us as we were both lost in our thoughts. Oddly, considering how the evening had started, I hadn't felt this close to my brother in years.

"How did you find out about this?"

Robert chuckled and shook his head. "A check bounced."

"Excuse me?"

"Dad had his personal slush fund set up on autopay to issue a check for ten thousand dollars a month to Beth's law firm. Without him around to add money to the account, it took two years, but it finally was depleted." Robert chuckled. "I got a call, from a bank I didn't even know we did business with, to tell me about the insufficient funds issue."

"Do you think Beth had anything to do with this?"

"No," Robert answered. "These payments started back when she was still in diapers."

"Where's the money now?" I asked.

"I have no idea," Robert answered. "All I know is it went to Beth's law firm, and if I have to, I'll subpoena their records to get some answers."

"Subpoena?" I said with a startled expression on my face. "You're actually going to try to sue Beth?"

"Not Beth," Robert answered. "Her law firm. But, I hope it doesn't come to that. They've been O'Connor Industries' lawyers for over five decades. They have a fiduciary obligation to us and I'm hoping to get some answers without it getting ugly. Until then, I have no idea where the money has gone or what it was used for."

"What is Bobby bringing over?"

"The smoking gun," Robert answered.

I nodded. "A copy of the bank records."

"Some of them," Robert corrected. "Some are so old they're going have to do a physical archive search in a warehouse somewhere." Robert pointed to the door, and a smile broke across his face when he saw his son Bobby. It quickly turned into a frown when he saw the person behind him.

Robert's ex-wife, Lilith O'Connor.

CHAPTER TWELVE

"WHAT THE HELL is she doing here?" I hissed at my brother as I felt all of the goodwill of the past forty-five minutes starting to quickly seep away.

"Certainly not my idea," Robert answered. "Bobby is living with her, and I specifically told him not to bring her with him."

"Then why is she here?"

Robert shook her head. "If I had to guess, she probably overheard me talking to him and bullied him to bring her along."

Sadly, that sounded exactly like something Lilith O'Connor would do and exactly the way Bobby would react. Like me, my nephew didn't like to make waves and had my go along to get along attitude as his default mode. In my case, I only had to deal with my brother; in Bobby's case, he had spent his life being double-teamed by Robert and Lilith.

For her age, Lilith O'Connor was an extremely attractive woman. Thanks to some rather extensive and expensive plastic surgery and a few hours a day at the gym, she looked at least ten years younger than her actual age. She was wearing a shimmering black cocktail dress and Christian Louboutin shoes with their signature three-inch red highlighted heels. It was clear now why it had taken Bobby so long to get here. Wanting to make a splash entrance, Lilith needed time to look that good.

I made eye contact with Angela then pointed in the direction of the hostess podium. As soon as my daughter saw Lilith O'Connor she muttered an obscenity that even I could lip-read from across the room. Angela quickly turned to Gabrielle and gathered her up along with Charles and Paige and headed toward the Wine Bar side of the restaurant. The group was giving Lilith a wide enough berth that they did not have to speak as they made their way to a side exit.

I leaned into my brother and whispered. "Angela is taking Gabrielle home."

Robert nodded his thanks but he couldn't take his eyes off the approaching duo. He was furious. "I told you not to bring her," he growled as he looked ready to strangle his only son.

Poor Bobby couldn't make eye contact with his father and seemed to be bracing himself for a verbal onslaught. "I'm sorry, Dad."

Robert started to speak but thought better of it and calmed himself before he made a scene. "We'll discuss this later," he said softly. "Do you have the documents?"

Bobby nodded, then put his briefcase on an unoccupied table and flipped the latches open. Inside was an oversized manila envelope, which he handed to his father.

"Hello, Allison," Lilith O'Connor said sweetly as she joined the group. "I haven't seen you in such a long time. We really need to do lunch sometime and catch up."

Yeah. Right.

Before I could respond, Beth joined us and nodded. "Lilith."

"Beth." Lilith answered coldly.

I wanted to pull Beth aside and give her a heads-up, but Robert handed her the envelope before I could say anything.

"What's this?" she asked.

"Proof that your law firm has been receiving substantial and off-the-record cash payments for nearly fifty years," Robert answered. "As the CEO of O'Connor Industries, I am formally requesting an explanation."

Beth carefully opened the envelope and pulled out the stack of document and quickly read the first few pages. It was a printed record from a small local bank that went back over a decade and indicated the payee was Bertram Ruggles, c/o Ruggles, Knapp and Woodrow, LLP. While her outward expression and tone of her voice never changed, I knew Beth well enough to know inside she was ready to explode.

Robert wasn't the only one who wanted an explanation.

"You won't be able to get any immediate answers from me, but I'll discuss it with my partner," Beth said as she returned the papers to the envelope, then glanced at Bobby. "Are these my copies?"

"Yes," Bobby answered meekly as he glanced at his mother for support. Lilith O'Connor was on top of the world as she watched Beth and Robert squaring off.

"I assume you have the originals and Photostats of the checks?"

"My company does," Bobby answered. "They are in our safe."

"I expect a full accounting of this," Robert said flatly, with a smug grin on his face.

I had often suspected my friend Beth has some kind of multiple personality disorder. One minute she was herself and then, like a switch had been flipped somewhere in her brain, she would mutate into Super Lawyer. Fortunately, since our relationship was strictly personal, I seldom saw the metamorphosis firsthand. But when I did, I always found it a bit unnerving to watch a warm, funny friend I'd known my entire life turn into a cold-blooded attack dog. As I watched her shift from "Beth" into "Elizabeth Woodrow, Esq.," I could almost feel the temperature in the room drop.

I was mesmerized as she shrugged and then tossed the envelope on the table next to Bobby's briefcase like it was a soiled napkin waiting for the busboy to pick up. "If you are entitled to a full accounting, then I'm sure my firm will be happy to provide it."

Elizabeth Woodrow's answer stunned Robert. It was not at all what he had expected. "How could I not be entitled to an explanation?"

"I have no idea at the moment," Elizabeth answered with a shrug as she took complete control of the discussion. It was easy to see why she was one of the most feared litigators in the country. I had heard just having her at the negotiating table was often enough to discourage her opponent from taking their chances with a jury.

"What the hell does that mean?" Robert demanded.

"I don't yet know the source of this money," Elizabeth Woodrow, Esq., replied with a disinterested shrug. "Is it O'Connor Industries?

If yes, then of course, with Ruggles, Knapp and Woodrow as your legal representatives, you will be entitled to a full and complete accounting."

"Where else could it possibly come from?" Robert said as his voice got louder as his frustration continued to build.

This reaction brought a small smile to Elizabeth's face and caused her to speak even more softly, forcing Robert to lean in closer to hear her clearly. "What if the funds were drawn from a different corporate entity which has no connection to O'Connor Industries? Or, from the personal account of Charlie O'Connor?" Elizabeth Woodrow, Esq., put her hand over her mouth to suppress a yawn to show exactly how seriously she took this matter.

Nice touch.

"I'll make some inquires at the firm and get back to you."

"When?" Robert demanded as his face started to flush.

"Give me a few weeks," Elizabeth Woodrow, Esq., answered in barely a whisper as she checked her watch. "I really need to be going, I have court tomorrow."

Lilith O'Connor cleared her throat and a wicked smile covered her face. "You might want to give it more of your attention."

"Why is that?" Elizabeth Woodrow, Esq., asked as she picked up the envelope again and roughly folded it in half so it would fit in her purse.

"No matter if the money came from O'Connor Industries, a different corporation or Charlie O'Connor's personal account, this was a clear effort to conceal money."

"We don't know that yet," Elizabeth Woodrow, Esq., answered.

Robert glared at Bobby. Clearly my brother had instructed my nephew to keep this information away from Lilith, but that had not happened. I didn't want to be around the next time father and son were alone.

"I spoke to my attorney," Lilith said triumphantly, "and he thinks we may have a case of asset concealment and we should explore the possibility of renegotiating my divorce settlement."

Elizabeth laughed out loud as she wiped a tear of laugher from her eye. "Really?"

"What do you mean?" Lilith asked defensively.

Elizabeth turned to Robert. "Did you know about this account at any time you were married?"

"No."

"Have you ever received any money from this account?"

Robert saw where this was heading and, for the first time tonight, looked like he now wanted to kiss Elizabeth instead of shoot her.

The enemy of my enemy is my friend.

"No," Robert answered.

"Did you ever do anything to conceal this account?"

"On the contrary, I'm the one who uncovered it."

Elizabeth Woodrow, Esq., wheeled on Lilith. "So you've found a lawyer who is willing to try to reopen a settled divorce proceeding from two years ago because your ex-husband didn't know his father had a checking account that he never received a penny from which may be perfectly legal and have a simple explanation?" Beth leaned in to Lilith. "Let me guess. Your lawyer is billing you by the hour instead of offering to take a percentage of the recovery?"

"How did you know that?" Lilith said with considerably less confidence than she had previously.

"Do you know why?"

Lilith squared her shoulders defiantly but didn't answer.

"You're hoping for a seven-figure judgment, and if your lawyer thought he had even the slightest chance of winning, he would have offered to take the case on a contingency basis instead of billing his hourly rate," Elizabeth Woodrow, Esq., said with a snort as she shook her head. "I always thought you were nothing more than a money-grubbing lowlife, but I was wrong. You're also a fool."

Elizabeth Woodrow, Esq., turned to Robert. "Why don't you share your good news?"

"What good news?" Lilith demanded.

Robert was beaming. "Gabrielle is pregnant," Robert answered triumphantly.

The look on Lilith's face was almost enough to make easily the worst day of my life worthwhile.

Almost.

CHAPTER THIRTEEN

ETH AND I were sitting at the table where we had had our initial chat with Robert. While she had held her emotions in check while eviscerating my brother and my former sister-in-law, now it was just the two of us. Beth was furious as she thumbed through the documents Bobby had given her.

"I'm a goddamn named partner at Ruggles, Knapp & Woodrow who brings in more billable hours every year than the other two named partners combined," she hissed as she reached for her wine glass again. "How is this even possible?"

From a lifetime of experience, I knew that at this point in her meltdown, all questions were rhetorical and my input really wasn't required or appreciated. My best option was to keep quiet, nod sympathetically and let her rant until the storm passed.

"I mean," Beth continued, "how does something like this not come up in a partners' meeting?"

I just shook my head and shrugged.

Beth did a double take when she saw the expression on my face, then burst out laughing. She gave my arm a pat and said, "Thank you."

"What are friends for?"

"Still," Beth said as she picked up her wine glass and clinked mine with hers before taking another sip. "This is so weird."

"Is this something I should be concerned about?"

"Yes and no," Beth said as she made a face then waved her hand back and forth in front of her. "You obviously have no legal liability for something your father did."

"I sense a 'however' in my near future," I said glumly.

"However," Beth said with a laugh. "I think I now know Robert's endgame."

"That sounds ominous."

"Yeah," Beth answered, then added, "It is ominous, and it could get very, very ugly."

I motioned for her to continue.

"Robert is absolutely desperate and is looking for any lifeline." She took another sip of wine. "I think this thing," Beth said as she pointed to the documents in front of her, "and threatening to challenge your mother's will are just a smokescreen to buy him time to right his finances."

"You lost me," I said.

"I think he's hoping to use multiple lawsuits where, at least on paper, he would have a chance to regain his personal financial footing."

"Why?"

"The bank will be reluctant to write off paper in the amount Robert owes if there is even a small chance they will be made whole or even close to it. This is especially true if the paper is so awful that there are no potential buyers of the note unless they practically give it away. Robert's loan may be bad, but for the bank it becomes smarter to hold on to the loan, let interest and fees accumulate, and hope for the best."

"Where does that leave me?" I asked.

Beth's eyes locked on mine as she took both of my hands in hers. "If there is even a chance of him getting a potential payday from Edna's estate, and no buyer of the paper on the horizon, the bank will be willing to let the loan ride. That would mean the longer Robert could drag out contesting Edna's will, the better it will be for him."

"And the worse it will be for me."

"Exactly."

"Is there anything I can do?" I asked softly.

"Are you financially in a position to make a low-ball bid to buy the bank notes?" Beth asked.

"I'm filing for divorce."

"How about after the smoke clears?"

"Why would I want to do that?"

"You already hold ten percent of the stock and Edna has already drawn up the papers to divide her thirty percent stake equally between Angela, Charles and Bobby. If you could acquire Robert's sixty percent, combined with the thirty percent you and your kids hold, you would control ninety percent of the company."

"Again, why would I want to do that?" I asked.

"It would keep the company in the family, it would get your brother out of debt and able to make a fresh start. But, most importantly, you could put Angela and Charles in charge of O'Connor Industries."

I made an involuntary snort. One of my least attractive habits. "You mean my twins who are still three years below the legal drinking age and off to college this fall?"

"I've been working around them for a couple of years now, and Charles has one of the best business minds I've ever seen. Angela is a force and would be the perfect new face for the company." Beth took another sip of wine. "O'Connor Industries couldn't afford to hire a senior management team at their level."

"What about college?" I asked.

"Overrated," Beth answered.

"Seriously?"

Beth shrugged. "About half of the richest people in the country are college dropouts. Bill Gates. Steve Jobs. Mark Zuckerberg. The Google guys."

I shook my head in disbelief. "You think my kids are at that level?"

Beth shrugged again. "I've been involved in some pretty heavy business transactions the past two decades and I've never seen anyone impress me more than that pair. With them, the sky is the limit."

I leaned back in my chair and let all of this sink in. While I had less than zero interest in being involved with O'Connor Industries, this was something to consider.

"How much would I need?" I asked softly.

Beth pulled out her phone and opened the calculator app and her fingers danced across the screen. Satisfied, she turned her phone around and showed me the number.

I almost fell off of my chair. "There is no way I could come up with that kind of money."

"We could talk to Edna...."

"No," I said before Beth could finish her thought. "Even if I had total control of my mom's assets, which I don't, it wouldn't come close to that number. Besides, Robert has always been her perfect little angel, and at this point her finding out he's really an asshole might be enough to kill her."

"I don't think you're giving Edna enough credit, Allie," Beth said.

I shook my head. "The answer is still no."

"Okay," Beth said. "I just wanted you to know all of your options."

"Thanks," I said weakly. "But that is way out of my league."

"Then I guess we'll just have to ride out the storm," Beth said. "I wonder if Edna realizes how much she has favored your brother over you for all of these years?"

"It has always been a blind spot for her," I said with a chuckle. "What I always thought was funny was how much she disliked you."

"In her defense," Beth answered, "we were quite the handful when we were younger."

I took a sip of wine and started laughing. "Remember when we stole that backhoe and drove it around all of those homes under construction? We were lucky we didn't end up in jail."

Beth shrugged. "I knew we would have avoided juvie."

"How can you be so sure?"

"We could have pled attractive nuisance since the driver had left the keys in the ignition."

"Gee," I said with a laugh. "You were born to be a lawyer, weren't you?"

"Pretty much," Beth answered.

"I am so glad the security guard called my dad instead of my mom."

"Charlie always thought we were hilarious," Beth said as she started packing up her things. "I think he liked me as much as your mom hated me."

"For whatever the reason," I added. "You were the only one of my friends my dad ever took a shine to."

"My mom did work for Charlie. I think since my dad had died so young he wanted me to have a father figure in my life."

I snorted. "Remember when my mom found out about the backhoe, assumed it was all your doing, and read your mom the riot act?"

Beth chuckled again. "I think my mom learned some new words that day."

"Speaking of your mom, how is Betty doing?"

"Unlike Edna, she really likes her assisted living facility." Beth made a face.

"What?"

"I forgot to call the facility this morning." She pulled out her phone and sent a text to her personal assistant, Wilma, to remind her in the morning.

"Is there a problem?"

"I doubt it," Beth answered. "Someone in their accounting department left me a message about a late payment. I only get nervous when one of the floor nurses calls."

"Is Betty still hustling the other old ladies at euchre?" I asked.

"They have a new rule that they can't play for money anymore," Beth answered. "But I've noticed my mom always has more than her fair share of pudding cups at meals."

"What's our next step?" I asked as I looked around to be sure I wasn't forgetting anything.

"I'll talk to Bertram Ruggles about these checks. He was your dad's personal lawyer for, like, forever."

"He's still around?" I said in amazement. "He has to be, what, a hundred-and-fifty years old?"

"He's ninety-three and still sharp as a tack," Beth said as she reached for her jacket and slipped it on. "He still comes into the office a few hours each week. I'll set up an appointment and see if we can at least get this part of the issue off the table."

"Will that be a possibility?" I asked.

"Unknown, but very likely," Beth answered. "You don't get to be the first name on the door of the largest law firm within two hundred miles by being either shady or stupid. If Bert set this up, you can bet it will be bulletproof and one hundred percent legit."

CHAPTER FOURTEEN

I DROVE THROUGH the gate at the Farm and as I headed around back, I noted that Charlie's GTO was parked in front of the doublewide and the lights in the trailer were out. Being a school night, I took that as a win and decided not to investigate it any further. I pulled into a spot next to Aunt Tillie's massive fire-engine-red crew cab pickup truck with tasteful flames painted on the doors and fenders. It dwarfed my sedan. With its oversized wheels, and the way the suspension was jacked up, I suspected I would need a step ladder to get inside.

Then I smiled as I imagined Aunt Jolene Marshall, author, self-help guru and academic, riding around in this gas-guzzling beast. Because of Jolene's career path, she has had to be careful about what she says and does, but the same rules do not apply to Aunt Tillie. Jolene can sit back and watch Tillie do outrageous things she can't and smile and shrug when her stick-up-the-butt Ivy League colleagues tut-tut and roll their eyes. Sometimes I thought that was the reason their relationship worked.

The house was quiet, but there was a flickering of blue light coming from the great room. I suspected Tillie was catching up on the late-night West Coast baseball score before calling it a day.

I entered through the kitchen and saw Tillie sprawled out on the L-shaped couch in the media end of the massive room with her feet up on the coffee table. She had a longneck in one hand and the TV remote in the other. She gave me a weak wave without taking her eyes off the screen. As I suspected, she had the sports channel on.

I dropped my purse and keys on the kitchen counter and opened the restaurant-sized refrigerator and smiled. Aunt Tillie liked to say she never arrived with a handful of gimme and a mouthful of much obliged. In addition to a case of beer, with two bottles missing, there were deli bags, blocks of gourmet cheeses, fresh herbs and vegetables that hadn't been there earlier. Knowing my aunts, if it had been up to Tillie, they never would have gotten past the beer and chips aisles. But Jolene loved to cook. Just the idea of one of her omelets was enough to make my mouth start to water.

I grabbed a beer and joined Tillie on the couch.

"Angela and Jolene already in bed?" I asked as I tried to twist the cap off of the beer bottle but failed. Tillie took the bottle away from me.

"Give me that before you hurt yourself." She effortlessly twisted the cap off and tossed it next to the other two caps and the empty bottle on the coffee table and handed me my beer.

"How's Jolene doing?"

"Good days and bad days," Tillie answered without taking her eyes off the screen.

Remembering Jolene's performance at the hospital, I asked, "Was today a good day or a bad one?"

Tillie, seeing this was going to be more than an aunt and her niece watching baseball highlights, used the remote to turn the volume down to barely a whisper and tossed the remote on the cushion next to her.

"Today was a very bad day," she answered. "On travel days, JoJo tends to sundown...."

"Sundown?"

"She gets worse as the day wears her down. By the time the dinner dishes are put away she is at her low ebb." Tillie sighed. "Seeing you and your kids really perked her up."

"I heard her muttering to herself a lot today," I said softly. "Should I be worried?"

Tillie laughed. "No. It's a coping thing she does."

"I don't follow," I said.

"Her memory works much better when she uses more of her senses. In lucid moments she'll make notes she can see and use later when she feels herself slipping. We've got Post-it Notes all over the house to remind her of things. It also helps her if she hears herself say things out loud." Tillie took a sip of beer. "It's a bit unnerving at first, but you'll get used to it."

"Plus," I said with a chuckle, "It helps when she's got someone gently giving her clues."

"Nice." Tillie clinked my bottle. "So you noticed the 'my favorite niece Allison' comment."

"Yeah," I answered with a smile.

"We worked on it on the drive over. We agreed that would be a trigger phrase for us and I had her write it down and say it out loud a few dozen times."

"It looked like you prepped Angela and Charles."

Tillie nodded. "There is nothing more unnerving, especially to young people, than to look at somebody you love and have known your entire life and realize they don't have a clue who you are." Tillie sighed. "I didn't want your kids to face that possibility without at least a heads-up."

"It must be tough on Jolene as well."

"Yeah," Tillie answered. "She can totally flip out when it starts to happen. By the way, it was really great the way Angela picked up on that when Charles' girlfriend came into the room and defused the situation before Jolene slipped into panic mode."

At the time, I hadn't noticed, but Tillie was absolutely correct.

"There's a lot of her granddaddy in that one," Tillie said.

"A little too much sometimes," I answered.

"Yeah, I hear ya," Tillie answered with a laugh. "My brother could really be a turd hammer when he wanted to."

I nearly choked on my beer. It had been a while since I had been around my aunt and I had forgotten some of what the family calls "Tillie-isms." The "t-hammer" was a perfect example. I wasn't exactly sure what it meant, but it was an image that would be hard to ever get out of my head.

"Do you know anything about Daddy making secret monthly payments to Beth's law firm?"

Tillie shook her head. "No. How much are we talking about?"

"Currently $10,000 a month."

"Currently?" How long has he been making these payments?"

"It's starting to look like maybe as long as fifty years."

Tillie shrugged and took another sip of her beer. "That certainly sounds like something my big brother would do."

I was a bit taken aback by Aunt Tillie's passive response. "How so?" I asked.

"Charlie was many things, but mostly he was a man of his word. If he made a promise and a commitment, then he would stick to it."

"So he lived by some special personal cowboy code of the West?"

"More like a Don Corleone code of the building trades," Tillie said with a laugh. "If you did business with your daddy, screw him once and he would never forgive or forget it. He was either your best friend or your worst enemy."

"So, what would be so important to him that he would be making large cash payments to a law firm for five decades?"

Tillie shook her head. "I have no idea. Have you talked to Bert Ruggles? If anyone would know, it would be him."

"No," I answered. "We just found out about this tonight. But since the checks were made out to Ruggles, it would be a pretty safe bet he knows."

"How did you find out?"

"From Robert. He's threatening to sue Beth's law firm to get the money back."

"This could get ugly," Tillie said softly then chuckled. "Beth tangling with your brother for a big sack of cash has pay-per-view potential. Have you told Edna?"

"God, no," I answered quickly. "The way she's always covered for Robert and his shortcomings his entire life; in her present health, it might kill her."

"There's more to the story about why Edna cuts your brother so much slack," Tillie said – then realized she had made a mistake. "But, I've already said too much."

82

"Tillie?" I said in disbelief. "You've never kept anything from me before."

"Oh, honey," Tillie said with a laugh. "If there were any more skeletons in this family's closet we'd need to be renting a storage unit."

"Like what, for example?"

"It's not my place to say, but you may want to have some serious conversations with your mother while you still can."

"Well," I said wistfully, "Mom and I have never been much good at communicating."

"Not your fault, kiddo. Edna can be pretty pigheaded," Tillie answered as her eyes focused back on the TV screen.

"I've always gotten the impression she was disappointed with me."

Tillie waved that thought off. "Naw. She loves you and is proud of you. She just wishes you were a bit tougher and made better choices."

"What does that mean?" I asked.

"Have you ever read any of Jolene's books?" Tillie asked.

I felt my cheeks darken. While I love a good novel, nonfiction puts me to sleep. I had tried multiple times to read Aunt Jolene's books but had never gotten past the first few pages.

Tillie glanced at me and snorted. "They have the same effect on me." She finished her beer and rose to her feet. "You ready for another?"

I shook my head. Tillie headed to the refrigerator and came back with a fresh bottle and fell heavily back on the couch.

"Jolene has this theory that we're all animals who have evolved too quickly and we're controlled by primal instincts."

"Controlled?"

"Yeah," Tillie answered as she twisted the cap off of the bottle. "Our lizard brain makes us act and react illogically."

"Lizard brain? Really?"

"It's her theory, not mine," Tillie answered with a laugh. "Old fight-or-flight instincts paralyze us and stop us from doing what is logical."

"For example?"

"In general or more personal?" Tillie asked.

I chuckled. "I've had a pretty rough day. Let's start in general and see how that goes."

CHAPTER FIFTEEN

"HAVE YOU EVER had the hair stand up on the back of your neck when you hear a strange noise?"

"Of course."

"That's your lizard brain sending up a red flag to get your attention to possible danger in the area. It's a self-preservation reaction that causes your old fight-or-flee instinct to kick in. The problem is, if you are unaware your lizard brain is making choices and don't override it with your intellect, then it goes crazy."

"For example?"

"Jolene believes millions and millions of people make unconscious bad choices every day because they don't realize their lizard brain is giving them bad advice." Tillie took a sip of her beer. "On the extreme, this bad advice can cause people to never leave their home, become hoarders and seldom, if ever, interact with other homo sapiens. In the middle, you have people who won't set foot on an airplane, drive a car during rush hour or who get stage fright. At the low end are people uncomfortable in a crowd or visiting new places."

"Interesting," I replied. "But the instant you became aware of the lizard brain, wouldn't it lose all of its power over you?"

"Not necessarily," Tillie answered. "Sometimes it stops you from doing something that keeps you from being injured or worse. It keeps you from walking off of cliffs. It's what wakes you up in the middle of the night when your house is on fire. After a few positive experiences, it builds up credibility. Because it has proven itself to be a guardian and on your side, some people mistakenly come to rely on it."

"So how do you separate the good advice from the bad?"

"Ah. That's the $64,000 question and where free will comes in." Tillie took another sip of her beer. "Ready for a personal example?"

"I shrugged. "Sure, why not?"

"Why have you put up with Lindsey's nonsense for so long?"

My bottle of beer stopped halfway to my mouth and my head snapped in Tillie's direction. "When you said personal, you meant it."

Tillie shrugged. "He makes you miserable and has humiliated you for years, but your lizard brain has always stopped you from kicking his sorry ass to the curb." Tillie glanced at me and saw the stunned look on my face but plowed on. "You've made what Jolene calls an 'unconscious choice' to keep him around."

I felt my temperature rising. "So toughing it out for my kids doesn't count?"

Tillie shrugged. "That's the argument your lizard brain made and you completely bought it."

"I don't think so," I protested.

Tillie shrugged again. "Would you have ended up in a homeless shelter without Lindsey in your life?"

"Of course not."

"Then it was something more basic, like primal fear, that kept you in the relationship." Tillie turned to face me. "There are probably two billion men of marrying age in the world, but you're afraid of being alone. You worrying about what your tribe would think has stopped you from doing the smart thing."

"Tribe?"

"You really need to read Jolene's books," Tillie continued. "Before Lindsey, you've let Robert verbally beat you up and manipulate you your entire life because your lizard brain considers him the tribal elder and male. You weren't willing to risk being exiled from the tribe, so it was always safer to let him win."

"Wow!" I said angrily. "Is that what everyone in the family thinks of me?"

"Naw," Tillie answered with a laugh. "We all love you and want to see you happy, but sometimes you seem to go out of your way to make yourself miserable so you can keep your lizard brain satisfied."

I was speechless.

Tillie shook her head and reached for the TV remote. "Read the damn book, Allison." Having known her my entire life, I took from Tillie's tone and body language that our bonding moment was over and it was time for me to move on. It was nothing personal, but Tillie only had so much touchy-feely in her in any twenty-four-hour period and she had obviously reached her limit for the day.

In a huff, I gathered up my purse and keys and headed upstairs to what had been my bedroom when I was a kid. It had been remodeled several times since my departure and now was a comfortable but seldom-used guest room.

I dropped my stuff on the dresser and headed into the bathroom. Leaning on the sink, I stared at myself in the mirror. What if Tillie was right? I had never even heard of this unconscious choice thing but vowed to learn more about it.

Squaring my shoulders, I headed back down the stairs to confront my aunt. As I stormed into the great room, her eyes were locked on the TV screen, but as she heard me coming, without looking in my direction, she held up a book. It was Aunt Jolene's book titled "Making the Right Choice."

I snatched the book out of her hand. "You can be a real turd hammer when you want to be."

"It runs in the family," Tillie answered with a laugh. "You can talk to JoJo about it after her treatment tomorrow."

"Treatment?"

"Hard to explain, easier to just see," Tillie answered. "If you don't want to talk to Jolene, you could probably discuss it with Charles's girlfriend. She looks like a true believer."

Right. I'm going to have a frank discussion about my lizard brain problem with my son's girlfriend.

I headed back upstairs, turned on the water in my bathtub to as hot as I thought I could stand and poured in a cup of coconut-scented Epsom salts. I undressed and checked the temperature with my toe and discovered it was too hot, so I added a bit of cold to the mix. I absently swirled the salts so they dissolved and glared at the book on the sink next to the tub.

The water was still too hot but was now at least bearable, so I slid in. With a sigh I opened the book and started to read. I immediately understood why Jolene was such a popular writer. She was able to take complex issues and put them in easy-to-understand language. What was baffling was why I had never been able to connect with her books before.

As I finished my fourth chapter, I realized I had been so engrossed with kicking my lizard brain's brains out that the water in the tub was now lukewarm. With a shiver I reached for a towel and stepped out of the bathtub.

That was when I saw it.

With a sigh, I picked up my phone for the first time in hours. I had put it on silent in the hospital and, with everything else swirling around me, I had completely forgotten about it. There were over twenty text messages, all basically saying that they were thinking of me and that Edna was in their prayers. Nice, but all things considered, none of them needed a late-night personal reply.

There were also two voice mails. One was from my current boss and former high school sweetheart, Bernie Williamson.

"Allie, Bernie. I just heard about your mom and just wanted to let you know if you need someone to talk to or a shoulder to lean on, I'm only a phone call away. Love ya."

I disconnected from the call and stared at the phone.

Love ya?

The last time I heard those words come out of Bernie Williamson's mouth I was eighteen years old and in the process of putting my bra back on.

Weird.

With D-Day – Divorce Day – on the horizon, maybe Bernie was looking for a match to rekindle the old flame. I made a mental note to make this a topic of discussion for the next time Beth and I had one of our chats. But I smiled because I already knew what she was going to say: "You were an idiot to let him get away the first time and you'd be an even bigger idiot if you do it again." She had never been a member of the Lindsey Clark fan club. I found out some years later it was because my soon-to-be ex-husband had hit on her while we were engaged. I wish she had mentioned it before the wedding; it would have saved me a world of pain.

The second voice mail was from the twins' school. I gave myself a mental head slap. I had forgotten to cancel my appointment. I drew in a cleansing breath then hit the play button.

"Ms. Clark, this is Ms. Taylor-Smith. You failed to show up or call to cancel our meeting this morning. It has also come to my attention that Angela and Charles were absent from classes today. Please call me or stop by my office before 11 a.m. tomorrow morning to discuss these pending matters. Failure to do so could result in your children being suspended and denied the opportunity to graduate with their class and forfeit the honor of being valedictorians."

What a passive-aggressive bitch.

Normally, something like this would make my heart race and I'd assume a submissive position like a small dog being confronted by a large, aggressive one.

This time, instead of panicking and worrying about how to deal with this awful woman who held power over me and my kids, I was enraged. Instead of "flee," I wanted to "fight." How dare she threaten my children? As I stewed in my anger for a moment, I felt a calmness settle over me. I glanced in the direction of Aunt Jolene's book and smiled.

My lizard brain can kiss the left cheek of my currently pruney butt, and Ms. Taylor-Smith can kiss the right cheek.

It's time I quit letting people walk all over me.

I dialed a number I knew by heart.

CHAPTER SIXTEEN

BEING TOO HYPED up to sleep, I finished Dr. Jolene Marshall's self-help tome and now understood why Paige had looked at my aunt like a goddess walking amongst mortals. After reading the book, my world had morphed into my personal version of "The Wizard of Oz." As in the movie, the opening scenes of my life were in black and white. When Aunt Tillie dropped the house on me, my reality exploded into Technicolor the same way it had when Dorothy arrived in Munchkin Land. I suddenly saw the world, and my place in it, very differently.

My days of living a life of fear and angst were over.

Despite only three hours of sleep, I got up early and showered, then put on a bit of makeup. Satisfied, I opened my closet and removed the garment bag I had hung there the day before. I had almost left it at home, but something told me I might need it.

As I had gotten older, I had learned to listen to that little voice.

This epiphany, along with the lessons I had learned from Aunt Jolene's book, brought a smile to my face. Maybe this little voice was my personal answer to the bad advice my lizard brain had been giving me. On an unconscious level I had already been making the choice to let my intellect, instead of my emotions, run my life.

I unzipped the bag and pulled out a dark skirt with a matching business jacket and a white silk blouse. This was as close to a power outfit as I owned.

With my battle armor in place I headed downstairs. Seeing me coming, Angela's fork, which was filled with a chunk of Jolene's amazing omelet, stopped halfway to her mouth. Tillie, with her back to me and the sports page spread out in front of her, saw the look on her grandniece's face. She pushed away from the table and turned to face to me.

"Oh, yeah!" Tillie said as she nodded her approval. "You got your big girl clothes on today. What's up?"

"I'm going to have a chat with Ms. Taylor-Smith."

Angela dropped her fork and terror filled her eyes.

"I've never trusted anyone with a hyphenated last name," Tillie said. "Who is she?"

"She's the head Nazi at the twins' high school."

Angela bolted across the kitchen, grabbed her phone and hit the speed dial. "Get your ass over here now."

Jolene, who was well-rested and more lucid than the night before, was in heaven in front of the huge six-burner gas range. She smiled at me over her shoulder. "Allison, would you like an omelet?"

I glanced over at Tillie, who smiled, then said softly, "A good night's sleep does wonders for her."

Tillie was right. Jolene looked and acted much closer to the way I remembered her. "I don't have time for breakfast, but I would love a cup of coffee," I answered as I gave Jolene's shoulders a gentle squeeze. "My friend, Beth Woodrow, will be here in a few minutes to pick me up."

As Jolene poured me a mug of coffee, she closed her eyes and repeated Beth's name to herself several times so it would be fresh.

"Aunt Beth is going with you?" Angela said with a relieved expression on her face. On cue, Beth's brand-new black Mercedes-Maybach S 650 sedan pulled up outside.

Tillie emitted a soft whistle then muttered, "Oh mama."

Before Beth even had the driver's side door open, Tillie was on her feet and headed in her direction. They met at the kitchen door. "Nice wheels, Beth," Tillie said loudly enough that Jolene could hear her name. "Mind if I take it for a spin?" Tillie held out her hand.

Beth started to drop her keys in Tillie's palm but shook a warning finger in her direction instead. "Allison and I have several meetings this morning and we can't be late. You get five minutes."

91

"I'll take it," Tillie said as she snatched the keys out of Beth's hand and trotted toward the big sedan.

Almost colliding with Aunt Tillie, a disheveled Charles, with his hair even messier than usual and his shirt tail hanging out, maneuvered around Tillie and charged into the kitchen. "What?" he demanded of his sister.

"Mom and Aunt Beth are having a meeting with Ms. Taylor-Smith," Angela answered.

"This can't be good," Charles muttered.

Beth, seeing my wardrobe selection, nodded her approval. Our outfits were almost identical and reeked, "I am woman, hear me roar."

Jolene smiled at Beth. "Your sister said you didn't have time for an omelet, but can I get you a cup of coffee or tea?"

Beth smiled and gave me a knowing look.

We saw no reason to correct Jolene about the "sister" mistake. Besides, with the way we were dressed, almost anyone could have taken us for siblings, if not twins.

"Coffee would be great," Beth answered before turning her attention to me. "Play the voicemail for Charles and Angela."

I put my phone on speaker and hit the play button and we all heard the nasally voice of Ms. Taylor-Smith.

"Ms. Clark, this is Ms. Taylor-Smith. You failed to show up or call to cancel our meeting this morning. It has also come to my attention that Angela and Charles were absent from classes today. Please call me or stop by my office before 11 a.m. tomorrow morning to discuss these pending matters. Failure to do so could result in your children being suspended and denied the opportunity to graduate with their class and forfeit the honor of being valedictorians."

Angela was stunned. "Can she do that?"

Beth rubbed her hands together and smiled. "Ask me that again in about an hour." Clearly, our little encounter with Robert and Lilith, and our pending meeting with Bertram Ruggles, had her fired up and feeling feisty. For maybe half a second I actually felt sorry for Ms. Taylor-Smith. She was probably blissfully planning her day and enjoying her coffee unaware of the tsunami that was headed in her direction. When I remembered all of the garbage she had heaped on me and likely countless others over the years, my pity for her faded.

"You two get a five-minute head start," Beth said forcefully. "Then get as many of your classmates on the front steps of the school as you can find before the class bell rings."

"What is going on here?" Angela demanded.

"With your grandmother on the sidelines," Beth said proudly as she nodded in my direction, "there is a new matriarch of the O'Connor family."

"And I'm not going to be pushed around by anybody," I added confidently.

The twins looked at me warily. They had heard this story before and knew how it ended. I don't know if it was my body language or what, but this time they both sensed something had changed. Their eyes locked on me and they both nodded their approval.

"About damn time," Angela said as she bolted upstairs to get her backpack.

"What she said," Charles added as he gave me a peck on the cheek before heading back to the doublewide.

Jolene, humming softly and seemingly oblivious to what was swirling around her, handed Beth a cup of coffee. "Here you are, Beth," she said, delighted that she got the name right without having to resort to her notes or Tillie's prompting.

"Thank you," Beth answered. As she took a sip of the coffee her eyes flew open wider in amazement. "This may be the best cup of coffee I've ever had."

"You're too kind, Beth," Jolene said as she turned blissfully back to her stove.

Angela flew down the stairs and out the door and had to slow down to bob and weave to avoid getting run over by Beth's Mercedes. Charles already had the GTO fired up and they sped away.

"Sweet ride," Tillie said as she handed Beth back her keys. When she saw the GTO roar away, she asked, "What the hell's going on?"

Before Beth or I could answer, we heard the sweet voice of Aunt Jolene. "Some awful woman at the school Angela and Charles attends has threatened them with suspension and revoking their valedictorian honor. Beth and Allison are on their way over to kick her ass."

There was a stunned silence as Tillie, Beth and I all stared open-mouthed at Jolene.

"I'm sorry," Jolene said. "Sometimes I get confused. Did I get that wrong?"

We all roared, then gave Jolene a group hug.

"I've been a lawyer for almost thirty years and that might have been the best summation I've ever heard."

CHAPTER SEVENTEEN

BETH WHEELED INTO the first available space in the visitors parking lot. As soon as we were out of the car, we were joined by four other people, three men and one woman. All four had expensive leather briefcases and all of them looked to be on the right side of thirty. In their black power suits and with their dark sunglasses, they looked like they were fresh off the set of the latest "Men in Black" remake.

"This is a little overkill, don't you think?"

"Shock and awe, baby," Elizabeth Woodrow, Esq., answered. "What's the point of having lawyers on staff if you don't use them?"

Elizabeth nodded and the quartet of young barristers fell in behind us as we headed to the main entrance of the school.

As Beth expected, pretty much the entire student body was waiting for us as we turned the corner. In the windows overlooking the main entrance we could see concerned teachers watching the proceedings. Like the Red Sea, the mass of students parted to allow us easy access to the front door. We were greeted there by a balding, middle-aged man who looked to be just a few years short of retirement. Behind him was a nervous, armed security guard in an ill-fitting uniform with his arms folded defensively across his chest. Milling even further back were a few teachers and the bulk of the office staff.

I spotted Ms. Taylor-Smith near the rear of the pack and trying her best to be invisible. Her normally smug expression was gone, and she looked pasty and pale.

"I'm Principal Maxwell," the man said in a squeaky tenor voice. "May I help you?"

"Yes," Beth said sweetly as she handed him one of her business cards. "I'm Elizabeth Woodrow of Ruggles, Knapp & Woodrow."

"I know who you are," the principal answered. "I've seen you on television. What I don't know is why you're here? Is this some kind of senior prank?"

"This is no prank, Mr. Maxwell," Elizabeth Woodrow, Esq., said firmly. "We are here to discuss the threats made by one of the members of your staff against Angela Clark and Charles Clark."

"Excuse me?" Principal Maxwell said. "Threats against two of my students? By someone on my staff!"

Ms. Taylor-Smith was getting paler by the moment, and I couldn't swear to it, but she also appeared to be shrinking. I wondered if someone had tossed a bucket of water on her.

Elizabeth motioned in the direction of the throng of students behind her. "Perhaps we should find a more private place to have this discussion."

A groan went up from the gathered masses. They had all been hoping for a ringside seat.

"Excuse me, excuse me," said a harried man trying to fight his way through the crowd of students.

"Ah, perfect timing," Elizabeth said. "I invited the Superintendent of Schools, Alex Peterson, to join our discussion." Elizabeth turned to me and I pointed at Ms. Taylor-Smith. "Vice Principal Ms. Taylor-Smith should join us as well."

A cheer went up from the student body.

Because of the number of people involved, we moved our meeting to the empty cafeteria, where Elizabeth took charge.

"I'm hoping we can make all of this go away without having to turn to the courts...."

"You're prepared to sue?" Superintendent Peterson asked.

"Considering the time-sensitive nature of this issue, I have two lawyers standing by at the federal courthouse awaiting my call. We're prepared to file for a temporary restraining order against the Superintendent of Schools, each member of the Board of Education and Principal Maxwell from taking any punitive action against my clients." Elizabeth's eyes locked on Superintendent Peterson. "Ruggles, Knapp and Woodrow also has an excellent relationship with all of the local media. Our public relations department is currently drafting a press release."

The superintendent jumped to his feet, his face flushed with anger. "What the hell is going on here?"

"Ms. Taylor-Smith, because the Clark twins missed classes yesterday, has threatened to suspend them and revoke their valedictorian status."

"I did no such thing," Taylor-Smith protested.

Beth motioned to one of her young lions, who put a tape recorder on a nearby table and played the voicemail. Another handed out a printed transcript of the call, on the very impressive letterhead of Ruggles, Knapp and Woodrow LLP.

"I'm not a jury," Elizabeth said. "But that sounds very much like a threat to me."

All eyes turned to Taylor-Smith.

"Mrs. O'Connor failed to show up or call to cancel a scheduled meeting and they had their fifth unexcused absence for the year yesterday." She folded her arm defiantly across her chest. "I was just following standard procedure and said I would wait until 11 a.m. before I took any action."

"According to your procedure manual, is a family medical emergency considered a valid reason for being absent?" Elizabeth asked.

"Of course."

"Are you aware that shortly before the beginning of the school day yesterday, the Clark twins' grandmother suffered a major cardiac event and was rushed to the hospital via EMS?" Beth waited for this news to sink in. "Are you also aware that Edna O'Connor is still in the hospital in guarded condition?"

The principal and the superintendent exchanged glances and shook their heads.

"No one notified me," Taylor-Smith said meekly.

"Sorry I didn't call," I said with a snippish tone in my voice. "I was a little preoccupied with my mother's health. Plus, with all of the sensitive equipment, they frown on cellphones in the emergency room and the Intensive Care Unit."

The superintendent cleared his throat. "Mrs. Clark, on behalf of my office, the Board of Education and Principal Maxwell, please accept our profound apology. No adverse action will be taken against your children, and we will be honored to have them as co-valedictorians at graduation."

"Thank you," I said. "Your apology is accepted." Superintendent Peterson and Principal Maxwell started to relax but froze when I added, "But there is one other thing I must insist upon."

Ms. Taylor-Smith closed her eyes and her chin fell to her chest as she waited for the executioner's axe to fall. I hesitated for a moment to allow Ms. Taylor-Smith to mentally replay all of the snide comments and passive-aggressive barbs she had thrown in my path for the past four years.

"What is that?" the superintendent asked stiffly.

"Seniors are exempt from any final exams, is that correct?"

"If the exam would not impact their final grades enough to determine whether or not they graduate, then they are not mandatory. In the case of your children, they are obviously exempt."

"So, since next week is finals week, counting today, there are only two days left in the school year."

"Yes."

"Considering my mother's condition, I would like to have my children excused from any additional mandatory classes and take them home with me." My eyes locked on Ms. Taylor-Smith. "If that is agreeable with all parties, then you'll never have to see me again and we will consider this matter closed."

"Agreed," Superintendent Peterson answered without even the slightest hesitation. Then he added, "On a personal note, with your twins being such high achievers, I've followed their progress the past few years. Let me say they are the kind of students that make public education look good." For the first time he smiled. "Also, thank them for the friends and family discount. My grandson loves his new sneakers."

CHAPTER EIGHTEEN

WITH MOST OF the students now in class, the large foyer near the main entrance to the school was nearly empty. Beth checked her watch. Again.

"We're meeting with Mr. Ruggles in less than half an hour."

"I know," I answered. "But this is important." I pointed at Angela and Charles heading in our direction.

"What happened?" Angela asked nervously. "Principal Maxwell jerked us out of class and told us to clean out our lockers."

"You are no longer students here," I said calmly, enjoying watching the twins sweat a bit.

Charles, who could always read me better than his sister, broke into a broad smile. "Do we still have to give the stupid speeches?"

"Yes," I answered.

"Damnit," Charles muttered.

"From this moment on," I continued. "You are considered graduates, and since the commencement is downtown, if you don't want to, you will never have to step foot in this building again."

"Sweet," shouted Angela as she gave me a hug.

"Plus," I said seriously, "I want to go ahead and give you both your birthday presents a few weeks early."

They were both a bit confused since I was empty-handed. "From this moment forward, consider yourselves emancipated."

Beth nodded her approval.

"Seriously?" Charles asked with an even broader grin. "No curfew, no checking in?"

"No curfew, no checking in." I repeated. "Consider me the provider of wise counsel, warm meals, the occasional load of laundry

99

and your number one cheerleader. But, from this moment forward, you call all of your own shots."

"Excellent," Angela said as she nodded her approval. "Now that we've moved to a parent-grown-child relationship, please do both of us a favor."

"Name it."

"File the damned divorce papers," Charles said.

"And move on," Angela added.

I could hear Beth chuckling next to me, but I had no intention of giving her the satisfaction of acknowledging her outburst and kept my focus on my twins.

"We appreciate you toughing it out until we graduated," Charles said. "But it wasn't necessary."

Angela glared at her brother.

"That didn't come out right," Charles said as he took a step back and turned the floor over to his sister.

"What my idiot brother should have said was, 'We really appreciate you toughing it out until we graduated' and then left it at that. Now," Angela said as she made a motion with her hands, "shoo, move along. You've done your job here, we'll be fine. Get on with your life."

"Yeah," Charles added. "What she said."

I glared at Beth, who was now laughing out loud, as Charles and Angela bolted out the door, giving each other high-fives.

I felt completely numb. I knew I had done the right thing but still, I felt a whipsaw of emotions. This was one of those defining moments in a mother's life. When I signed the divorce papers, the nest would be officially empty.

It would be me against the world.

Beth wrapped her arm around me as I wiped a tear from my eye. "Is it too early to get a drink?" I asked.

"It's too early to even get lunch," Beth answered. "Besides, we've got a meeting with Bertram Ruggles."

I nodded and we headed out the main entrance of the high school. It was my turn to laugh out loud. The GTO, with the top down and the bass of the sound system bumping with enough authority to rattle all of the windows in the school, rumbled into the front circle where the buses normally park.

"See ya!" Charles yelled at the top of his lungs.

"Wouldn't want to be ya!" Angela answered just as loudly.

Charles floored the gas on the old-school muscle car and it fishtailed as it laid a sixty-foot batch of rubber that left a cloud of blue smoke from the tires in his wake.

We could hear a dull, muffled whoop coming out of the bowels of the school, and, turning, we saw students pounding on the windows and flashing victory signs.

"The Clark twins' legend continues to grow," Beth said with a chuckle.

We headed toward the visitors parking lot without speaking, but once we were back in Beth's car, she asked, "Well?"

"Well, what?"

"Please," Beth said. "Are you going to do it?"

"Yeah."

"Today?"

I drew in a deep breath and let it out slowly. "I think so."

"Think, or know?"

"Back off," I snapped. "I just cut the cord with my kids and now I'm pondering ending twenty-eight years of marriage. That's a lot for one day."

"Okay, okay," Beth said with a chuckle. "It's just you're on a heck of a roll and I'm trying to keep the momentum going."

We rode along in silence for a few minutes with my mind racing and the streets around me nothing more than a blur. I knew the twins were right. I knew Beth was right. And, to her never-ending credit, she, as usual, knew what I was thinking and left me alone in my thoughts. One of the things I loved the most about Beth was she never felt the need to fill time with witless conversation. To her there was no such thing as an awkward silence.

I closed my eyes the way Aunt Jolene had taught me years ago, drew in another cleansing breath and then released it. As the air escaped from my lungs, I felt oddly lighter, as if a weight had been lifted off me. I felt all of the anger and hurt I had felt toward Lindsey vanishing into the ether.

I smiled and chuckled to myself.

At that moment, I knew Lindsey no longer had the power over me to evoke even the slightest emotional response. He, because of our children, would always be a part of my life. But from this moment forward it was "my" life and no longer "our" life.

Any and all obligations to him were marked "paid in full."

It was time to move on.

I fished my phone out of my purse and found a number in my contacts and turned to Beth. "Can you put this call on speaker?"

"This is a Mercedes," she answered with a snort. She pushed a button on the steering wheel and the background music died and we could hear a phone ringing on the elaborate sound system. "Who are you calling?"

The question became moot the moment the line was answered.

"Spence and Moore, how may I direct your call?" said a friendly female voice on the speakers.

"Morey Spence, please. Allison Clark calling."

"Hold please."

Beth gave my knee a squeeze.

An old Eagles song I hadn't heard in a while began play on the speaker. We only got about eight bars in before Morey picked up. We had been friends for years, and he even owned one of the biggest homes in Charlestown Reserve. Being the top divorce lawyer in town had its perks.

"Hey Allison," Morey said cheerfully. "You ready to pull the trigger?"

"I am," I answered. "I'm in the car with Elizabeth Woodrow."

"Hey, Elizabeth," Morey said. No one in the local legal profession ever called her Beth, and very few had the right or courage to call her Elizabeth instead of Ms. Woodrow. Morey Spence, also being a named partner of a major law firm, was an exception. "How are Derek and the boys?"

"Michael is just about to start a year walkabout and everybody else is fine."

"Nothing a divorce lawyer hates more than a happy marriage."

"Coming from a guy with zero first-hand knowledge," Elizabeth said with a laugh. "How's wife number four doing?"

"Fine so far," Morey answered.

"How's the pre-nup?" Elizabeth asked.

"Ironclad," Morey answered with a laugh.

"Do you have the papers Allison needs to sign?"

"Yup," Morey answered. "If she could swing by…"

"We're on our way to my office," Elizabeth said with authority as she cut across him. "I'll have one of our couriers pick them up. We'll have them executed and notarized and back to you before the end of business."

"Sounds good," Morey said.

"Timeline?" Elizabeth asked.

"We've already done all of the groundwork, and both parties are in full agreement on all of the settlement issues." We heard the sound of papers rustling. "Here we are," Morey said. "Lindsey has already signed the papers. So, unless Allison wants any changes, we are good to go."

"Excellent," Elizabeth said.

"Thanks, Morey," I added as I disconnected.

Beth hit a button on the steering wheel and said in a clear voice, "Call Wilma."

The call was answered on the first ring.

"Yes, ma'am," said one of Elizabeth's assistants.

"Send a courier to Spence and Moore and pick up some documents from Morey Spence for Allison Clark and have them brought to me immediately."

"Yes, ma'am." The line went dead.

I guess when you bill at Beth's hourly rate, brevity is an asset.

Beth slowed as she approached the entrance to her office building, which was next door to the county courthouse and across the street from the federal courthouse. She turned and headed down a ramp to the underground parking garage. The electronic sensor recognized her car without having to bother with a touchpad or swipe card and the gate lifted. She pulled into the second spot away from the elevator with Woodrow stenciled on the wall. As we approached the elevator, Beth pointed to a vintage Bentley in the only spot closer to the elevator than hers.

"Bert is here."

"Where does Knapp park?" I asked, thinking I was being funny since she was the third name on the letterhead but she had the second-best parking spot. My joke fell flat. She had already put back on her humorless, "I'm a named partner at the biggest law firm in town" face.

"Thankfully for pedestrians everywhere, he has a driver," Beth answered in a cold, controlled monotone. It was always a bit unnerving to see the transition from my BFF to the most feared litigator in a five-hundred-mile radius. There had been flashes of it at the school earlier today, but that was just for show. Now, she was deadly serious and had her game face on.

Beth pushed a button on the elevator panel and we were whisked upward.

CHAPTER NINETEEN

R UGGLES, KNAPP & WOODROW owned the building. The penthouse, where Beth's office was located, only had three private offices on the top floor. The rest of the space was multi-functional with moveable walls and could handle anything from a three-hundred-person, invitation-only Christmas party with a spot for a live band to being reconfigured into a small auditorium that could seat the entire staff.

Ruggles and Knapp had claimed the only available corner offices, and Beth's was between them. The space around Knapp's office was empty and dark. Apparently, he wasn't in today. The space in front of Beth's office was a madhouse. There were four workstations, but six people needed a place to work, so two of her staff had poached empty desks in Knapp's space.

A secretary I had met before approached Elizabeth but was waved off. "I'll be in Mr. Ruggles' office," Beth said without breaking stride.

Ruggles, like Beth, had four workstations outside his office, but only one was occupied at the moment. Guarding the door was a woman who appeared old enough to have been the spouse of one of the signers of the Declaration of Independence. She saw Beth approaching and waved her into the office.

"You're late," she said sternly. "Mr. Ruggles does not like to be kept waiting." From what I had seen from my previous visits to Beth's office, I would be willing to give long odds that old biddy was the only one in the building who took that tone with Elizabeth Woodrow, Esq.

Beth saw the bemused look on my face. "That's Helen. She's been Bert's secretary for the past fifty-eight years. When Bert dies, I'll bet she'll move her desk to the cemetery and you'll have to get past her before you can put flowers on his grave."

Bert Ruggles was behind a heavy walnut desk slightly larger than a ping-pong table. When he saw me, his face lit up and he bounded around the desk in my direction. He was as adorable as I had remembered. He had hung his jacket on the back of his chair and was wearing his signature red suspenders and floral bowtie. As my father's personal lawyer and close friend, he had been a regular fixture at all of the events held at the Farm for as long as I could remember. The last time I had seen him was the day of Daddy's funeral.

"Allison O'Connor," he said as he held me at arm's length and examined me from head to toe.

"I've been Allison Clark for the past twenty-eight years, Uncle Bert."

He waved me off. "You'll always be an O'Connor to me."

Then a thought hit me. Should I revert back to my maiden name? I shook my head and put that thought out of my mind. I had other, more pressing things on my plate at the moment.

"Sit, sit," he said as he motioned to chairs opposite his desk. "Beth tells me you have some questions about your father's finances," he said as he moved back to his chair.

"Yes," I said. "We have recently learned that my father was making rather large and regular payments to Ruggles, Knapp & Woodrow for about fifty years."

"Forty-nine years and four months," Bert corrected.

I glanced at Beth, but she looked like she was about ready to come across the desk and strangle Bert Ruggles with his floral bowtie then string him up from the rafters by his red suspenders. I decided it was probably best if I did all of the talking.

"So you're familiar with the account?"

"Of course," Bert answered. "I'm the one who set it up."

Elizabeth had heard enough and turned her full ire on Bert Ruggles. "I am a named partner. Why am I hearing about this from an outsider?"

"I'm surprised you heard about it at all," Ruggles said calmly. "This agreement was executed long before this partnership was formed and was grandfathered into my partnership agreement as a separate entity. It has absolutely nothing to do with Ruggles, Knapp and Woodrow."

"Does anything in your agreement put this firm in any legal jeopardy?" Elizabeth demanded as she tried to control her temper.

"I can't imagine how," Ruggles answered calmly. "I am merely a conduit. The funds come in each month. We subtract a modest fee for our services, then distribute the funds."

"Distribute the funds how and to whom?" Elizabeth asked as she continued to struggle with the sense she had been betrayed by one of the few people on Earth she thought she knew and could trust.

Ruggles shook his head. "Sorry." Then he smiled. "May I ask how you discovered this arrangement?"

"There were insufficient funds in the account to cover the latest scheduled debit. Since the banker had known my dad and didn't want to bounce a check he thought could easily be covered, he contacted the O'Connor Industries accounting department," I answered.

"Interesting," Ruggles said. "I wonder why they didn't contact me?"

"They may have tried," Elizabeth said coldly. "You're not in the office that much anymore."

Ruggles glanced at Elizabeth, who was glaring back at him.

"My brother believes," I said, wanting to get this meeting back on track, "my father may have been embezzling money from the company."

"That's absurd," Ruggles answered with a laugh. "Charlie O'Connor was possibly the most ethical human being I ever came across in my entire life."

"So these funds were acquired legally?" Beth barked.

"Of course," Ruggles answered calmly.

"You should prepare yourself," Beth said dryly. "I doubt Robert O'Connor will be willing to take you at your word for that and will likely sue to see the records."

"I wish him luck," Ruggles answered with a shrug.

"Are you going to tell me where the funds are going?" I asked.

"Absolutely not," he answered with an odd grin on his face.

"Can you tell me the purpose of this account?" I continued.

"No," Bert answered sweetly.

"Why not?" I asked.

"Attorney-client privilege."

"But my father is dead," I protested.

"Privilege doesn't end with the death of the client...." Beth said but stopped when she saw the grin on Bert Ruggles' face. "Of course," she muttered.

"You did not hear it from me," Ruggles said.

"Hear what?" I asked.

Beth abruptly stood up and motioned for me to follow her. "Come on," she said as she walked toward the door.

Caught off guard by the sudden conclusion to the meeting, I was slow to get up and found myself lagging behind. I took a couple of quick steps to catch up with Beth.

"What's going on?" I asked as I tugged on Beth's arm to slow her down.

"We're talking to the wrong person."

"Who should we be talking to?" I asked.

"Bert's client. Edna O'Connor."

CHAPTER TWENTY

LIZABETH'S SECRETARY WASN'T exactly hovering just outside Bert Ruggles' office, but she had obviously not taken her eyes off the door. As soon as her boss popped out, she was on her feet and headed in our direction with a manila folder in her hand.

"These are the documents you requested from Spence and Moore."

Beth nodded in my direction and her secretary handed them to me.

For some reason, I had expected twenty-eight years of my life to weigh more.

"What does my day look like?" Elizabeth asked.

"I've rescheduled everything from this morning and we're still on schedule for the rest of the day," Wilma answered.

"Exactly the way I like it," Elizabeth said flatly.

Beth looked around and saw all of the desks in front of her office were occupied, so she grabbed my arm and guided me in the direction of Mr. Knapp's private office. Of course, the lights immediately came on the moment we entered the room. I had met Knapp several times at social functions I had attended with Beth when her husband, Derek, had respectfully declined to go with her.

One of the reasons I think the Woodrows had made their marriage work was that Derek would attend any function his high-powered wife requested, but Beth seldom made the request.

I had never been in Knapp's office before and it was intimidating. Not wanting to push the limits of even her authority, Beth parked me in one of the two visitor's chairs in front of Knapp's Louis XVI desk instead of in Knapp's spot behind it.

Once seated, the first thing I noticed was that the wall behind his desk was a shrine to a powerful lawyer who had been a mover and shaker for decades. In addition to some very impressive diplomas, it had framed photos of Knapp with politicians, including three presidents, local sports stars and celebrities. The second thing I noticed was that the pictures were carefully placed so they were impossible to miss if you were in one of the visitor's chairs.

Nice.

I opened the envelope and started looking for a pen.

"You need to read those before you sign them," Beth said.

"I've read them a dozen times," I protested. "And they are always the same."

"Those were drafts," Beth said bluntly. "This is the real deal. Once you sign these, there is no going back."

"But…"

"Shhh," Beth said as she gave me the big eyes. "I'll have someone come in and notarize your signature in a few minutes."

This was Beth's home turf and she was the best in the business, so I did as I was told and started to reread the document. As I had suspected, nothing had changed since the last time I had read them except at the bottom of the last page, in dark blue ink, was Lindsey's notarized signature. He and I had been fair with each other and there was no animus and the document reflected that. With the twins now almost eighteen there were no child support or custody issues. The house was in my name before the marriage, so it was off the table. In lieu of alimony, I had accepted a rather nice one-time cash payout and further agreed to make no claims on Lindsey's IRA or other retirement accounts. Morey said I should have asked for more and he was probably right. Lindsey didn't bother with a counter offer and accepted my terms the same day they arrived at his attorney's office.

After I finished rereading the documents, through the door I saw a steady stream of people going in and out of Beth's office.

She was definitely the Queen Bee of this hive. I smiled when I saw David Woodrow step off the elevator and head in my direction with a notary seal embosser in his hand.

"Hey, Aunt Allison," he said brightly as he joined me in Knapp's office.

"Hey, David," I answered without bothering to get up.

"I'll need to see your driver's license."

"Seriously," I said with a laugh. "I changed your diapers when you were a baby."

"Sorry," David answered with a smile. "Mom makes the rules and all of us just follow them."

"It must be awkward working here sometimes," I offered, as I fished my driver's license out of my purse and slid it across the desk in his direction.

"Not as awkward as you might think," David answered as he took a picture of my license with his cellphone and slid it back to me. "She's fair to everybody and we all know the firm wouldn't last a year without her at the top."

I had always suspected Beth was a huge asset to the firm or they wouldn't have put her name on the door. "Proud son?" I asked.

David shrugged and smiled. "Old man Ruggles comes in for about six hours a week but has nothing to do with the day-to-day business. I don't think I've ever even met or even seen Mr. Knapp and I've been here almost a year."

"Really?"

"Yeah," David said as he pointed to a line that needed my signature. "We've got a great team of partners that keeps the place humming, but Mom's the glue that holds it all together."

"My daddy used to say if you want to run a successful business, hire people better than you and stay out of their way."

David laughed. "That's one of my mom's favorite lines and pretty much the prevailing philosophy around here."

"Does she have you on the partner track?" I asked.

"Of course," David answered with a sigh. "But sometimes it is tough when you live in the shadow of a legend."

I laughed out loud for the first time today and it felt good. "Remember. You're talking to Charlie O'Connor's daughter."

"True," David Woodrow answered with a chuckle. "But you never had to work in the same office with him."

My mind immediately leapt to my brother and his situation with our father. "That's a problem?" I asked.

"The expectations are tough to live up to and any mistake is amplified. Plus, just being Elizabeth Woodrow's son, with office politics, puts a target on my back."

"I had no idea," I said as I accepted the offer of a pen. It was heavy, probably gold, and felt good in my hand. It was exactly the kind of instrument you would want your client to use to sign important documents.

I signed my name and David blew on it to be sure the ink was dry then added his name underneath mine. Next he put the signature page in the notary seal embosser and clamped down on it. Finally, he took a picture of the signature page with his cellphone.

"We're all done," David said.

"That's it?"

David rechecked the document. "Your ex-husband has already executed the document so that's it."

Ex-husband.

David picked up the divorce decree and rose to his feet. "I'll make you some copies and get the original back to Mr. Spence. With it being a Friday, they may not be officially registered in the courthouse until Monday."

As I sat alone in Mr. Knapp's massive and cold office, my heart was racing and I was struggling under a flood of emotions.

"You okay?"

I looked up and saw Beth standing in the doorway.

"Is it still too early to get a drink?"

Beth closed the door to Knapp's office and headed to a wet bar in the corner I hadn't noticed and came back with a pair of Waterford crystal high ball glasses and a bottle of Johnnie Walker Blue Label. "Won't Mr. Knapp mind?"

"It's been so long since anyone has seen or heard from Knapp we're starting to suspect his wife has his body in the freezer in her basement so she can keep getting his partnership checks."

Beth poured about two fingers of scotch into each glass then pushed mine in front of me. "You've had a heck of a morning."

"Tell me about it." I picked up my glass. It was heavier than I expected and had the same heft of authority as David's pen. I brought the glass slowly to my mouth so I could smell the aroma before tasting the golden nectar. The first sip was wonderful as I felt my body starting to relax.

"David confirmed Lindsey had already executed the decree."

I smiled. That was so Beth. Morey Spence had already told her Lindsey had signed, but until she had confirmation it was an open issue.

"Yeah," I answered wistfully. "When Bert called me Allison O'Connor it made me think about going back to my maiden name."

"I don't know," Beth said as she took a sip of scotch. "You've been Allison Clark longer than you were Allison O'Connor and it would be kind of weird if your kids had different last names than you."

"Both good points," I said as I felt myself starting to relax even more. "I got a weird voicemail from Bernie Williamson last night."

"How so?" Beth asked.

"It was the usual heard-about-your-mom message but he signed off with 'love ya,' which I thought was kind of odd."

Beth laughed. "What's odd about that? The man has carried the torch for you since tenth grade." Beth leaned in closer and lowered her voice. "You'd be nuts to not give him another shot."

I took a second sip of scotch and it was even better than the first one. "I knew that was what you were going to say."

"Of course it's what I'd say," Beth said as she refreshed my glass but with only about half as much this time. Such a good friend. She figured me being falling-down drunk before noon on my first day back in the dating pool might be a bit unladylike and give potential suiters the wrong impression.

"Can I have a few days to get used to being single again before you start fixing me up?"

"Tick. Tock," Beth answered.

"Meaning?"

"He's single. You're single." Beth said as she pretended to take another sip of scotch, hoping I wouldn't notice the volume in her glass had not gone down. "But most of the good ones are already married off."

There was a soft tap on the door.

"Come!" Beth barked with an edge to her voice that said this had better be important. Her mood immediately lightened when her son popped his head in.

"I have your copies, Aunt Allison," he said.

Beth glared at David. "You want to try that again?"

"I have your copies, Ms. Clark," he said as he tried unsuccessfully to keep from smiling.

"Much better," Elizabeth said. "Leave them on the desk and get a driver for Ms. Clark to take her to the hospital to see her mother, then to take her home."

"Yes, ma'am," David said as he dropped the manila envelope on the desk, winked at me then left Knapp's office.

"Is David too young for me?" I asked mischievously. "I mean, he's single. I'm single."

Beth smiled sweetly. "Would you do me a favor? Get the hell out of my office, I've got work to do."

This time we got to our feet at the same time and I gave Beth a hug then whispered in her ear. "I don't think I could have gotten through all of this without you."

"I know," she said as she patted me on the back. "But, Mrs. Robinson, if you make a pass at either one of my sons, I'll have you assassinated."

"Love you too," I said as I headed toward the elevator where David was waiting to take me to the car Beth had ordered for me. When I was sure his mother was still watching, I hooked my arm inside of David's and guided him into the elevator.

"Are you flirting with me, Aunt Allison?"

I seductively leaned in and whispered in his ear. "No. I'm making your mother crazy."

"I'm in," David answered as he pretended to smell my hair.

When we turned around, I gave Beth a finger wiggle and pulled David closer. I could hear her growl from forty feet away.

CHAPTER TWENTY-ONE

I FELT GUILTY riding in the middle seat of an SUV that could comfortably seat eight and would have blended right in with a presidential motorcade. Fortunately, the windows were so heavily tinted that no one could see I was the only passenger and think I was a jerk for leaving such a massive carbon footprint.

The driver was an enormous specimen with a thick Eastern European accent named Roman. From his size and demeanor, I had to wonder if he occasionally doubled as a bodyguard. He wasn't much of a talker, which was fine with me since I was on the verge of a mental overload. When we arrived at the main entrance of the hospital, he had my door open before I had even figured out how to unfasten my seatbelt. When I told him I was uncertain how long I would be, he gave me a business card and told me to text him when I was ready to go.

I already knew my mother's room number, so I breezed past the reception desk in the lobby and headed straight for the elevators. The sixth floor was quiet and there wasn't much activity in the corridors. The nurses' station was unoccupied as I headed for room 618.

I was feeling pretty good about myself for the moment. I had spent the last few years as a "tweener." In addition to a disintegrating marriage, I was stuck between an aging and sometimes difficult parent, and difficult kids who weren't aging fast enough. With the kids emancipated and Lindsey now in my rearview mirror, things should, hopefully, start to be a bit less complicated so I could focus on Mom.

When I entered the room, a plump Hispanic woman was changing the sheets on my mom's bed.

"Hello," I said.

"Housekeeping," the woman answered with a cheerful smile.

"I can see that," I answered as I pointed to the bed. "Where is Mrs. O'Connor?"

"Housekeeping," she repeated.

I pointed to the bed and tried to remember some of my high school Spanish. "*Donde Señora?*"

Apparently I was close enough as the housekeeper's eyes lit up. "*Señora* gone."

"Gone?" I repeated as I felt panic starting to build. "What do you mean, gone?"

"Housekeeping," she answered with a smile.

I felt a tightness in my chest and instantly wondered if my mother's health problem was hereditary. Before a full-blown panic attack set in, I thought I should find someone whose first language was English. I returned to the corridor and saw Dr. Frazier standing at the nurses' station scribbling notes on a chart. Nurse Johnson was standing next to him. I bolted in their direction.

"Where is my mother?"

"Who is your mother?" Dr. Frazier asked without looking up from the note he was making.

"Edna O'Connor," Nurse Johnson said, "room 618."

Frazier kept writing. "She wasn't a surgical candidate, so I referred her back to her primary care physician."

"She has been discharged," Nurse Johnson said.

"Why wasn't I notified?"

Dr. Frazier ignored me and kept writing.

I leaned in, snatched the pen out of his hand and hissed. "I asked you why I wasn't notified."

Frazier turned to me and started to answer but stopped when he caught a whiff of the scotch on my breath. He snorted as he tagged me as not only irrational but the kind of broad who needed a drink before noon to take the edge off. He took his pen back. "Nurse

Johnson would be better equipped to answer your questions," he said as he started writing again.

Nurse Johnson motioned for me to follow her around to the other side of the nurses' station, a good twenty feet away from the incredibly arrogant and rude surgeon. Nurse Johnson made a "don't get me started face" as she thumbed through the rack of patients' charts hanging in a file until she found my mom's. "Let me see here." She read through the file and flipped a few pages. "Who is Robert O'Connor?"

"He's my brother."

"Well, he also has your mother's medical power of attorney and he is the first name on the notification list."

"So that was why I wasn't notified?"

Nurse Johnson ran her finger further down the chart. "Are you Allison Clark?"

I nodded.

"You're the second name on the notification sheet, but since Robert agreed to pick your mother up, there was no need for us to call you."

"What was my mother's prognosis?"

Nurse Johnson shook her head. "With the HIPAA privacy rules, since you're neither the patient nor the POA designee, I can't tell you anything."

"Can you at least tell me how long ago Robert picked her up?"

"He didn't," she said as she found the discharge paper and checked the signature. "His daughter, Gabrielle O'Connor, took her home over an hour ago."

Nurse Johnson thinking Gabrielle was Robert's daughter instead of his wife brought an odd smile to my face. Nurse Johnson noticed the grin but I think she had also noticed the aroma of scotch.

I waved my hand in front of my mouth. "Sorry," I said. "I just signed my divorce papers."

Nurse Johnson patted me on my arm. "Been there," she said sympathetically. "Bad timing with your mom and all."

"Yeah."

Nurse Johnson opened a drawer and found a plastic Tic-Tac container and offered it to me. I popped one in my mouth, thanked her then headed for the elevator. I waited until I got back to the lobby before I texted Roman. He immediately texted back that he was in line at Starbucks and asked if I would like a coffee. I texted back two words.

"Grande, black."

Despite the emotional storm swirling around me, the actual weather was beautiful. I wandered outside and found a bench to sit on to wait for my Roman chariot. I didn't have to wait long before I saw the massive Cadillac Escalade turning in my direction and rolling to a stop under the drive-through portico by the main entrance.

I waved Roman off and opened my own door. My coffee and a napkin were in one of the pair of cup holders in the backseat. In the other was a small plastic cup filled with ice chips in case my coffee was too hot. Which it was. When I pulled the lid off my Grande, Roman had clearly told them to leave space for the ice and the fill line was low enough it was unlikely normal road bumps would cause a spill. I was really starting to like this guy.

"What do I owe you for the coffee?" I asked.

He just shook his head. "We'll bill the client."

I poured some ice in my Grande and got just the right temperature before putting the lid back on. As we approached my mother's house, I was just about to give Roman the security code when I noticed the gate was standing wide open. That was odd. Even odder, as we approached the Farm, there were at least a half-dozen pickup trucks parked haphazardly along the driveway. They were of various age and condition, but all looked like workhorses and not show horses. I could also hear the sound of a power saw and several hammers coming from the backyard.

If Roman went much farther it would be a tight fit. "This is fine right here," I said.

Roman nodded and, despite me releasing my seat belt before we had come to complete stop, he still had my door open before I could reach the latch.

"I'm new at this," I said sheepishly. "Am I supposed to tip you?"

"Only if you want me to get fired," he said with a laugh before climbing back behind the wheel. He waved just before doing a perfect "Y" turn without bending a single blade of my mom's grass.

As I headed around to the back of the house, I started seeing familiar faces of men obviously well past retirement age who used to work for my daddy. Aunt Tillie was supervising a trio working on building a ramp from the patio to the backdoor.

When Daddy was still alive, he loved to have huge summertime parties and considered himself a BBQ master. Hardly a weekend from Memorial Day to Labor Day would go by without a major event. To accommodate the parties, his crew had built a flagstone patio that covered nearly a half-acre that included an oversized swimming pool about halfway between the house and the garage where Daddy kept his vintage cars. For some reason, all of the lawn furniture, except for a few solo chairs that were spread out and left at odd spots on the stone, had been pushed onto the grass. I had no idea what was going on until I pulled up short when I saw my mom. She was sitting in the shade in the back corner of the patio astride a battery-powered wheelchair. When she saw me heading in her direction she put her drink down on the table next to her. Next, she grabbed the joystick on the chair and it started doing terrifying high-speed figure eights, then began weaving her way through the few chairs left on the deck like a skier running a slalom course. I had to jump out of the way as she hummed past me.

Aunt Tillie came over and put an arm around me. "Ain't she a dandy!" she said as we watched Mom flying around the huge patio cackling like a schoolgirl.

"What is she doing?"

"I thought it was better for her to get used to how it handled out here instead of taking hunks out of the furniture inside."

"Is that thing safe?" I asked.

"Oh, hell, honey," Tillie said with a laugh. "That's her indoor wheels. I'm going to pick up a farm-level quad bike for her so she can still get to her garden." Tillie was warming up to the idea of the quad. "Honda makes a two-seat model with a 675cc liquid-cooled OHV single-cylinder four-stroke engine. Fuel injection…"

"Tillie!" I said sharply, cutting her off. "Have you lost your mind?"

Tillie laughed. "The doctor said she shouldn't bend over and pick up anything and keep her walking to a minimum. He didn't say she couldn't have any fun."

We both saw Mom heading in our direction and coming at us full speed. Tillie pulled a red shop rag out of her back pocket and waved it out in front of her.

"*Toro! Toro!*" she shouted and as Mom sped past, Tillie side-stepped her and pulled the rag away like a matador. "*Olé!*" she shouted.

This has all of the makings of a long summer.

Then a thought occurred to me as I looked around. "Where's Jolene?"

"She's inside with Gabrielle," Tillie said as she never took her eyes off of Mom, who was gearing up for another pass. "She's a real sweetheart, and she and JoJo connected immediately."

"Really?" I said.

"Yeah," Tillie answered. "They've been as thick as Venezuelan crude since she got here."

I usually bat around .500 with the Tillie-isms and this was a swing and a miss. I had no idea what that one meant.

"They're in the house making lunch," Tillie said as she sidestepped Mom again. "I haven't seen JoJo this happy and so fully engaged in years."

Maybe I had been selling my sister-in-law short.

We both turned when we heard a loud bang like a cooking pan hitting the floor followed by loud shouting.

"This can't be good," Tillie said as she made a "time out" signal with her hands in the direction of my mom. Mom nodded then headed back to her shady spot and her pitcher of "lemonade." I suspected, since it was a bit darker than usual, it had been "improved" by my Aunt Tillie.

Tillie and I made our way around the men who had been building the ramp but now were chuckling as they stared inside the kitchen.

Through the years, I've seen many odd and wonderful things in the kitchen of the Farm, but I had to admit, I never thought I would see anything like this.

Gabrielle and Jolene were standing nose to nose in front of Mom's massive Viking range, waving their hands and shouting at each other.

In French.

Chapter Twenty-Two

AS I MOVED to separate Gabrielle and Jolene, Tillie put out a hand to stop me. This was a day for firsts. Looking up at her, I saw something else I had never seen before. A single tear was running down the cheek of my, to use a Tillie-ism, *tough as a two-dollar steak*, aunt.

"Give it another few seconds," she said softly.

Suddenly, Jolene stomped her foot, folded her arms across her chest and turned her back to Gabrielle. Not to be outdone, Gabrielle shouted something that I'm pretty sure they didn't teach in any high school French class, folded her arms across her chest and turned her back to Aunt Jolene.

"Okay," Tillie said. "Now we can separate them."

I pulled her back as she started to walk away. "What is going on?"

"I'll bet dollars to doughnuts it involves onions," Tillie answered.

"Excuse me?"

"I'll get you Jolene's book on how to attain a state of enlightenment."

"Enlightenment?"

Tillie saw the expression on my face and chuckled. "If you buy into her theory, if you release all of the BS in your life, there are multiple levels of enlightenment. Location One is part time and people will sometimes revert back to their old ways and drop completely off the scale. Location Two can be more permanent. By the time you get to Location Three you're pretty much like the Dalai Lama. Location Four, all emotions slip away and you basically turn into Mr. Spock. Jolene is what she would call a 'traveler' who can move from one location to another, seamlessly." Tillie chuckled again. "There are only two things in the world that will get JoJo riled up enough she drops completely off her location matrix and she blows her stack. One is stupid drivers, but since I don't let her drive anymore, that one is a non-issue. The only other thing that can set her off is onions."

"Onions?"

"Mine is not to reason why," Tillie said with a laugh. "I'm guessing Gabrielle must have wanted to put onions in something."

I shook my head and approached my sister-in-law. "Gabrielle," I said softly. "Is everything okay?"

Gabrielle immediate started rapidly speaking in French but quickly changed to English. "This old woman is impossible."

"This child has no palate," Jolene said with contempt dripping on every word. "She wanted to put onions in my soup."

"My soup," Gabrielle corrected. "And since the leeks were dreadful at the market, I wanted to substitute sweet Vidalia onions. And she went out of her mind."

"An onion is an onion," Jolene said defiantly.

"She won't even try it," Gabrielle said.

"I don't need to," Jolene said defensively. "I can smell them."

"Jolene Anabel Marshall!" Tillie's voice cracked like a whip. "You are being a rude and inconsiderate guest. You should at least try Gabrielle's soup and quit being a stubborn jerk."

Jolene made a face then snatched a spoon out of Gabrielle's hand and slowly dipped it in the saucepan on the stove. Reluctantly, she tried the soup and sneered. "Passable, but it would still be better with leeks."

"Of course, but the Vidalia are sweet enough to use when the leeks were as awful as those at the market."

"They were dreadful," Jolene said as she got a fresh spoon out of the drawer and dipped it into the soup for a second taste. "It needs more pepper."

Gabrielle made a face, grabbed a clean spoon and tried the soup. "I think you're right," she said as she nodded her approval. "Three turns?"

"I would start with two turns, then check again." Jolene answered. "We can always add more but we can't take it out."

"Agreed," Gabrielle said as she reached for the pepper mill.

Tillie leaned in and whispered in my ear. "When this is over, we're going to want to take Gabrielle home with us." Tillie, hoping I wouldn't notice, casually wiped another tear from her eye. "I haven't heard Jolene cussing anyone out in French in years."

I turned when I heard a thud on the staircase behind me. Two men, both O'Connor Industries alums, were struggling with my mom's mattress as they maneuvered it down the steps. I turned to Tillie. "What's going on?"

"So Edna doesn't have to deal with the stairs, we're converting the den into a bedroom."

I was so glad Tillie was here. Her take-charge, no-nonsense approach to life was exactly what this family needed right now. Plus, Tillie was just as ornery as my mom and she would not take no for an answer. Converting the den was a masterstroke. It didn't have much of a closet and was about half the size of Mom's bedroom. But it had a private full bathroom and a door to the patio.

Looking around the great room, I noticed some of the furniture had been rearranged to give my mom and her new toy extra room to maneuver. I felt myself starting to tear up. Between Beth and Tillie, it made me appreciate the true meaning of friends and family. It is nice to have people who love you and will stand by your side when things get rough.

I leaned over and gave Tillie a kiss on the cheek.

Caught off guard, she shot me a strange look. "What was that for?"

"Just for being you," I said as I gave her a squeeze. "I don't think I could have gotten through this without you."

Tillie pulled away from me and gave me a dismissive wave of the hand. "Sure you would have. You're an O'Connor girl." Then she chuckled. "Of course, you wouldn't have done it as well as me."

"Of course," I answered as more workmen appeared in the kitchen with some oddly shaped pieces of stainless steel tubing in their hands. Tillie pointed them toward the former den.

"What's that?" I asked.

"I'm having safety grips installed in the bathtub and next to the toilet so that crazy mother of yours doesn't do a face plant after taking a shower or taking a dump."

"Where did you find all of these people?"

Tillie shrugged. "I made a few calls, and when word got out that Charlie O'Connor's widow needed some carpentry help, some of the old-timers just started showing up."

On cue, a silver-haired man with hands that looked like they were made out of walnuts came over. "Hello, Allison. Remember me?"

At first I didn't, then my eyes flew wide open when I recognized him. "Oh, my God! Freddy Nash!" I squealed as I gave the old man a hug. He had been one of my daddy's foremen for over thirty years and had even lived for a few months in the doublewide. I remembered him and Daddy down by the pool late at night smoking nasty cigars and drinking whiskey and telling tall tales.

"You grew up nicely," he said softly, then turned his attention to Tillie. "We've got the bed for the ramp in place. You want to take a look at it before we install the handrails?"

"Will it hold the weight of her and the chair?"

"Hell, Tillie," Nash said with a laugh. "We built it strong enough you could park that monster truck of yours on it."

"Good enough for me," Tillie said as she pointed to the door leading to the patio as Edna hummed into the room. "And it looks good enough for Edna. Do you have a solution for opening and closing the door without her having to get off that damn thing?"

"Workin' on it," Nash answered. "We're thinking maybe putting in a commercial sliding door with motion sensors, but to do that we'll have to enlarge the opening and run some electric."

"Timeframe?"

"If I can get into the warehouse for parts, I'm sure I can jerry-rig something." Nash scratched his head. "Two days, three, tops."

"Before we destroy the kitchen, take a look at the door in Edna's new bedroom. It already has a sliding door so it has a bigger opening."

As Freddy Nash walked away, Mom whirred to a stop next to me. "What are you all dressed up for?" she asked as she eyed my business suit with suspicion.

"I had to deal with an issue at the twins' school this morning."

Edna sighed and shook her head. She was expecting to hear how I had been cowed.

Tillie jumped in and said, "I talked to Angela and apparently our little Allison here left the place in a smoldering heap."

"Really?" My mom said in disbelief.

I fought the urge to smile and instead added as I reached for the envelope in my purse. "I filed my divorce papers today." I held up the envelope.

"Well, I'll be damned," Mom said. "I didn't think I'd live long enough to ever see you show any O'Connor grit."

"Be nice, Edna," Tillie hissed. "Just because you're rounding third and are heading for home doesn't mean I won't smack you one."

Edna shrugged but let it drop.

Freddy Nash returned. "The new bedroom will be easier. We can knock out the patio door and replace it with a commercial sensor job without any cutting."

"Great," Tillie said brightly. "How long will it take?"

"Depends on parts," Nash answered. "And I need your guidance on the electric hook-up."

"Show me," Tillie said as she pointed a warning finger in my mom's and my direction. "You two play nice."

As Aunt Tillie walked away, I leaned into Mom and said, "We need to talk about something important."

"So talk," Edna said bluntly.

"Robert thinks Daddy was stealing money from the company."

"Why would he think that?" Edna asked.

"Apparently monthly checks have been going to Beth's law firm for nearly fifty years and it was off the books...."

"Off the company books," Mom said, cutting me off. "It has nothing to do with O'Connor Industries."

"So you know about it?"

"Know about it? Hell, I'm the one who insisted your daddy set it up."

Wow! Beth, as usual, was right.

Chapter Twenty-Three

"I'LL TALK TO Robert about it," Edna said.

I snorted. "But you won't talk to me?"

"None of your damn business."

"Well," I said, "since it affects my inheritance, I guess I'll just have to make it my business."

"Oh, is that right?" Edna said as she shifted her weight so she could look me straight in the eye. "How are you going to do that?"

"You either tell me right now what the money was for, or I'll have Beth draw up papers and have you declared incompetent and have you committed to a nursing home."

"You wouldn't dare."

For my entire life my mother had always treated me like an annoying child that she either humored or dismissed.

That ends today. Thank you, Aunt Jolene.

"Like you said, I'm finally showing some O'Connor grit. You think your precious Robert can protect you from Beth and me?" I leaned in closer and rested my hands on her motorized wheelchair until we were nose to nose. "Try me."

At that point, my mom did the most remarkable thing. She began to quiver and a single tear ran down her cheek. "Tillie!" she shouted. "Tillie!" she shouted even louder.

"What do you want, you crazy old bat?" Tillie answered as she came charging out of the new bedroom.

Mom pointed to me. "Repeat what you just said to your aunt so I'll have a witness."

In for a penny, in for a pound.

I squared my shoulders and turned to face Tillie. "I want to know about the missing money, and I told her if she didn't give me a satisfactory answer, I would move to have her declared mentally incompetent and commit her to a nursing home."

"And." Mom motioned for me to continue.

"I told her if she thought her precious Robert could protect her from Beth and me, she should try me."

"Son-of-a-bitch!" Tillie said as she fished some bills out of her front pocket while Mom did the same.

"Can you believe this?" Mom said.

"I've seen it every day of my life for the past sixty years," Tillie answered.

"How the hell does she do it?" Mom asked.

"No idea," Tillie answered as she took Mom's cash and combined it with hers, then shouted, "Jolene!"

Aunt Jolene glanced over her shoulder at Tillie, who was waving the cash over her head. "Winner, winner. Chicken dinner."

Jolene squealed, knocked some flour off her hands and bounded across the room. She snatched the cash out of Tillie's hand and said, "A pleasure doing business with you." Jolene counted the cash, then tucked the bills into her bra.

I closed my eyes and shook my head. As my Aunt Tillie, or maybe it was Yogi Berra, might say, 'It's déjà vu all over again.'

"What was the wager this time?" I asked.

"When I saw you this morning," Jolene said, as she gave my cheek a pat, "I knew today would be the day you would finally stand up to your mother."

"That was the bet?" I said with a horrified expression on my face as I wheeled on my mother. "That I would stand up to you?"

"She was even giving odds," Edna added dejectedly. "We've been waiting for this for a long time," my mom said as she gave my hand a squeeze.

Tillie pounded her forehead with the heel of her hand three times. "Stupid, stupid, stupid," she said with each impact.

"What?" I demanded.

"Honey, here's words to live by. If Jolene Anabel Marshall is willing to bet she can spit in your ear from twenty feet in a wind storm and you're dumb enough to take the bet, you'll end up with a wet ear."

Gabrielle, who had been hanging around the fringe of the conversation, handed Jolene a wad of cash.

"You were in on this too?" I shouted in disbelief.

Gabrielle just shrugged and muttered something under her breath in French.

"I heard that!" Jolene shouted.

Tillie gave Gabrielle a pat on the shoulder. "Now that she's pregnant, she's a full-fledged member of the O'Connor Sisterhood."

"Pregnant," Jolene gasped. "Oh. That explains that."

We all watched as Jolene went over to her knitting basket and came back with a crib blanket. "I just finished this," she said as she handed it to Gabrielle and gave her a hug.

Gabrielle blinked a few times as she examined the blanket. "Pink?"

Tillie laughed as she glanced at Jolene. "I'm giving ten to one that Gabrielle's baby is going to be a girl."

Hardly surprising, with Jolene's track record, Tillie didn't get any takers.

"Okay," I said. "About this O'Connor Sisterhood thing. How come you never invited me into your little secret society when I got pregnant?"

"We all hold veto power for new members," Edna said.

"And my own mother vetoed me?" I said in disbelief.

"Not me," Mom said.

"That would have been me," Aunt Jolene said sweetly.

"Why did you keep me out?" I demanded.

"You weren't ready yet, dear," Jolene answered, then added brightly, "but now you are."

"What the hell does that mean?"

"We all knew you'd made a mistake with marrying Lindsey," Tillie stated flatly.

"You were still your father's little ray of sunshine and oblivious to the world," Mom added.

"That's why I voted to withhold membership until you came to your senses," Aunt Jolene said gently.

"Took you long enough," Tillie mumbled to herself.

"After your performance at school this morning," Mom added. then continued, "and finally kicking Lindsey to the curb...."

"Finally," Tillie interrupted.

"And," Mom said more loudly than necessary to draw the focus back to her. "Since you finally stood up to me, you're now a member of the Sisterhood as well."

I folded my arms across my chest and glared at the other women. "And what exactly are the benefits of being a part of this Sisterhood?"

"We open the family skeleton closet," Tillie said.

"No more secrets?" I asked.

"For the moment; you're still in your probationary period. We'll see how you handle some of the small secrets," Mom answered with a laugh. "Then move on from there."

"Give me one of the small secrets," I said with an impatient tone.

Edna sighed. "For your entire life I've treated you and your brother differently."

I put both hands on my cheeks and leaned back with my eyes and mouth wide open. "Really?" I said in disbelief. "I never noticed."

Tillie burst out laughing. "Yeah, but do you know why?"

That stopped me. I had always assumed Mom loved Robert more than me and had never contemplated that there might be a more rational reason.

"I'm listening," I said softly.

"Your father and I always wanted children, but for the first ten years we were married we had no luck."

"It wasn't for lack of trying," Tillie muttered. Edna glared at her. "What?" Tillie protested. "You two were hotter than the sidewalk in Panama in August in the early days. I was tempted to keep a fire hose handy to cool you two off."

I felt my cheeks darken slightly. While I had zero interest in being updated on my kids' sex life, I really didn't want to know anything about my parents', either. "Way too much information," I said.

Tillie shrugged, then motioned for Mom to continue.

"We had given up," Mom said as she continued to glare at Tillie. "Then, when I was thirty-five, I got pregnant with Robert."

Jolene grabbed the glass out of Edna's wheelchair's cup holder and headed to the refrigerator to freshen up Mom's drink. "I lived through this nightmare," she said softly. "I don't need a recap."

Gabrielle, like me, was on pins and needles waiting for Edna to continue but was too polite or too intimidated by the rest of the Sisterhood to say anything and held her peace.

"It was a tough pregnancy," Edna said.

"Brutal," Tillie added.

Edna glared at Tillie. "If you don't mind, I'd like to tell this without any additional running commentary."

Tillie held up her hands in mock surrender and took a step back. "You have the floor."

"It was so bad," Mom continued. "I was bedridden for the last two months before the delivery. Then, after twenty-three hours in labor, Robert was born. He was a sickly baby." Edna shook her head. "It seemed like he never stopped crying. I don't think I got more than two straight hours of sleep for the first year." Mom got a wistful look in her eyes. "I ended up with post-partum depression that got so bad they had me on a suicide watch."

I was stunned. I had never heard any of this before and was baffled as to why, after all of this, she had always favored my brother over me.

Then a horrible thought struck me.

"Was your pregnancy with me even worse?"

"Heaven's no," Mom said with a laugh. "I had the first labor pain when I was working in the garden and we barely made it to the hospital before you arrived. Then you were the dream baby. Never sick, barely ever cried."

"Then I don't understand," I said. "Then why did you always favor Robert over me?"

Edna sighed. "We needed balance in our family," she said. "Your father worshiped the ground you walked on, but he always hated your brother."

CHAPTER TWENTY-FOUR

"HATE IS A pretty strong word," Tillie said softly as Jolene returned with Mom's lemonade. "I would say Charlie deeply resented Robert and the way he impacted your marital relationship with him."

"Fair enough," Edna said. "He resented Robert, and it colored everything about their relationship. To Charlie, since they were so different, Robert was a huge disappointment. Charlie wanted a wheeler-dealer extrovert of a son, but Robert was none of those things." Mom sighed. "As Robert got older, things only got worse with each passing year. He saw the different way your father treated you as opposed to him, and Robert started to bully you, which infuriated your father even more."

"I'm surprised Robert went to work for the company," I said.

"I talked him into it," Edna answered. "Charlie would never admit it, but he had limitations, and O'Connor Industries had grown to be too big to be run out of a cigar box and with a handshake. Robert added the structure and discipline that was sorely missing. The battles they had were what made the company work. Unfortunately, Robert lacks the vision and dynamic personality of your father, which is why the company hasn't done as well since your daddy passed."

"Wheels within wheels," Aunt Jolene said gently as she handed me a lemonade. "Life and family relationships can be complex."

I found myself lost in thought. This was a side of my mother that, while in plain sight my entire life, I had never seen from her perspective. She didn't favor Robert over me because she loved him more. She felt I was getting all of the love I needed from my daddy, including Robert's share. She was just keeping the family books balanced.

Damn.

I took a sip of the lemonade and my eyes widened as I gasped for breath. "Holy moly! What is this?"

"It's your mother's recipe," Jolene said sweetly. "I believe she calls it Lynchburg Lemonade."

"Lemonade with a splash of Jack Daniels," Edna said.

"A splash?" I said in disbelief. "Keep that away from open flames," I suggested as I put the spiked drink down on the table next to me. "I thought liquor and your medication didn't mix."

"Allie," Mom said as she took a big pull from her glass. "There is absolutely nothing the doctors can do, and my countdown clock is ticking. I'm not going into the ground sober or on a damn diet."

Aunt Tillie clinked her glass with Mom's. "For once, you and I are on the same page, Edna."

I was thunderstruck.

"Don't you want to live?" I demanded.

"Yes," Edna answered in a matter of fact tone. "And I intend to live every day like it might be my last. I'm not going to spend the time I have left moping around and feeling sorry for myself or whacked out on some damn drugs."

Tillie clinked Mom's glass again. "Allie, the senior members of the O'Connor Sisterhood have all lived long and happy lives. None of us," Tillie motioned first to Edna and then Jolene and then to herself, "have time for regrets. While we all want to live, when our time comes, we will meet death as an old friend with the hope there is new adventure on the other side just waiting for us."

I shook the cobwebs out of my head and moved back to my original question. "What about the money?" I asked.

"What money?" Jolene asked.

For the first time Gabrielle spoke. "Robert discovered the company has been making large monthly payments for years without any record of what the money was for or where it was going."

"How much money?" Jolene asked.

"As best we can tell," I answered, "several million dollars."

A soft whistle escaped from Aunt Jolene's mouth. "Let me guess," she said as she grinned at my mom. "These payments started about fifty years ago?"

"Exactly," I answered. How did you know?"

Jolene ignored my question. "Penitence?" she asked Mom.

My mom shrugged and nodded.

"Oh, you dog!" Tillie said as she gave my mom a knuckle bump. "You never told me that part!"

"Penitence?" I asked. "Penitence for what?"

"Your daddy was tighter than an enlarged prostate. There was only one thing he loved more than you and your mother," Tillie said as she continued grinning at my mom. "And that was his money."

"I think we've shared enough family secrets for one day," Edna said as she took another pull from her Lynchburg Lemonade.

"That's not fair, Edna," Tillie protested. "You can't tease them like they're teenagers on a porn site and then leave them hanging."

"How about this," Edna said as she turned to me. "Years ago, before you were born, your father did something terrible, and I made him pay for it for the rest of his life." Next, Mom turned to Gabrielle. "If you see him before I do, you can tell Robert all of that money came from Charlie and my personal account and was paid by after-tax income."

"Oh, my God!" Tillie shouted as she burst out laughing. "After-tax income? You didn't even let him write it off? That must have killed Charlie."

"In hindsight, I may have overdone it and should have let him off the hook," Edna said with a sigh. "The first of every month Charlie got a slap-in-the-face reminder so the wound never got a chance to heal." Edna squared her shoulders then turned back to Gabrielle. "Tell Robert the money had absolutely nothing to do with O'Connor Industries." Edna's eyes narrowed and she waved a warning finger in Gabrielle's direction. "Also, tell him to back off. At this point in his life, nor mine, does he want me as an enemy."

CHAPTER TWENTY-FIVE

BEFORE GABRIELLE COULD answer, Charles and Angela bounded into the kitchen.

"We heard Aunt Jolene was making lunch," Angela said as she eyed the stove and sniffed the air and wasn't disappointed.

"Actually," Jolene said sweetly, "Gabrielle did most of the work."

"Really?" Charles said, an odd expression covering his face as he glanced sideways at his sister. "Gabrielle is a good cook?" he asked.

"Other than having an inexplicable onion fetish," Jolene said with a laugh, "she's every bit as good a chef as me." She glanced at Gabrielle and smiled. "Possibly even better."

A light clicked on in Angela's eyes when she figured out why Charles was so interested in Gabrielle's culinary skills. "Oh my," she muttered as she nodded in her brother's direction to indicate she had caught up. "Where did you study?" Angela asked.

"I received my Grand Diplôme from Le Cordon Bleu in Paris three years ago," Gabrielle answered hesitantly, not sure where this was headed.

"What is a Grand Diplôme?" Angela asked as she reclaimed her position as the spokesperson for the twins.

"It means she is certified in both cuisine and pastry," Jolene answered.

"And that's a big deal?" Angela asked Jolene.

"It is a very big deal," Jolene answered as she gave Gabrielle's arm a gentle squeeze. "Any kitchen in the world would welcome her with open arms."

"I wouldn't go that far," Gabrielle said modestly.

"Have you ever done any commercial cooking?" Angela asked.

"When I was studying in Paris, I worked part time in a small bistro. The summer after graduation, I worked in Tuscany, then a few months in Barcelona, before coming back to America. Why?"

Angela glanced at Charles and his head moved maybe a quarter-inch from side to side. "Just curious," Angela answered with a smile. "What's for lunch?"

"We'll show you!" Gabrielle answered cheerfully as she motioned for Aunt Jolene to follow her.

As Charles started to walk away, I pulled him back. "What was that all about?"

"Hard to say at this point," my son answered with a laugh.

"Enigmatic as always," I answered with a sigh.

Angela pointed to the oversized envelope on the table with the Ruggles, Knapp & Woodrow return address in the upper left corner. "Is that what I think it is?"

I nodded.

Angela gave me a huge hug and whispered in my ear. "You okay?" she asked.

I drew in a deep sigh. "A bit overwhelmed at the moment. But I'll be fine."

Tillie shouted at Charles and Angela. "I want the play-by-play of what happened at school today, and don't skip any of the juicy details."

"Best day of our lives!" Charles said with a rare burst of enthusiasm. "Mom and Aunt Beth were awesome."

Before he could continue, the front doorbell rang. It took a minute for it to register. Everyone who knew us or worked for us always went around to the rear of the house, where there was an abundance of parking, and came in the back door. I hadn't heard it ring in years.

"Who the hell is that?" Edna asked as she glanced in the direction of the foyer.

"Probably a delivery person," I answered as I headed to the door.

It wasn't a delivery person or anyone I had ever seen before. On the front porch, with two oversized suitcases, was a small, dark-skinned man who, if I had to guess, was either Indian or Pakistani.

The man bowed briefly. "Please forgive the intrusion," he said politely. "I'm Sridhar Singh and I'm looking for Dr. Jolene Marshall."

"Steve!" Aunt Tillie's voice boomed behind me.

Steve?

Tillie bumped me out of the way, grabbed one of the suitcases and wheeled it into the house. "Did you have any trouble finding the place?"

"No ma'am," Sridhar "Steve" Singh answered uncomfortably. Being six inches shorter and at least thirty pounds lighter than my aunt, he appeared to be completely intimidated by her.

"Sridhar!" Aunt Jolene said enthusiastically as she gave the visitor a hug. "Did you have any trouble finding us?"

"No, ma'am," he answered as he looked around at the ultra-modern and roomy interior. I had seen that look before. With the old facade still facing the street, the interior of Chateau O'Connor was nothing like what he was expecting when he rang the bell.

"We were just about to have lunch, Steve," Tillie said. "Have you eaten?"

"No ma'am," he answered hesitantly when he saw Gabrielle walking toward the patio with a large tray of sandwiches for the crew doing the work on the house. They were overflowing with an abundance of meats that made Sridhar blanch. "I do not wish to intrude," he said politely. "Perhaps I should come back later."

"Don't be silly, Sridhar," Jolene said as she hooked her arm under his and pulled him in the direction of the kitchen. "I thought you might be showing up, so I made some of that curry with tofu you like so much."

At the sound of that, Singh's eyes lit up. Like everyone else who had ever sampled Jolene's cooking, he knew he was in for a treat. "That would be wonderful."

She motioned in the direction of Gabrielle as he headed out the back door. "My niece suggested we garnish it with fresh mint."

"That sounds amazing, Dr. Marshall."

We all moved outside to the patio, where the work crew had already filled their plates with Gabrielle and Jolene goodness and were busy locating shady spots to enjoy their meals.

I smiled when I noticed how quiet the backyard had become. It is always a good critique of the food when people were too busy chewing and swallowing to bother with polite conversation.

After I helped myself, I noticed that Charles and Angela had Gabrielle cornered well out of earshot and appeared to be grilling her with questions. I found a spot to sit where I could watch the interplay of my kids and my child-bride sister-in-law. I had no idea what they were discussing, but at first Gabrielle's body language was defensive and guarded. As the conversation continued, Gabrielle started to relax and her answers became less cryptic and more detailed.

Finally, the huddle broke up and Gabrielle headed back into the kitchen with a faraway look in her eyes, like she was deep in thought. The twins headed toward Charles' GTO, which was parked directly behind me. As they passed the buffet table, they each grabbed a sandwich wrapped it up in a paper towel, and Charles grabbed an extra one to eat later.

"What was that all about?" I asked as the twins approached.

"Nothing," Angela said with a smile as she stopped next to me.

"It didn't look like nothing to me," I said.

Charles cleared his throat and tapped his watch.

"We have an appointment and we really need to go," Angela said as they started back toward the GTO.

"An appointment? What kind of an appointment?"

Charles looked around with a befuddled look on his face. "Angie, where did you leave our Emancipation Proclamation?"

I laughed out loud and clapped my hands together. "You're right. You're right," I said "None of my business."

Charles gave me a wink as he walked by. "Thanks," he said softly.

All heads turned as Charles fired up the GTO and the powerful V-8 rumbled like only a muscle car could. With the top down, the twins waved to everyone as it rolled out the driveway.

At that moment, Aunt Tillie wandered over. "What are they up to?"

"Not a clue," I answered with a sigh.

"Sometimes being stupid is smart," Tillie said as we watched the GTO disappear down the driveway.

"Yeah," I answered with a chuckle. "Especially with that pair."

"You about finished with your lunch?"

"Why?"

"I thought you might want to sit in on one of Jolene's mind game sessions."

CHAPTER TWENTY-SIX

AUNT TILLIE LUGGED one of the two suitcases up the stairs while "Steve," as Tillie continued to call Sridhar, dealt with the other one. Once we were inside the bedroom Tillie and Jolene were sharing, Steve opened one of the oversized suitcases and began removing his hardware. As Jolene sat passively in the chair Tillie had placed in the center of the open floor space, Sridhar applied an odd electronic device on her head that looked like a flexible plastic spider web. At the junction where each one of the wires strands crossed in the web was a small electrode

I had an "aha" moment and leaned into Aunt Tillie. "That explains the haircut."

"The better the contact, the better the result," Tillie answered as she started to remove her hearing aids.

With her hair covering them, I had never seen the hearing aids before. "When did you get those?" I asked.

"The day I discovered my 'silent but deadly' farts weren't as silent as I thought." Tillie put the hearing aids into a small case. "The EMF some of Steve's stuff puts out make these damn things buzz like a bumblebee."

I chuckled and pointed to the thing on Jolene's head. "What exactly is that?"

"No idea," Tillie answered. "Jolene tried to explain it to me a couple of times, but it just made my eyes glaze over. Apparently Steve and his buddies used an MRI to map JoJo's noggin and locate any problem areas. The best I can figure, that contraption focuses on the plaque that causes Alzheimer's and other blockages. Steve uses his laptop to triangulate problem areas, then uses a highly focused ultrasound thingy to try to break up the obstructions and stimulate circulation."

"Is it safe?" I asked.

"Jolene says it is and it's her head Steve is messing with and not mine," Tillie answered with a laugh. "Personally, you couldn't pay me enough to get me to let Steve start microwaving my brain."

Sridhar shot Aunt Tillie a look.

"Ignore her," Jolene said.

"Does it work?" I asked as I watch Sridhar connect two plugs from the back of the spider web to a black box about the size of a small inkjet printer, which was also connected to his laptop.

"Jolene swears by it," Tillie answered.

"But you're not convinced?"

Tillie shrugged. "Some days after a treatment she's clearly better. I mean all the way back to the way she used to be. Other times, not so much." Tillie sighed. "You'll be able to judge for yourself in an hour or so."

"What happens in an hour?"

"Sometimes the treatment will disorient her so I'll tuck her in bed for a short nap."

Sridhar fired up his equipment and hunched over his laptop. It didn't take long for me to get bored watching Sridhar type on his keyboard and Jolene sitting with her eyes closed in a trance-like state. I nudged Aunt Tillie, who showed no indication she was leaving, and I pointed toward the door. Tillie nodded.

After making my quiet exit, I headed back downstairs. With Edna's ramp outside the kitchen door finished and handrails in the bathroom installed, and the bulk of the crew out foraging for parts to install an automated door in the den, it was fairly quiet and calm. Gabrielle was in the kitchen cleaning up from lunch. She had already figured out the great room sound system, which put her light years ahead of me, and was softly singing along with a song I had never heard before. I stood at the bottom of the stairs and watched her as she happily went about her work.

Aunt Tillie likes to say, *Youth is wasted on the dumb*, but in Gabrielle's case it didn't seem to apply. I had known Aunt Jolene my entire life and I knew she did not suffer fools easily and was incredibly intuitive when it came to reading people. For Gabrielle to have bonded so deeply and quickly with Jolene told me volumes about her.

I wandered into the kitchen, picked up a dishrag and started to help with the cleanup.

Gabrielle smiled at me and softly said, "If you have other things to do, I've got this."

And clearly she did. I make a bigger mess opening a can of soup and burning grilled cheese sandwiches for the twins than she had let accumulate while preparing a feast for twenty. Gabrielle knew her way around a kitchen.

"Where's Edna?"

"She rode along with one of the men to the warehouse."

"Really? Why?"

"She said something about wanting to be sure the people at the O'Connor warehouse didn't give her crew any problems."

I laughed. "I imagined she may have phrased it a bit stronger than that."

"Indeed," Gabrielle answered. "She is quite a handful."

"And you're quite the chef."

Gabriele puffed out her cheeks and made an odd snort. "Compared to my mother, I'm a novice."

"Really?" Then it dawned on me. I realized I didn't know her at all. She and Robert had eloped and I wasn't invited to come along so I had never met her parents. I didn't know she was a world-class chef until recently – which certainly explained why Marko sought her advice. Plus, I had always carried a chip on my shoulder about her. At best, I thought she was a brainless snuggle bunny, and at worst, another Lilith. I had never given her a chance.

That all changes today.

"When things calm down a little bit, I think we should get to know each other better."

"I'd like that," Gabrielle said with a radiant smile. "I'd like that very much."

With Gabrielle apparently not needing any help inside, I went outside and gathered up stray dishes and silverware and emptied the trash cans. After I came back in, I emptied the massive dishwasher. Gabrielle glanced around the kitchen; she puffed out her cheeks again and shook her head.

"What?" I asked. "The kitchen looks perfect."

"I have to tell my mother I'm pregnant."

"Is that a problem?"

"She's French, so there is no telling."

I had no idea what that meant but I smiled and offered, "Would you like some backup?"

"No," Gabrielle said with a smile that quickly faded. "It's just this should be the happiest day of my life, and all of this tension with you and Robert..." She let the thought drift away.

"Robert and I have been at each other's throats our entire lives; sometimes I think it's how we show we love each other." I gave Gabrielle a hug and whispered in her ear. "This storm between Robert and me will pass." I released her and pointed her toward the door. "Go tell your mother. I'll finish up here.

I watched Gabrielle leave and was just about to put the finishing touches on the kitchen cleanup when I heard a voice behind me.

"Very nice."

Chapter Twenty-Seven

I TURNED AND saw Aunt Jolene on the bottom step of the staircase. She was a different person and had completely reverted back to the woman I remembered my entire life. Brilliant, more than a bit intimidating and dripping with self-confidence. She had changed clothes and now wore a well-cut black pantsuit combination with a silver-gray silk blouse. Her hair, what little there was of it, was brushed. And, though I couldn't swear to it, she might have on a touch of makeup. She stood tall and erect and her eyes were taking in everything in the room.

Aunt Tillie was one step up behind Jolene on the stairs. "Steve hit the X ring today," she said, beaming with a massive smile on her face. "She didn't even want her nap."

"You've come a long way in a very short time, Allison," Aunt Jolene said proudly. She looked over her shoulder at Aunt Tillie. "Why don't you finish tidying up the kitchen? I'd like to have a chat with our niece."

Tillie leaned forward and kissed Jolene on the top of her head, then maneuvered around her on the stairs. "My thoughts exactly."

As Tillie brushed past me, she leaned in and said, "I haven't seen her this good in two years. I think she willed herself to come back because she wants to talk to you. You may not get another chance to speak to the Oracle. Don't waste this."

I nodded and felt a shiver go down my spine. While she had always just been Aunt Jolene to me, I knew she had a massive worldwide following, and had helped millions of people improve their state of well-being. Unlike my mother and my Aunt Tillie, she had never once pushed me to read any of her books. She had never commented on my life nor ever made any suggestions.

I had a feeling that was all about to change.

Unlike the unsteady stride Jolene had the previous day and this morning, she walked confidently to the L-shaped couch in the media wing of the great room and sat down and waited for me. Before I had even gotten settled in, Jolene started talking. She had the tone of a professor addressing an overflowing auditorium. "You read one of my books," she stated and not asked.

"Yes," I answered meekly. "I read…"

Jolene cut me off. "I know which one you read. It was obvious when you walked into the kitchen this morning. You were no longer intimidated by an authority figure, so that woman at the school held no power over you. You had moved from making unconscious choices to managing your choices."

I blinked a few times. "How did you…"

"That is not important," Jolene said as she cut across me again. "Do you have any idea why I blackballed you from the Sisterhood for all of these years?"

I shook my head.

"You have spent your entire life trapped in a vicious, self-reinforcing cycle. First, because you had lived such a generous and blessed life, you never had to make the hard choice between confronting your primal fear and your intellect. For you the rewards of going along far outweighed the unknown risks of rejection. Because of this, on some level, your decision to be cowed by men made a great deal of sense."

I started to protest but she held up a single finger and, almost magically, it completely silenced me.

"Your fear of offending the dominant men in your life, first your father, then Robert, then your husband, caused you to make bad choices."

"I'm not sure…"

Jolene held up her finger to stop me again.

"The intuitive need to please your male elders and not be exiled from the tribe is one of the strongest primal fears to overcome. It is why battered women return to be abused again and again." Jolene smiled and patted me on the knee. "When I saw you this morning in your battle gear and ready to come to the defense of your children, I knew then, even if you didn't, you had absorbed the lessons of my book and crossed a personal threshold. I suspected that a victory over that awful woman at your children's school would motivate you to take the next step and finalize your divorce. When that occurred, I knew you were never going back to your old ways and would likely challenge your mother. At that point I withdrew my veto."

"And made your bet."

"And made my bet," Jolene repeated.

"I'm not sure I completely grasp what's going on," I said softly.

"The women of the Sisterhood are strong and self-reliant and all make conscious choices. We do not respond to peer or social pressure that will negatively impact our lives. Have you ever seen your mother or Tillie react well when anyone tried to manipulate or bully them?"

I laughed. "Exactly the opposite."

"Precisely," Aunt Jolene replied. "We don't go along to get along. We don't make decisions out of an undefinable fear or the need for positive reinforcement of others. We evaluate each situation and use our intellect." Jolene patted my knee again. "If you had been allowed in the Sisterhood any earlier, it would have been a disservice to you and to us. You would have been confused and might have retreated even deeper into the illusionary safety of the cave guarded by the men in your life. Our goal has always been to show you the light and not have you retreat further into the darkness."

I stared at Aunt Jolene as I tried to gather my thoughts, but I was distracted by the throaty rumble of Charles's GTO as it pulled up outside. Charles and Paige Thompson came in the back door. Paige, fresh from being picked up from school, had her backpack slung over her shoulder and a confused expression on her face.

"I need to get back to my meeting," Charles said as he gave Paige a peck on the cheek before making his exit.

Paige's eyes locked on Jolene. "Charles said you wanted to see me," Paige said cautiously.

Jolene rose effortlessly to her feet. "Yes, and thank you for coming." Jolene extended her hand, indicating that Paige should join us. "I need to apologize, Paige." Jolene said her name without the aid of notes or verbal clues. "Last night I was tired and I did not give you the attention you deserve."

"Okay," Paige said reluctantly as she dropped her backpack on one of the other chairs in the great room. She came around the end of the couch and slowly sat down.

Out of nowhere, Aunt Tillie arrived with a stack of books and a heavy fountain pen and put them on the coffee table in front of Jolene. Jolene glanced up at Tillie and smiled at her. "Thank you." Tillie disappeared just as quickly as she had appeared. Jolene removed the cap off the pen and opened the cover of the book on the top of the stack. "Thompson. T-h-o-m-p-s-o-n?"

"Yes," Paige answered and was getting more confused instead of less.

"The copies you had me sign yesterday, being dog-eared and with notes in the margin, were obviously your much-loved personal copies."

"Yes," Paige said with a twinkle in her eye as she tilted her head to read the names of the titles of the books on the coffee table. In the short time I had known her, I had never seen her smile like that before.

"These are all first editions of my books," Jolene said as she leaned back a bit further before attempting to sign them. Out of nowhere, again, Tillie arrived with Jolene's reading glasses. Jolene nodded her thanks, put the glasses on her nose, scooted closer to the coffee table and began writing.

Tillie leaned into Paige and whispered. "Several of these editions are quite rare and she seldom adds a personal note." Jolene finished signing the first book and slid it across the table in Paige's direction before opening the cover of the second book in the stack.

With quivering hands, Paige pulled the book in front of herself, spun it around and, with Tillie looking over one shoulder and me looking over the other, read the inscription.

To Paige Thompson

From one Traveler to another.

May your life be filled with peace, love and joy.

Beneath it was a dramatic signature that only a fine fountain pen would do justice.

Dr. Jolene A. Marshall
(AKA) Aunt Jolene

Paige was stunned and speechless as she wiped tears from her eyes. "You think I'm a Traveler?"

Jolene did not answer but glanced up at Paige with a knowing smile.

"Thank you so much," Paige said meekly.

Jolene made eye contact with Aunt Tillie, then Tillie gently tugged on my arm and whispered in my ear, "Let's give these two some space."

When we got to the other side of the room and out of earshot, I asked softly. "Aunt Jolene thinks Paige is a Traveler?"

Tillie snorted. "JoJo knows she is, even if Paige hasn't figured it out yet."

"So exactly what does all of that mean?"

"Luke Skywalker just met Yoda."

CHAPTER TWENTY-EIGHT

AUNT TILLIE NODDED that we should take our conversation outside and I quickly agreed. We found a four-seat table in a shady spot and sat down opposite each other.

"I can't believe the difference in Aunt Jolene," I said as I shook my head in amazement.

"Because of who she is, she has access to all of the cutting-edge technology that is available on enhancing brain function. The way she explains it, with MRI, ultrasound, light frequency, and other things I barely understand, they are making massive strides. She doesn't think she'll live long enough to see it, but she believes Alzheimer's and dementia will soon join polio and smallpox on the ash heap of medical history."

"Wow!"

"Plus," Tillie continued, "There are promising studies on PTSD and even drug addiction." Tillie shook her head. "The things your kids and grandkids are going to see are going to be amazing."

"Thanks for motivating me to finally read Aunt Jolene's book."

Tillie shook her head. "Your mom and I have been pushing it in your direction for years with no luck. I once asked Jolene to suggest it and she flatly refused."

"Why?"

"She said it would be meaningless to you if you weren't ready. She said your lizard brain would rationalize everything and cause you to dismiss the book. As usual, JoJo was right."

"I wonder why I resisted for so long?" I asked absently.

Tillie let out one of her famous roars of laughter that can fill a room and turn heads half a block away. She wiped a tear from her eye then said, "It was because your lizard brain knew if you ever found out what it was up to, its days would be numbered."

"You're kidding."

"Okay," Tillie said. "Let me ask you this. After reading the book, how obvious was it your lizard brain was making bad choices for you your entire life?"

"Pretty obvious," I answered with a sigh.

"How does that make you feel?"

"Like an idiot for taking so long to see it."

"Are you ever going to let it control you like that again?"

"I certainly hope not."

"But it was able to do it for over fifty years of your life. How do you think that happened?"

I leaned back in my chair and stared at Tillie for a few moments. "That's an excellent question."

"According to most accepted research, the lizard brain is very primitive, with its vocabulary limited to the big four, Flight, Fight, Freeze or Fawn. Jolene thinks it goes deeper than that and includes things like sex drive, an unwillingness to resist temptation such as drug abuse, overeating, etc." Tillie reached across the table and tapped me on the forehead. "It was your modern brain that heard the crude and simplistic warnings; then you created a rational response based on your reality at the time."

"So you're saying, after hearing the warning bell go off, I talked myself into reacting a certain way."

"Exactly," Tillie said. "Like Jolene said in her book, once you are aware of this little saboteur lurking deep in your brain, you can either figure out how to manage it or go fully enlightened and start to control it."

Tillie reached across the table and squeezed my hand. "While this is a major breakthrough for you, you need to take it slow. Before you say the word 'no' about anything, take a few seconds and think about it. Ask yourself, is it me or my lizard brain talking?"

"Okay," I answered. "What's going on with Jolene and Paige?"

"JoJo is looking for someone to continue her work after she's gone."

"Wow!" I said. "Isn't Paige a little young?"

Tillie sighed. "Jolene has given up on trying to find anyone in academia."

"Why?"

"We're pretty much not welcome on any campus anymore."

"What happened?"

"You know your Aunt Jolene is humor challenged."

"She is pretty serious."

"Well," Tillie continued. "A few years ago she cracked a joke that I thought was hilarious but some of the delicate darlings on campus had to retreat to their 'safe space' and locate their fainting couches and smelling salts."

"What did she say?"

"You familiar with the term LGBT?"

"Sure," I answered. "Lesbian, Gay, Bisexual and Transgender. Right?"

"Right. But these days they keep adding letters and it is difficult to keep track of what each letter means without a score card. So one day Jolene and I are on a campus and somebody handed us a flyer that was in support of, I kid you not, 'LGBTTQQ2SIAAP.' Jolene laughed and asked the young lady if her cat had walked across her keyboard while she was typing up the flyer."

I chuckled. "Okay," I said, "for Aunt Jolene that is pretty funny."

"Right," Tillie answered. "Then all hell broke loose. Here were two octogenarian lesbians who were openly gay when it could end a career instead of enhance it like today. I mean, we had our skulls cracked open on a bridge in Selma, Alabama. We burned our bras on the White House lawn and had opened and funded one of the first battered women's shelters in the country. Now, because of a clever throwaway line, we were suddenly ostracized."

"That sounds like a bit of an overreaction for such a harmless joke."

"Well," Tillie said. "There was the other thing."

"Oh, God," I said as I shook my head. "What did you say?"

Tillie shrugged. "I suggested being born with a penis should automatically disqualify anyone from ever competing in women's sports."

"Who did you say that to?" I asked.

"That coffee-maker named reporter."

I started to ask, then it hit me. "Katie Couric?"

"That's her," Tillie answered.

"That's not that bad."

Tillie made a face.

"What else did you say?"

"I might have suggested if transgender athletes want to compete, they should set up their own competition, you know, like the Special Olympics."

"So you compared transgender athletes to Special Olympic athletes?"

"Pretty much."

I ran my hand back and forth in front of my mouth. "You were born with no filtration system."

We both turned when we heard a car pull into the driveway and take one of the spots near the door. It was a late model Lexus coupe, so it clearly wasn't one of the work crew's rides. The driver's side door opened and I felt an involuntary smile break across my face.

Bernie Williamson waved in our direction before leaning back into the car to retrieve something from the backseat.

"Isn't that your old business partner?" Tillie asked.

I nodded and kept smiling. Knowing Bernie's screwball sense of humor, I couldn't wait to see what he was up to. He emerged from the car with a half dozen helium-filled balloons in one hand and a pastry box in the other. He must have had his production department create the writing on the balloons, because I don't remember ever seeing any at the grocery store with the same message. Two of the balloons were facing the wrong direction but the four I could read from where I was sitting said, *About Damn Time!, Free At Last!, Kiss Me I'm Single, Divorcees Do It with Style.*

Tillie gave Bernie a round of applause. "Brilliant!" she shouted in his direction before leaning in to me. "I always liked him." Tillie bounded to her feet and relieved Bernie of the pastry box. "Since Allison is on a perpetual diet, I assume these are for me."

"Edna, actually," Bernie said as he handed Tillie the box and then tried to give her a hug, but the balloons had a different idea. "When I heard Jolene Marshall had moved in, I figured if I showed up with a macaroni and cheese casserole it would just end up in the landfill. No one can compete with her."

"Stick around," Tillie said. "Gabrielle O'Connor is giving her a run for the money."

Bernie snapped the fingers on his empty hand. "She studied in Paris, if I remember correctly."

Am I the only one on the planet who didn't know Gabrielle was a chef?

The balloons were all attached to a weight, which he put in the middle of the table before giving me a hug.

"How's Edna?"

"Still hanging in there and as ornery as ever." I glanced at the balloons. "I take it you heard about my divorce being finalized."

Bernie made an odd face. "Really," he answered, deadpan. "What makes you say that?"

Other than putting on a few pounds and having a bit less hair, Bernie hadn't changed much since high school. He was the kind of guy you instantly liked. He always had a smile on his face and a joke on his lips and had a photographic memory for faces and personal details. He could bump into someone he hadn't seen in years and ask about the person's spouse and kids by name. Self-effacing, he always took the attitude that it was amazing what you could accomplish when you didn't care who got the credit. Working with large egos that demanded the spotlight be only on them, he possessed a combination of strengths and attitude that made him a perfect public relations person.

Bernie was basically the anti-Lindsey.

My ex-husband always wanted the limelight on him. If he wasn't at that moment trying to get into your pants or your wallet, it was unlikely he would remember your name. Still, even at his age, he was the vigorous Alpha Male. Power, intellect and confidence oozed out of every pore in his body. It was easy to see why so many young women were lining up in the hope of being the trophy wife or at least a member of the next wives club.

Thinking back, I wondered how different my life might have been if I had married Bernie instead of Lindsey. I immediately dismissed that thought.

No Lindsey, no twins.

On balance, putting up with Lindsey's nonsense for three decades in exchange for Charles and Angela, while unpleasant at times, was a tolerable trade.

Besides, the timing was all off. Bernie and I dated in high school but we went to different colleges. We always stayed close; close enough that even after I married Lindsey we started a business together.

Who was I kidding?

The reason I married Lindsey was sex. With Bernie it was cuddly and playful and he was always attentive to my needs. With Lindsey it was intense, animal, primal....

Son-of-a-bitch.

I picked Lindsey over Bernie because my ex was exactly the kind of man my lizard brain preferred. Strong, aggressive, protective. That would certainly explain why so many women end up with lousy men. Speaking from personal experience, the bad boy sounds good on paper and can be exhilarating in the bedroom, but the trade-offs can be brutal.

"I heard you laid waste to your kids' high school this morning."

I tried my best to keep a smile off my face but failed badly. "I'm going to kill Beth. Did she tell you to stop by?"

Bernie waved me off. "I heard Edna had been discharged from the hospital and planned on swinging by anyway." He pointed to the

157

array of balloons fluttering in the breeze next to us. "This was just a bonus." Suddenly, he turned serious. "You okay?"

"Actually," I answered. "I'm better than okay."

"Excellent! Do you want to have dinner with me tonight?"

"Really?" I shook my head and chuckled to myself. "How about we at least let the ink dry on my divorce papers before you start hitting on me?"

"Look, I'm unattached and you're unattached. You've known me forever and we've always enjoyed each other's company and neither one of us is getting any younger."

"What does that mean?"

"I figure we have maybe twenty-five to thirty good years left in us before we start getting fitted for a walker." Bernie grabbed my hands and looked me straight in the eyes. "I want to travel the world and I don't want to do it alone, and I certainly don't want to do it with anyone but you."

I burst out laughing. "Who in your copywriting department wrote that and how many times did you practice that line in front of a mirror?" I asked.

"Too much?" Bernie asked with a snort and I nodded. "I never could pull anything over on you." His smile vanished. "Seriously, Allie, if you tell me to back off, I will. If you tell me there is no chance for us, I'll back off forever. But I think we would be idiots if we didn't give us another chance."

I could almost hear my lizard brain screaming that this was the wrong time. You need to heal. Go find a well-endowed younger man with incredible endurance who will curl your toes in bed, etc.

I reached across the table, grabbed Bernie's hands and looked him straight in the eyes. "Pick me up at seven, and it had better be white tablecloths, soft music, an expensive bottle of wine, and not a sports bar for wings and a beer."

Take that, lizard brain.

CHAPTER TWENTY-NINE

BERNIE HUNG AROUND for about fifteen minutes. When there was still no sign of my mother, and no ETA, he said he needed to get back to work and headed out. Before he left, we made a reservation at Gino's for dinner. Bernie was never a big fan of Italian, but, because of our personal connections, it was the only place we could get a short-notice reservation on a Friday night.

As I watched him drive off, I reached for my cellphone. It rang long enough that I thought it was about to kick to voice mail, but just before I hung up, Beth breathlessly came on the line. "What?" she demanded in an irritated tone. I could hear voices and people moving around in the background. She was in a meeting, but when she saw my name on the caller ID, and unsure if something had happened to Edna, she took my call.

"What did you tell Bernie?"

Beth laughed. "I'm in the middle of something. I'll call you back in two minutes."

We both hung up without a goodbye.

I tossed my phone on the table and tapped the balloons Bernie had brought me. Cute, clever and sweet. At one hundred and nineteen seconds after I had hung up, my phone rang. I glanced at the caller ID then barked before Beth could say anything. "Who the hell do you think you are?"

There was a long silence, then the voice on the other end said, "This is Wilma, Elizabeth Woodrow's personal assistant. She told you she would call you back in two minutes but she is going to need about ten more minutes."

My chin dropped to my chest and I shook my head. "I'm sorry, Wilma. I thought you were Beth. Please tell her there is no urgency, I'll be willing to strangle her whenever she can work me into her schedule."

"Excuse me?" Wilma said.

"Just tell her to get her affairs in order." Before Wilma could respond or call 911, I broke the connection.

Tillie walked out with a pastry in her hand and offered me a bite, but I declined. "I always liked that one," Tillie said. "Funny as hell."

We both looked at the balloons and chuckled.

"Well?" Tillie said.

"Well, what?" I asked.

"Did he ask you out or not?"

"He asked me to go to dinner with him tonight."

"Whoa!" Tillie said with a cackle. "He doesn't mess around." Aunt Tillie gave me a sideways glance. "What did you say?"

"God, Tillie," I said with a deep sigh. "There are a thousand reasons this is the wrong time."

Tillie, obviously disappointed, nodded that she understood and wasn't going to argue the point.

"So, after spending last night cuddled up with Jolene's book, I thought spending time with a warm-blooded biped would be fun. I told him to pick me up at seven."

"Outstanding! What are you going to wear?"

"I hadn't really thought that far ahead," I answered. "I think I'll run down to my house and see what's in the closet."

"Need any company?"

"Naw," I answered. "You should probably stay here and keep an eye on Jolene...."

"The way she and Paige are going at each other in there, a bomb could go off in the great room and neither one would notice."

"What do you mean?"

"Paige has been hitting Jolene with questions that she would have had trouble fielding twenty years ago."

"Should I go in and break it up?" I said with a hint of panic in my voice.

"You'll have to go through me to do it," Tillie answered. "The more Jolene uses her brain these days the better she gets. Paige is a godsend."

"What are they talking about?"

"It appears Paige Thompson has read every word Jolene Marshall has ever written and heard every word she has ever uttered on YouTube. She is in there challenging Jolene's theories and making Jolene defend them. Apparently Paige has some ideas of how to make Jojo's theories more appealing to a younger generation and Jolene is not buying it." Tillie wiped a tear from her eye. "Jolene is mopping the floor with Paige, but that girl will not back down. Jolene is having the time of her life."

"Okay," I said. "But I still think you should hang around here."

"Why?'

"One of us should be here when Edna gets back."

"Good point."

"I won't be gone long," I said as I headed to my car.

I was still backing up when my phone rang and my car picked it up. I tapped a button on the steering wheel. "Hello."

"Hey," Beth said cheerfully. "You know Wilma has no sense of humor and wouldn't recognize sarcasm if it bit her on the butt. I thought she was going to have a heart attack. What the hell were you thinking?"

"What the hell were *you* thinking?" I demanded.

"I was thinking the first person I should tell you'd signed your divorce papers was Bernie Williamson."

"He showed up at the Farm."

"And?"

"And he asked me out to dinner tonight."

"And?"

"Gino's at 7:30."

"That's right," Beth said enthusiastically. "Who's the matchmaker?"

As I arrived at the end of the driveway, I looked both directions before making my turn. "I don't think it took a lot of manipulation on your part to get Bernie to ask me out."

"Granted," Beth said. "It wasn't my toughest close ever, but I'm still claiming it as a win."

"Would you and Derek like to join us?"

"Oh, hell no," Beth answered instantly. "All we would do is complicate things."

"How so?"

"Sweetie, you've known Bernie forever and you don't need a buffer. Besides, after the second glass of wine, you'll both know if you two have a future or not. You may not be ready to get naked with him tonight, but you'll know if it's worth moving forward."

Get naked? Yikes!

As I approached my house, I was surprised to see two cars in the driveway. One was Charles's GTO and the other one was a late-model, fire-engine- red Porsche Boxster sports car with vanity plates that had "ACQUIRE" embossed on them.

"I need to go."

"Why?"

"I'm just pulling up to my house and the twins have company."

"Who?" Beth asked.

"My ex-husband."

CHAPTER THIRTY

I PULLED IN behind the GTO instead of Lindsey's car for two reasons. One, I didn't plan to stay long because I only needed to pick up an outfit for tonight and I would probably leave before the twins. Two, if Lindsey saw me and immediately wanted to skedaddle, I didn't want anything standing in his way.

I sat in the car and gathered my thoughts for a moment. Since Charles, Angela and I had officially moved into a "don't ask, don't tell" relationship, it was absolutely none of my business if they wanted to see their father. Besides, this could be completely innocent. Lindsey still had some things at the house and maybe he stopped by to pick them up and simply ran into the kids.

Right.

This was prearranged. In twenty-eight years of marriage, I can count on one hand the number of times Lindsey was home on a weekday before six o'clock, and usually he didn't roll in until after eight. Plus, manual labor was not in his vocabulary. He would have one of his personal assistants who, strangely, were always attractive young females, pick up his stuff. This was obviously the meeting the twins were in such a hurry to get to, and the third sandwich was for their dad.

I got out of my car, opened the front door and entered my house. I could hear voices coming from the dining room at the other end of the hall. I slammed the front door with enough authority they all immediately knew they had company. I gave them a few seconds then headed down the hallway.

Lindsey was sitting in the chair at the head of the table and smiling innocently in my direction. Charles and Angela had hurriedly gathered up some papers that I suspected had a moment earlier been spread out on the table. They had just finished cramming them into a file box when I reached the doorway to the dining room.

"This is an unexpected surprise," I said coldly.

"Daddy was just helping us with a business problem," Angela said hopefully.

"You two are moving quickly if you're already seeking the advice of an international mergers and acquisitions negotiator," I said with even less warmth in my voice.

"I am sorry, Allison, I should have called," Lindsey said without the slightest hint of embarrassment or sincerity in his voice or regret on his face. "The kids had some questions and I had a cancellation, so here I am."

"Don't let me interrupt," I said as my eyes narrowed on my ex-husband. "I just needed to stop by to pick up some clothes for my date tonight."

Angela gasped. Charles had a silly "good for you" grin on his face and Lindsey didn't react at all.

I immediately turned and headed up the stairs to the master bedroom. Before I even got to the top landing, I heard the front door open and close and I also heard footsteps taking the stairs behind me two at a time and closing fast.

"Do you really have a date tonight or were you just messing with Daddy?" Angela asked, catching up with me just as I was about to enter my bedroom.

At that moment, I was so pleased with myself for not letting my lizard brain stop me from saying yes to going out tonight that I was having trouble keeping a smile off my face. "I have a date."

"Please tell me it's with Bernie Williamson."

"Okay," I said as I stopped and leaned back and looked in Angela's direction. "My date is with Bernie Williamson."

Angela made a fist with both hands then jerked them backward. "Yes!"

"I take it Bernie has the O'Connor twins' official seal of approval."

"Absolutely," Angela answered as she did a happy dance. "What are you going to wear?"

"That's why I'm here."

"Great, I'll help," Angela said as she dashed ahead of me in the direction of my walk-in closet.

I glanced out the window and saw Charles and Lindsey in a deep conversation with each of them leaning on their respective cars. Hardly surprisingly, Lindsey was doing all of the talking. The index finger of his right hand was touching first one finger then the next on his other hand as if he was laying out bullet points and the right sequence in which they should be applied. I could see my son taking mental notes and nodding his agreement.

Angela emerged from my closet with an armload of outfits and tossed them on my bed. She saw me staring out the window and joined me.

"It looks like you're missing the climax of the meeting."

"Mom…"

I held up my hand and stopped her. "It is none of my business what you two are up to, and I'm delighted that you have a close relationship with your father."

Angela grabbed me and turned me away from the window to face her. "He will always be our daddy and you'll always be Mom. We have decades of holidays and birthdays ahead of us and neither Charles nor I want this to be awkward or painful for either one of you."

As I gave Angela a hug, I felt a single tear run down my cheek. "When did you get so old and wise?" I released Angela from the hug but held her at arm's length. "There is no animosity between your father and me, and being around him doesn't trigger any emotional response on my part or, apparently, his." I pulled Angela back into a hug. "You don't need to sneak around to see him."

Angela patted me on the back. "That's what we thought, but considering today was the day you filed your divorce papers we didn't want to chance it."

"So, tell me one thing." I said with a chuckle as we separated. "How did you get him to come to you instead of you going to his office?"

Angela's voice suddenly went soft and little girlish. "Daddy. Charles and I have a business problem and you're the only one we can talk to about it. We don't want to get too far away from Grammy and we really don't want Mommy to know. Could you possibly meet us at the house this afternoon?"

"Evil!"

Angela giggled. "He knew I was playing him and we didn't care where we had our meeting. It was just a power play by Charles and me to establish our future working relationship with him. Considering everything that had happened the last couple of days, he didn't dare say no to me, so we had our first sit-down on our turf and not his."

"You do realize up until a few hours ago this was his house too."

Angela giggled again. "This was never his house. The yard guy spent more time here than he did. This was our house and we made him come to us. That will put us on equal footing for the rest of our lives."

"Where did you learn all of this?" I asked, already knowing the answer.

"Charles wasn't the only one who spent time with Grandpa in the garage. At that point in my life I was too dainty to actually get down and dirty with Charles and Grandpa, but it didn't stop me from sitting on the sidelines and listening."

I laughed out loud. "He gave you the 'first meeting' speech."

"You heard it too?" Angela asked.

"I got it the day Bernie and I opened our new business."

Angela sighed. "I think toward the end he wanted to share as much of his wisdom as possible with Charles and me."

"Including setting you up in your own business?"

Angela, with a faraway look in her eyes, chuckled. "I think he expected us to crash and burn and was shocked, but more than a little proud, when we actually made it profitable from the get-go."

"He was quite the man." I felt tears forming in my eyes and quickly turned my attention to the outfits Angela had laid on the bed.

At that exact moment, Charles appeared in the doorway and stopped dead in his tracks when he saw the tearful expression on my face and all of the dresses on the bed.

"I'm guessing you don't need any input from me," he said with a laugh.

"I think we've got this," Angela answered.

"Mom, have you seen Paige? She's not answering her phone or responding to text messages."

"The last time I saw her she was in a deep conversation with your Aunt Jolene."

"Outstanding," Angela said and Charles nodded his agreement.

"What is outstanding about that?"

"Sometimes I think the only reason she dates me is because of the chance to meet Jolene." Charles turned and started to make his exit. "I'm going to check up on her." He waved and then disappeared down the steps.

After Charles was out of sight, I picked up a slinky red cocktail dress with a slit up the side and a plunging neckline and tossed it aside.

"I've never seen you in that dress before," Angela said as she picked up and held it against herself.

"And you never will," I answered as I foraged through my other options. "Your father got that for me a few years ago and actually expected me to wear it to his company Christmas party. I really didn't want to go as Santa's slutty girlfriend."

"Can I have it?" Angela asked as she pressed it against her body and looked at herself in my full-length mirror.

I slowly turned and glared at her.

"What?" She demanded. "Would you rather I sneak in when you're not here and borrow it?"

I gave her a dismissive wave. "All yours, just promise me you won't wear it when there is even a slight chance I might be around."

"Done," Angela answered as she rehung the dress in my closet so it wouldn't get wrinkled. She picked up another selection. "What about this one?"

I glanced up and immediately dismissed it. "Too come-hither," I said.

"So slutty and come-hither are out; exactly what are we going for here?" Angela asked.

"The perfect dress that says I got divorced today and this is my first night out with any man other than my ex-husband in three decades."

"Ah," Angela answered. "Got it."

We settled on a tasteful, age-appropriate, dark blue cocktail dress with a lovely pale blue over the shoulder shawl.

"With that settled," Angela said with a mischievous grin on her face. "Top-drawer or bottom-drawer underwear?"

I shot Angela one of my famous big-eye, open-mouth looks, which I had, until this moment, always thought would stop my rebellious daughter in her tracks. Apparently, with her emancipation, it had lost all of its magical powers.

"What?" she demanded. "Do you think in the nearly eighteen years we've lived under the same roof I hadn't gone through your drawers before?" She made a dismissive snort. "Please."

The top drawer of my dresser contained my everyday undies; those in the bottom drawer, how to put it, were a bit more exotic. They were mostly gifts from my perpetually horny ex-husband and most had never even been worn.

I thought about it for half a beat. While it was unlikely my date with Bernie tonight would end up in a passionate embrace, he was one of only five men I'd ever had sex with in my entire life.

What the hell.

"Bottom drawer."

"Atta girl," Angela answered.

CHAPTER THIRTY-ONE

THE ARMY HAD returned to the Farm and my mom was out on the patio, with her lemonade, supervising the installation of the auto-open door in her new bedroom. I waved and she waved back, but she made no indication she was either coming over to see me or needed my attention. Fine with me. I entered the kitchen with an outfit over my arm and Angela in tow.

"Is that what you're wearing tonight?" Tillie asked as she wiped pastry crumbs off of her chin. I nodded and she motioned to see my selection of attire for the evening. I held the dress up against my body and Tillie nodded her approval. "Nice."

Charles was sitting on one of the bar stools in the breakfast nook of the great room that faced the swimming pool and was busy eating one of the sandwiches left over from lunch.

"Where's Paige and Jolene?"

Charles, with his mouth full of ham and Swiss on dark rye, pointed in the direction of Edna's garden. Moving my head slightly to the left, I could just catch a glimpse of them deep in conversation on one of the many benches mom had in her garden. Edna had placed them so that no matter the position of the sun, there would always be a shady place to sit.

"Thick as thieves," I muttered as I headed upstairs to hang up my outfit and begin the ritual of preparing my face and hair for an evening out. As I stepped from my bathroom in a robe and towel-wrapped my wet hair, I was delighted to discover Angela fussing around in my makeup bag.

"God, Mom," she said. "It has been so long since you used most of this stuff, it's dried out and worthless." She held up two handfuls of cosmetics. "Thankfully you have a dating-aged daughter with the same skin tones as you and a wonderful sense of style."

Just a bit before seven, we decided I was as good as I was going to get, and we headed to the stairs. "Oh, Lord," I muttered as I saw the reception committee waiting for me at the bottom of the steps. I felt like a high school girl going to her first prom. Edna and Tillie were in front with Jolene and Paige behind them. Charles was grinning at me from the couch.

"You look fabulous, Ms. Clark," Paige said.

Aunt Tillie licked her thumb, then touched her butt like it was hot.

Jolene, obviously tired from her mental workout with Paige, was starting to fade and simply smiled.

"I expect you home by eleven o'clock, young lady," Edna barked as she handed me a twenty-dollar bill. "Here's your 'mad' money, in case he gets fresh." Edna wagged a finger in my face. "No drinking and driving, and if you feel uncomfortable I'll come and get you, no questions asked."

We all laughed.

"How many times have I heard that speech?" Angela added.

"You're all enjoying this, aren't you?" I said with a smile.

"Pretty much," Charles answered for the group.

In fact, I was enjoying this too.

When the doorbell rang, Tillie answered it and the entire room fell silent.

Standing in the doorway was Bernie Williamson. He was wearing a blue suede tuxedo jacket with a paisley bowtie and matching cummerbund. He had a white carnation pinned on his extra-wide lapel. In his hand, he had a box with a wrist corsage. "This is as close as I could get to what I wore to our senior prom."

The room exploded as Edna motored into the great room and returned with a picture in a silver frame of Bernie and me on these very same steps from thirty-two years ago. Paige insisted we try to duplicate the original.

Bernie still had the same silly grin he had always had, and I tried to mimic the original "too cool for school" look I had on my face in the original picture, but I couldn't keep from breaking up.

"Don't worry, Mrs. O'Connor," Bernie said with a deadpan expression on his face. "I'll have Allison home earlier than last time."

Everyone started laughing again.

Charles, the only other man in the room, approached Bernie with a stern expression on his face. "Young man. What are your intentions with my mother?"

Bernie thought about it for a few moments, drew in a deep breath then let it slowly out. "Marry her and have kids that aren't pains in the ass."

Angela gave Charles a shove. "You should know better than to try to out trash-talk Uncle Bernie."

I leaned into Bernie, "I hope you really don't plan to wear that tonight."

He leaned in even closer. "Don't worry, I have another coat in the car and a real tie."

I cleared my throat. "This has been fun," I said, "but we have a reservation."

"Where are you going?" Angela asked innocently.

"Gino's," Bernie answered and winced when I slugged him in the arm. "What?" He demanded as he rubbed his arm.

"Why would you tell her that?"

Angela batted her eyes in our direction and we headed toward the door.

"Anything that happens at Gino's is now all on you."

"Sorry. Sorry," Bernie said as he tossed the tux jacket on the backseat of his car and came up with something more appropriate. "I had forgotten how sneaky Angela can be."

"She prefers 'crafty,'" I said with a laugh. "I think you can skip the tie."

The short drive to Gino's was uneventful, but I knew we were in trouble when we entered the restaurant and Marko was at the hostess station waiting for us.

"Right this way," he said, very professionally, as he guided us to one of only two very private and very intimate booths in the restaurant. It was in the far back corner and well away from all of the other diners and the people in the Wine Bar.

"I've picked a special wine for you that I think you'll enjoy." Marko snapped his fingers and the wine sommelier appeared out of nowhere. With a flourish, he opened a bottle and poured a sample for Bernie. Bernie made a big production out of swirling the wine in the glass and checking its bouquet but he wasn't fooling anyone.

"You know less about wine than me," I said, with a snort.

"I know," he answered as he swallowed the sample in a single gulp then wiped his mouth with the back of his hand. "This is a nice place, but the drinks are a little skimpy."

The wine sommelier sighed as he filled our glasses. While this was a new joke for me, apparently that wasn't the first time he had heard it.

"Now I know why Marko put us over here by ourselves. He knew you'd do something to embarrass yourself."

"Or he knew you would."

Suddenly our waiter arrived with an iced platter with a dozen oysters on the half shell.

"Subtle," I said with a chuckle.

"Don't look at me," Bernie answered.

"Angela," we said in unison.

That pretty much set the tone for the entire evening of playful back-and-forth banter. After the second bottle of wine, I was a bit tipsy as I gave Bernie's arm a squeeze. "Thank you," I said.

He wasn't sure if I was setting him up for another verbal volley, so he eyed me with suspicion.

I slugged him again. "I'm serious," I said. "I haven't had this much fun or laughed this much in years."

"Okay," he answered. "Now let me be serious." He cupped his hands over mine. "Marry me."

I burst out laughing again.

"I'm dead serious," he said.

I reclaimed my hands. "No."

"Why not? Right now. We can find a justice of the peace."

I leaned back in my chair and looked at him hard. "You're serious."

He nodded. "First off, I would be arrested for bigamy. While all of the paperwork has been signed, they haven't been registered in the courthouse yet. I'm still technically married to Lindsey at the moment."

"Details," he answered with a dismissive wave of his hand. "We can fly to Vegas after everything is finalized."

"Bernie. No," I said forcefully. "I'm coming out of twenty-eight years of marriage. I need time before I'll be ready to get back in the saddle."

"Okay," he said playfully.

"You didn't expect me to say yes, did you?"

"Of course not," Bernie answered. "It was all part of my plan to set the mood for my real question."

"Which is?"

"Will you come home with me tonight?"

I burst out laughing. "Wow!"

"I didn't hear a no in there anywhere."

"I'm a little out of practice, Bernie."

"You and me both," he said with a sigh. "Performance anxiety is a bitch."

I shrugged. "Yeah."

"I really like you. You really like me and we've always had fun together." He shrugged and gave me a wicked little smile. "Besides, we've seen each other naked before. So what's the big deal?"

My lizard brain starting throwing up warning signals left and right. "You're still married." "What would your kids think if they found out?" "What about birth control?" "What if I got an STD?" "Is Edna's bad heart hereditary?"

I drew in a deep breath and used my intellect instead of my primal emotions. How many times had I thought how different my life would have been if I had married Bernie instead of Lindsey? After Beth, he was my best friend and he could always make me laugh. What the hell. There was only one way to see if we could reignite the spark.

I caught the eye of our waiter.

"Check, please."

CHAPTER THIRTY-TWO

"SO," BERNIE SAID as he draped his arm around me in the back seat of the Uber Marko insisted we call. "You want to make out?"

This comment got us a glance and a grin from the driver, who was a slightly overweight woman who looked barely old enough to drive. She had the perfect appearance for an Uber warrior. She was dressed in business casual and was extremely polite.

"Are you still eighteen?" I asked as I pushed Bernie so we were still touching but he wasn't leaning on me.

"I'd like to think so," Bernie answered with a laugh. "I'm baffled by this old guy I keep seeing in the mirror every morning when I'm shaving." He leaned back in again and gave me a nudge. "So, what do you think?"

I cupped my hand over my mouth and exhaled.

"What are you doing?" Bernie asked.

"Checking to see if my breath smells as much like garlic and wine as yours."

"Ah," he said as he gave me some additional space. "Good point. FYI, I bought you a toothbrush."

"Wow! Am I that easy?"

"No," he answered with a laugh. "The power of positive thinking on my part."

It seemed like I had known Bernie my entire life. When we were growing up, he lived five doors down from Beth. My daddy had always liked him, and after he had gotten married, Daddy had given him an amazing deal on a house in Phase Two. With his business thriving, he had been one of the original Phase Three buyers. His current house was just two blocks down from mine in Charlestown Reserve. Even after his wife, Maryanne, had been killed by a drunk driver, his roots in the neighborhood were too deep to ever consider moving.

As an awkward silence settled over the backseat my mind began to drift.

"To change the subject…"

"Why would we want to do that?" Bernie asked seductively, drawing another glance in the rear-view mirror from our amused driver.

"I'm serious," I said forcefully.

"This doesn't sound good. Should I have saved the receipt for the toothbrush?"

I laughed and shook my head. "Nothing like that," I answered. "Have you read any of my Aunt Jolene's books?"

"I've read all of them. Why?"

"What do you think of her concept of people making unconscious choices based on their lizard brain?"

"Her theory is bulletproof."

"Really?"

"Remember, I was a psychology major."

I made a face. "That's right." I shook my head. "I never really understood that."

Bernie shrugged and moved a bit further away since he figured this conversation might take a while. "I knew I wanted to go into sales and I figured the better I understood people, the more successful I'd be."

"So you completely buy into the theory that people make unconscious bad choices based on primal instinct?"

"Man," Bernie said as he slid further away and shook his head, "You really know how to kill the mood. So you think I'm a bad choice?"

I burst out laughing. "Exactly the opposite. If I hadn't read Aunt Jolene's book last night, it is unlikely I'd be here with you right now."

"In that case," he said as he moved back closer. "What kind of perfume does she like?" Bernie asked with a chuckle.

"After reading the book, I realized I had spent my entire life afraid to do things for no rational reason."

"You and millions and millions of other people," Bernie said. "Everyone from advertisers to politicians play to people's basic fears but also capitalize on the other side of the coin."

"What does that mean?"

"The same force that froze you up can drive others, especially men, to do bad things. Keep up with the Joneses. Drink the right liquor. Spend money you don't have for appearances' sake. That kind of stuff."

"Explain that 'especially men' part."

"I'll do even better. I'll give you the perfect example: your ex-husband."

"Lindsey?" I leaned away. "Now who's killing the mood?"

Bernie chuckled. "He's the classic Alpha Male and he has spent his entire adult life trying to fit the stereotype."

I turned slightly in my seat to face Bernie and motioned for him to continue.

"When you two first met, you were the classic Alpha Female. Smart, beautiful, rich. He zeroed in on you immediately, and since you were susceptible to unconscious choices, you never had a chance." Bernie shot me a mischievous grin. "So, did he start cheating on you when you were pregnant, or after your kids were born?"

I was stunned and momentarily speechless as Bernie continued. "When I was pregnant," I finally answered. "How did you know?"

"It is classic Alpha Male to seek other sexual partners and spread his DNA, and Lindsey has the same lizard brain the rest of us suffer from. He knew when it was just the two of you, if he cheated and got caught, you would likely have kicked the bastard to the curb and he would lose status with the tribe. That was a risk he was unwilling to take. Once the twins came along, the dynamics of the relationship changed." Bernie shook his head. "At that point he had all of the leverage. He knew you didn't want your kids growing up in a single-mom household, so he started pushing the boundary further every year but never crossed a line by throwing it in your face."

"He never did," I answered with a sigh. "But that didn't stop the Bimbo Brigade from calling."

Bernie sighed as he saw the pained look on my face.

"We can change to a more uplifting subject than your husband, if you would like."

"So, what would you consider a step up from talking about my ex-husband?"

"Toe fungus. The heartbreak of psoriasis. Plastic killing the oceans. Ebola."

"As tempting as all of those sound," I said. "Your insights so far have been pretty good, so let's stick to Lindsey."

"Okay," Bernie said. "Let me guess, things started to really go downhill two years ago."

I had never really thought about it, but he was absolutely correct again. I didn't want to give him the satisfaction of letting him know he had hit a bullseye, so I tried to keep a straight face.

"What happened two years ago?" I asked.

"Your father died, and the true Alpha Male in the family hierarchy, and the man he feared, was no longer there. Lindsey quit on your marriage the day of your father's funeral. He no longer had anyone around whom he feared. Plus, the twins were fast approaching graduation, so the clock was ticking on the hold he had on you. He let his primal instincts take over and began pursuing younger women in the open and without regard to how it humiliated you." Bernie's eyes locked on mine. "Am I right?"

I sighed, rolled my eyes and reluctantly nodded my head maybe half an inch. "Maybe a little," I answered softly "Well, Dr. Freud, how did you figure all of this out?"

"Psychology major doing public relations work, remember? I do damage control for lots of borderline sociopaths like Lindsey who have been caught with either their pants down or their hand in the cookie jar, or both. But, I had some pretty big clues." Bernie, seeing

I was taking this better than he had imagined, was starting to warm up to the topic and was really hitting his stride.

"First, every time you threw a party or there was one of your father's shindigs at the Farm, I'll bet you ten to one Lindsey always wanted to be sure I was coming."

Again. I was stunned. "How did..."

Bernie waved me off. "Lindsey knew I loved you and it was his way to assert himself at the head of the pack by rubbing you in my face. 'Ha. Ha. I'm sleeping with the love of your life and you can't do anything about it.' It was a classic passive-aggressive Alpha Male move on his part. And, it cost him nothing with your father."

"And you went along with it?"

Bernie shrugged. "What was I going to do? I was happily married to Maryanne and it is in neither of our natures to cheat on our spouses. I've always had, and always will have, strong feelings for you, and I'm pretty sure you feel the same way. But we both had to play the hands we were dealt." Bernie laughed softly. "It was like that old Stephen Stills lyric. *If you can't be with the one you love, love the one you're with.*"

Bernie pulled me close.

"The big clue was the way your dad acted around Lindsey. Charlie O'Connor could read people better than anyone I've ever met. When I heard he made Lindsey sign a prenuptial agreement and put your house in your name only, I knew he was seeing the same thing in your soon-to-be-ex-husband that I was."

"If you knew all of that," I said as tears welled up in my eyes. "Why didn't you stop me? Why didn't you fight for me?"

Bernie laughed. "You needed to have read your aunt's book thirty years ago. Your lizard brain bit you in the ass. You were completely smitten. You had landed the big dog. You got the man all of the other women wanted. You were convinced you were marrying Prince Charming and you were going to live happily ever after. Anything I could have said would have just looked like sour grapes and have made you angry. You would have looked at me as weak and pathetic and made you even more determined to marry Lindsey." Bernie shrugged. "I'm guessing your dad saw it the same way. I knew I was beaten, and then Maryanne came along and the rest is history."

"What if Maryanne hadn't…"

"Died?" Bernie shook his head, then said, "I would be home with her right now and we wouldn't have gotten a second chance." Bernie gave me a rare serious look. "I would never have cheated on Maryanne the way Lindsey cheated on you. Never."

I leaned my head on his shoulder and put my hand on his chest. What a sweet and wonderful man. Then it hit me and I chuckled softly.

"What?" Bernie asked as he held me close.

"Before today, such a frank and earnest conversation about my relationship with Lindsey would have wound me up like a top. Now, I feel nothing. It is almost as if we were talking about someone else's life."

"Outstanding," Bernie said as he pulled me even closer. "Your Aunt Jolene would say you have made a huge personal breakthrough. You've completely released Lindsey and he no longer has the power to pull your chain or generate any kind of emotional response."

"Charles asked you an interesting question earlier. What are your intentions with me?"

"Pretty simple," he said as he stroked my hair. "I want your last name to be Williamson longer than it was O'Connor or Clark." He chuckled. "And I really like the symmetry of me being the first man you ever had sex with and the last man you had sex with."

As the Uber pulled to a stop in front of Bernie's house, the driver, who had been silently hanging on every word, reached around and handed me a small plastic Tic-Tac box.

"What's this for?" I asked.

"You were worried about your breath, but honey, you really need to kiss that man before you let him get away again."

CHAPTER THIRTY-THREE

"WHY IS YOUR hair wet?" Angela asked as Bernie and I tiptoed through the backdoor at the Farm. We had hoped the flickering light in the great room meant that only night owl Tillie was still up watching "SportsCenter." We weren't expecting both of my kids to be sitting on the oversized L-shaped couch with her.

"Busted," Bernie muttered.

Tillie lowered the volume on the TV, turned around and gave us the eye. "What have you two kids been up to?" she demanded.

Feeling like a teenager who had been caught breaking curfew, I couldn't make eye contact with my aunt, much less my children.

"Gee, Mrs. Loopner," Bernie said in his best Bill Murray "Saturday Night Live" voice. "Because we did not want to drink and drive, your lovely niece and I walked here from my house. It was a delightful and warm summer's evening, so Allison and I decided to take a quick and refreshing dip in the swimming pool." He batted his eyes at Tillie. "When we realized how late it was, we rushed right over to apologize and didn't bother to dry our hair."

"Oh! My! God!" Angela said with a disgusted expression on her face. "Since I notice neither of you have a bathing suit with you, that means you two went skinny dipping!"

"Huh," Tillie said as she suppressed a yawn. "I thought I heard something in the backyard."

"You were naked in OUR swimming pool!" Angela made a horrified face. "Ewww."

"What she said." Charles seconded as he rose to his feet and headed toward the door as Angela stomped up the stairs.

"That went well," Bernie said cheerfully.

Tillie picked up the remote and turned her attention back to the television. "The pastries were great and there's beer in the refrigerator."

"I think we've had enough to drink for one night."

"And then some," Tillie answered in a distracted voice.

"You're not going to grill me?" I asked in disbelief.

Tillie waved me off without taking her eyes off the screen. "I'm your aunt and not your mother. Besides, you're both consenting adults." Tillie chuckled. "I do think you may have scarred your children for life, though."

I leaned in and whispered to Bernie. "I told you that was a bad idea."

Bernie just shrugged then tried, unsuccessfully, to suppress a yawn, with little success. "I think I should head home. You wore me out."

I slugged him in the shoulder, gave him a dirty look and nodded in the direction of my Aunt Tillie.

"I still have my hearing aids in," Tillie said to no one in particular.

I grabbed Bernie's arm and roughly pulled him toward the door and back outside. "In less than twenty-four hours I've gone from long-suffering but loyal wife, to divorcee, to swimming pool slut."

"Great!" Bernie said. "And today is only Friday. What are we going to do the rest of the weekend?"

I started to punch him again, but halfway into my windup I got a bad case of the giggles and fell into his arms instead. "I haven't had this much fun in years." I gave him a big kiss that lasted embarrassingly longer than I expected. "Thank you."

"Noooo," Bernie answered. "Thank you. You've learned some moves since high school."

"Lindsey may have been a lousy husband and absentee father, but he was good in bed."

Bernie let out a wicked, borderline-evil, cackle.

"What?"

"Revenge is a dish best served cold," Bernie replied with a satisfied grin on his face. "I'll be sure to thank him the next time I see him. It won't make up for all times he threw his sex life with you in my face, but it'll be a start."

I just shook my head and laughed. "Goodnight, Bernie."

"Goodnight, Allie. I'll call you tomorrow."

I watched him walk out of sight before turning back toward the house. How did I ever let that man get away the first time?

As I walked passed Aunt Tillie, I gave her a kiss on the top of her head. "Good night."

"Oh, I almost forgot," Tillie said as she turned the television completely off. That alone stopped me cold. "Jolene wanted me to ask you if she could have a few minutes of your time tomorrow after her nap."

Yikes!

In all of the years I had known Jolene Marshall, I had always found her to be more than a little intimidating. I knew she had very strong beliefs and a massive and rabid following, but she had never tried to sway or influence me. In fact, to the best of my memory, before this afternoon we had never had a private one-on-one conversation. "Is there a problem?" I asked with a slight quiver in my voice.

Tillie just shrugged. "One way to find out." Aunt Tillie's eyes locked on mine. "So can I tell her you'll see her?"

I drew in a cleansing breath and released it. "Yes."

CHAPTER THIRTY-FOUR

THIS EMANCIPATION THING was turning out great. With my kids' problems now theirs and not mine to worry over, I slept better and later than I had in years. Of course, two hours of endorphin-inducing cardio with Bernie and the release of years of sexual frustration were also likely contributing factors. Throw in that Lindsey was now the problem of every female under thirty who happened to stray into his line of sight and no longer of any concern to me. I felt like a great weight had been lifted off me.

As I trotted to the bathroom, I smelled coffee. A shower and preening could wait. After I finished my necessaries and ran a brush through my hair, I headed to the door in my PJs. Before I even reached the top of the stairs, I could hear rowdy laughter from the kitchen.

I heard Angela, much more animated than usual, defending her position. "All I'm saying is, I'm never getting in that swimming pool again."

Aunt Tillie and my mom roared with laughter.

It didn't take Sherlock Holmes to figure out what they were discussing. I knew I had to eventually face the music, and my need for caffeine convinced me there was no time like the present. I padded barefoot into the kitchen as inconspicuously as possible. Despite my best efforts at stealth, all eyes still turned in my direction. Including those of an unexpected visitor, Paige Thompson.

Through the glass I could see one of the doors was up on Daddy's garage. I assumed the estrogen level in the kitchen had exceeded my son's tolerance level and he was down working on the testosterone-fueled muscle cars. My suspicion was confirmed when the 1971

Barracuda convertible with the Hemi engine rumbled out of the bay and, with Charles behind the wheel, headed out for a spin. As his grandfather had taught him, the cars needed to be driven regularly, and Charles was more than happy to oblige.

"Oh, Angie," Tillie said as she wiped a tear from eye. "If you knew half the stuff your grandparents had done in that pool...."

Angela put her hands over her ears and closed her eyes. "I can't hear you!"

I shrugged and pulled a mug out of the cabinet and poured myself a cup of coffee from the carafe on the counter. Instead of waiting for all of them to start in on me, the new me took the offensive. "You might want to check the calendar, Angela," I said as I blew across the top of my mug.

Angela, in no mood for riddles, shot me a nasty look. "What are you talking about?"

"Your birthday is June 11th."

"So?" she snapped.

"You and your brother were born nine months and one week after the annual Labor Day weekend party," I said as I took a tentative sip of coffee.

Mom's head immediately sagged to her chest as she softly chuckled.

"Well spank my butt and call me red!" Aunt Tillie shouted as she laughed so hard she nearly fell off her chair.

Aunt Jolene caught up next and started laughing as well.

"Oh, jeez," Paige said as she started to giggle.

My daughter was so agitated her brain had ceased to function properly. "What?" Angela demanded.

With a deadpan expression I said, "There is better than a 50/50 chance you and your brother were conceived in that swimming pool."

That did it. Angela bounded to her feet and stormed out of the kitchen.

After Angela was safely out of earshot, my mom said, with a quizzical expression on her face, "I thought Lindsey hated that pool."

"I don't think he's ever been in it," I said as I took a long pull of my coffee. "But Angela doesn't know that."

Paige leaned back in her seat and began clapping. "Good one, Mrs. Clark. Not many can get the best of Angela."

"I've emancipated the twins, so by extension you're emancipated too, Paige. Please call me Allison."

Paige nodded.

"What's gotten into Angela?" I asked Paige. "She's always been wound a bit tight, but this moves the bar even for her."

"She's worried about her valedictorian speech," Paige answered, then continued, "and Charles really set her off."

"Oh, God." I closed my eyes and rubbed my forehead. "What did he do?"

"The program went to the printer and she's scheduled to go first. She has really been pestering Charles to see a draft of his speech. To get her off his back, he handed her a piece of paper and told her it was what he planned to say right after her." Paige started to giggle.

Tillie and the rest of the Sisterhood leaned forward in anticipation.

"This is going to be good," my mom said.

Paige got control of herself and pretended she was reading from the paper and cleared her throat before continuing. "What she said."

We all roared with laughter.

Paige shook her head. "She's been bouncing off of the walls ever since."

"Charles could always wind her up," I added.

Paige studied me for a moment, made a face then turned her attention to Aunt Jolene. "I think most of the issues have already been resolved."

"Indeed," Jolene answered. "The transition is quite remarkable."

"I assume you two are talking about me," I said as I stretched and yawned before pulling up a chair. I winced and made a face as I sat down, which didn't escape the notice of Tillie.

"Use some muscles you haven't used in a while last night?" Tillie asked.

"Shut. Up," I said as I rubbed a knot out of a muscle in my lower back, then glanced across the table at Jolene and Paige, who were sitting side by side. "What transition are you talking about?"

Jolene glanced at Paige and nodded that she should take the lead. "Dr. Marshall." Paige closed her eyes, took in a cleansing breath and started again. "Jolene was deeply concerned with all of the negatives that hit you yesterday...."

"Negatives?" I interrupted and took another sip of coffee.

Paige was a bit flustered and glanced at Aunt Jolene, who motioned she should continue.

"First, there was Ms. Taylor-Smith..."

"Who?" I asked as I suddenly realized I was starving and I looked at Tillie. "Are there any of those pastries left?"

"Too late," Tillie answered as she nodded in Edna's direction.

I glared at my mother then turned my attention to Jolene. "If it's not too much trouble, I would love one of your omelets."

"No trouble at all," Jolene said as she slowly rose to her feet.

When I turned my attention back to Paige, she had a stunned, open-mouthed expression on her face and her hand clutching her chest.

"What?" I demanded. "I know I slept in, but asking my aunt to make one of her special breakfasts doesn't seem like an unreasonable request."

Paige turned to Jolene, who was already turning on a burner. "She's completely released it."

"I know, Paige," Jolene answered before turning her attention back to me. "Any special requests, Allison?"

"Nope," I answered. "I trust you."

Paige shook the cobwebs out of her head. "I've read about this in your books but found it nearly impossible to believe."

"After hearing about the exploits at the high school and then her date last night, I told you this morning it was a possibility and she wouldn't need any guidance from us." Jolene smiled. "For some, it is like a light switch."

"What are you two talking about?"

Jolene's mind had moved on to cooking and Paige was still busy trying to get her head wrapped around what had just happened, so Tillie took over. "Jolene wanted to talk to you about using some of her releasing techniques to help you cope with the avalanche of negativity that hit you yesterday." Tillie smiled at me. "You not even remembering the name of the vice principal at the high school who tried to mess with your kids…"

"That's right," I said as I snapped my fingers and then waved a finger in Tillie's direction. "The odious Ms. Taylor-Smith." I shook my head. "I had completely dropped her down the memory hole."

"Precisely," Tillie continued. "Then with you moving on from your ex-husband so, ah, vigorously, with Bernie last night has made your talk with Jolene unnecessary."

As I kept my eyes on Paige, I leaned in to Tillie and softly asked, "What's up with her?"

Tillie gave Paige a dismissive wave. "Some people spend a lifetime trying to do what you did in the past twenty-four hours, and you don't even have a clue as to what happened."

"I spent three years," Paige muttered to herself.

"What the hell did I do?" I asked then thought about it for a moment. "Okay. Okay. I showed a little spine at the high school. Big whoop. I signed my divorce papers and got laid for the first time in nearly three years. What's the big deal?"

"By you not even remembering Ms. Taylor-Smith's name," Paige answered as she regained her balance. "It indicated you had released her so completely she not only no longer had the power to evoke an emotional response, you had filed her away permanently." Paige shook her head. "Next you signed your divorce papers; then a few hours later walked in on the twins in a secret meeting with your ex-husband and you completely blew it off."

"Again," I said. "What's the big deal?"

"When you no longer allow anyone to have the power to evoke an emotional response from you and you take complete control over your own life…." Paige stopped and looked at Jolene. "I could use a little help here."

Jolene smiled. "Allison, without trying or even being aware of what was happening, you have attained a state of enlightenment that millions of seekers would envy."

I started laughing. "You either need a tune up by Steve, or maybe you should hold off trying to keep up with Mom in the mimosa department."

Edna, hearing the word "mimosa," picked up her empty glass and motioned for a refill. Aunt Tillie got up and brought over the pitcher, which was still half full, and set it in front of my mom.

"Let's cut out the middleman," Tillie said.

I got up and got a tumbler out of the cabinet and poured myself a mimosa before sitting back down. "I think we're both going to need this if Aunt Jolene is going to do one of her lectures."

Edna clicked my glass with hers. "Here, here."

Jolene smiled first at Edna and me, then at Paige. "See. They are both perfect examples of unconscious enlightenment. Allison has no clue the gift she has received." Jolene began whisking eggs. "But she still has one more hurdle to overcome." Jolene pointed her whisk at Edna. "How will she handle the death of her mother?"

Edna blew a raspberry in Jolene's direction. "I'm going to dance on all of your graves!"

CHAPTER THIRTY-FIVE

THE NEXT TWO weeks went off without a hitch. The twins gave their speeches. Angela's was brilliant, but I could see Charles's heart wasn't really into it. His mind was clearly elsewhere.

My life had really changed for the better. I was spending my nights with Bernie and my days with Mom. For maybe the first time ever, Edna and I were actually having real conversations.

After Mom had threatened to lower the boom on Robert, he had backed off on his legal threats, at least for the moment. But I heard he had quietly hired a forensic accountant to try to ferret out more about the missing money. Our mom was furious with the bank for contacting Robert instead of notifying her. She ordered the bank to deny any further access to her account information by my brother. Meanwhile, her lawyer, Bertram Ruggles, was stonewalling every maneuver Robert attempted.

Lately the twins were spending more time with their father than with me. I had no idea exactly what Charles and Angela were cooking up, but I had never seen Charles so intense and Angela so unsettled.

Tomorrow was the twins' birthday, and a landscaping crew was manicuring the backyard of the Farm for the big event. The highlight was going to be the distribution of Daddy's muscle car collection. I understood that four of the nine cars were quite valuable. In Daddy's will he had decreed that, when the twins came of age, they and Robert, Jr., would each get three of the nine. The order of selection was still up in the air.

Edna was busy in her garden and Tillie and I were camped out on the patio, watching the activity while Jolene had her post-treatment nap. We both turned when we heard an odd and unexpected sound from the direction of Daddy's garage.

"What's that?" I asked.

Tillie started to her feet with a concerned expression on her face. "An air impact wrench."

"In English, please," I said as I got up as well.

Tillie started toward the garage with a deliberate stride. "It's the kind of tool you use to remove lug nuts on a car's tires," she answered absently.

One of the bay doors was open and I saw Paige Thompson carrying a box and heading inside. If Paige was there, it meant Charles was probably the one using the air wrench.

What are my twins up to now?

I picked up my pace. Since Tillie had lost a step or two in the last few years, I beat her to the door.

What I saw stunned me.

The usually pristine garage where Daddy kept his cars was a disaster area. Paige was tossing trash around and Charles was kneeling next to the jacked-up rear end of Daddy's 1967 L88 Corvette and was busy removing a tire.

"What the hell are you doing?" shouted Tillie in a horrified tone as she muscled past me.

Angela came around from behind the 1971 'Cuda she had been covering in dust and glared at her brother. "I told you to use the tire iron and not the air wrench."

Charles just shrugged as he pulled the tire off the Vette and tossed it on the floor.

"I repeat," said Tillie with her cheeks flushed. "What the hell are you doing?"

Charles just grinned and glanced at Angela, who took charge.

"Cousin Bobby and his mother are coming over to view the cars in a few hours."

Tillie's eyes moved around the garage, and then she started laughing so hard she had tears in her eyes. Tillie moved to a shelf and grabbed an old alternator and put it on the garage floor next to the 1967 Ford GT40 Mark 4, then fiddled in the grille for the release latch and raised the hood.

"Nice touch," Charles said as he headed to the shelf for more stray parts and started spreading them around.

I didn't get the joke. These old cars were my father's pride and joy, and seeing them being trashed by my own children caused my blood pressure to rise.

Tillie, seeing the look on my face, came over and gave me a shoulder squeeze. "Relax," she said. "After the viewing, the twins will put everything back in order with no harm done."

My eyes narrowed on Charles and Angela. "What are you two up to?" I demanded

Angela glanced at Charles and he shook his head maybe half an inch.

"You just need to trust us here, Mom," Angela said reassuringly. "Like Aunt Tillie said. A couple of hours after Bobby views the cars, we'll have everything back to normal."

"Not good enough," I said softly as I tried to control my anger. "You will tell me exactly what's going on here and do it right now."

"I thought we were emancipated," Charles said softly, but with a cold edge to his voice I had never heard before. I felt my jaw drop. Charles had never spoken to me that way in his entire life. He sounded so much like my father it made me do a double-take.

Then it hit me. Up until now, emancipation had just been abstract talk; now it was reality. My children were no longer kids; they were full-grown adults.

"At the stroke of midnight tonight," Angela said, "we'll both be eighteen and these cars will legally be ours and Bobby's to do with as we see fit."

"We need you to take a step back," Charles said softly. "We'll explain everything tomorrow."

Tillie came up and gave me a good-natured shoulder bump. "I've got a pretty good idea what's going on here, Allie," she said gently, then looked at Charles and Angela. "But I don't have a clue what the endgame is." She put her arm around my shoulder. "For the moment at least, I think we really need to trust your kids."

CHAPTER THIRTY-SIX

"SO THESE ARE the famous cars," Lilith O'Connor said as she majestically entered the garage and sneered at the collection of muscle cars. The place was a complete mess and, except for Charles' GTO, which was pristine, the other cars appeared to not even be drivable. Spare tires and odd motor and transmission parts were spread randomly around. The entire space, which was normally as clean as a whistle, was now coated in a layer of dust and grime.

Tillie and I exchanged glances. Lilith was on her "A" game. Her makeup was flawless and between her summer dress and jewelry, the value of her designer wardrobe and accessories would be a good start on reducing the national debt. I still had no idea what the twins were up to, but if it meant taking the obnoxious Lilith down a peg or two, I was all in.

Angela was nowhere to be seen and I had been instructed to stay mute, so, for once, Charles was forced to do all of the talking.

"I can't believe neither one of you has ever been in here," Charles said as he wiped his hands on a rag.

"Fifty-year-old rusting pieces of metal aren't really my thing," Lilith answered as she surveyed the garage and was, well, less than impressed.

Cousin Bobby was hanging well back and only nodded in the direction of the twins. As usual, he was cowed by his domineering mother.

Charles made eye contact with Paige and she began taking a video of their conversation. "Did you hire an appraiser like I suggested?" Charles asked Bobby.

Bobby just shrugged as he looked at the mess of partially assembled cars, dust and oil stains.

"We're doing the division of the cars tomorrow, Bobby," Charles said.

"I prefer Robert," Bobby answered gruffly. "Did you have an appraisal done?"

"Absolutely," Charles answered as he nodded in the direction of a nine-by-twelve manila envelope on the work bench. Handwritten on the outside of the envelope, in bold red block letters, was "APPRAISAL."

Lilith O'Connor eyed the envelope. "How much did your appraisal cost?" she asked casually.

Charles puffed out his cheeks and slowly let out some air through his lips. "You have to ask Angela the exact amount. She wanted honest numbers and not someone blowing sunshine up her skirt about how much they might bring at auction. For that appraisal," Charles nodded in the direction of the envelope on the workbench, "she asked for the number they would be willing to write a check for today." Charles motioned around the room. "Exactly as they stand."

Lilith raised an eyebrow at Charles. "That's fascinating, but I asked how much you paid for the appraisal?"

Charles shrugged. "Including airfare and two nights in a hotel, I think we spent over $10,000," he answered. "If you want an exact number, you'll need to ask Angela."

On cue, Angela stuck her head into the garage. "Charles. Can you give me a hand?" she asked. "You, too, Paige," Angela added.

Charles wiped his hands on a rag, tossed it on the workbench next to the envelope then headed toward the door. Paige stopped recording and was about a step behind.

"Mom. I could use you and Aunt Tillie as well," Angela said in our direction and we joined the exodus. We didn't go far. We went out the bay door and immediately entered another, much smaller, room just a few steps off of the main garage. Inside was the security console for the garage and the surrounding area. The oversized monitor on the wall had nine different angles, one for each of the

HD security cameras mounted in and around the garage. Paige sat down in front of the console and eliminated eight of the cameras, leaving the one in the garage aimed at the work bench as the only one playing. Next she blew it up so it filled the entire screen and turned up the volume so we could not only see, but also hear, everything that was going on.

On the screen, Lilith O'Connor craned her neck, and when she was certain they were alone, she hustled over to the workbench and picked up the envelope.

"What are you doing?" Bobby hissed as he glanced at the open door to see if his cousins were returning.

"Why should we pay $10,000 for an appraisal when they've already done one?"

Lilith O'Connor opened the envelope and quickly read the contents.

Paige zoomed in on the letter, and it was so clear, it was almost like I had it in my own hand.

> Dear Mr. Charles Clark:
>
> Thank you for the opportunity to view your grandfather's car collection. As one of the largest classic car auction houses in the country, we would be very interested in either placing your vehicles in our next major event or purchasing some of them outright.
>
> If you wish to avoid the risk and uncertainty of placing your vehicles on the auction block, below is a bid for an outright purchase for 5 of the 9 cars we appraised. Note: We only make cash offers on vehicles which are fully restored, drivable and immediately ready for auctioning. If a vehicle is not fully operational or has an appraised street value above $250,000 dollars, we are unable to make a cash offer. If you select this option, we will issue a certified cashier's check upon the receipt of the transfer of title and will arrange to have the vehicles picked up.

Chevy 1957 Belair	Offer $31,000
Chevy 1967 Corvette L88	No Offer
Chevy 1969 Camaro SS	Offer $38,000
Chevy 1969 Camaro ZL1	No Offer
Ford 1955 Thunderbird	Offer $23,000
Ford 1965 Mustang	Offer $12,000
Ford 1967 GT40 Mark 4	No Offer
Pontiac 1971 GTO Judge	Offer $95,000
Plymouth 1971 Cuda `	No Offer

Please feel free to contact me at the number below if you have any questions or wish to discuss this further.

Sincerely,

Matthew Border, VP Sales
You're Not Getting Older, You're Getting Better Classic Car Auctions

There were handwritten notes next to the cars that had not gotten an offer.

Chevy 1967 Corvette L88	No Offer. Bad rear end, suspension shot, serious oil leak.
Chevy 1969 Camaro ZL1	No Offer. Transmission shot, bad tie rods.
Ford 1967 GT40 Mark 4	No Offer. Needs new drive shaft and rebuilt carburetor.
Plymouth 1971 Cuda	No Offer. Bad universal joint and camshaft.

Lilith motioned Bobby over, and he reluctantly joined his mother by the workbench. "What do these notes mean?"

Bobby read the appraisal. "I have no idea," he answered. "But none of them sound simple or cheap to fix." A nasty smile formed on Bobby's face when he saw the GTO his cousin Charles drove was worth nearly as much as the combined value of the other four cars that they had made offers on. He spread the letter out on the workbench then used his phone to take a picture of the offer sheet. Next, he returned the offer letter to the envelope where his mother had found it.

"We won't have to waste any time on the internet tonight looking at boring old cars, Robert," Lilith said triumphantly. "We know everything the twins know."

"Let's go," Angela said briskly as she headed to the door of the security room.

Hearing us returning, Lilith and Bobby stepped away from the bench and pretended to be interested in one of the cars.

Paige immediately started filming again.

"Any questions?" Charles asked. "You want to go over any of the vehicles?"

"I don't think so," Bobby said confidently.

"You really should get your own independent appraisal. Some of these cars are quite valuable."

"Naw," Bobby said with a satisfied look on his face as he patted his phone. "I'm good."

"Okay," Charles answered. "We'll see you tomorrow."

CHAPTER THIRTY-SEVEN

SINCE WE HADN'T had a major event at the Farm since Daddy had passed two years ago, Mom had decided the grieving process for Charlie O'Connor was over and insisted it be a first-class affair to rival anything previous. The twins would have preferred a few friends and family over for a cookout, but they didn't protest. While unspoken, we all knew Mom didn't have that much time left. If this was going to be her last hurrah, then, by God, it was going to be a doozy.

The caterers were busy setting up the food on the patio. Tables were being added and a tent was being erected in case it rained. Edna had even booked a four-piece cover band, and there was going to be a top-shelf-only open bar.

Aunt Tillie and I were sitting in a corner of the patio, in the shade of a massive oak, sipping lemonade and watching the show. Edna was driving the caterer crazy as she wheeled her scooter around the backyard barking orders and giving instructions.

Tillie sighed. "I hope I go down like that."

"What do you mean?" I asked.

"She's going to still be fighting the undertaker as he tries to nail the box closed."

"I think she'll be too drunk to put up much of a fight."

Tillie chuckled. "When did you get funny?"

"I've been hanging around Bernie."

"Speaking of Bernie," Tillie looked around for him.

"He's not here yet, but he's on his way."

"Is this going to be the first time your ex and your new squeeze have been in the same room since you started doing the no-step two-step with Bernie?"

"Yeah."

"Do you expect them to play nice?"

"We'll see," I said with a sigh. "We'll see."

After most of the guests had arrived, the patio had self-segregated into five distinct groups. The biggest crowd was friends of Edna, Tillie and Jolene. Because of all of the older women in the group, and the level of backbiting and gossip, Aunt Tillie kept referring to them as the "Blue Hair Mafia." Next in size was a group of my friends, and the third-largest group was Robert's friends. Surprisingly, the twins' friends were few and far between, at least early in the evening. I learned later the birthday boy and girl planned an after party to start as soon as all of the old codgers had made for the exit. The last and smallest group was Lilith and Bobby. It consisted of exactly two people. The pair had claimed a small corner of the patio with the table farthest from the other guests. Lilith was wearing a fire-engine-red "look at me" dress that highlighted her great figure. Still, with the combination of a sour and regal expression on her face, I thought she looked like the Queen of Hearts an inch away from ordering a beheading.

My brother and I, mostly for our mom, had declared an unconditional truce for the evening. He was being civil and, with the radiant Gabrielle on his arm, he was happily accepting congratulations on his pending fatherhood. That combination really helped to keep the tone of the party light.

Bernie, as usual, was cracking me up. Whenever Lindsey was nearby, he would make a big deal of holding my hand or putting his arm around my waist. Lindsey knew exactly what Bernie was doing, and I had to admit I was kind of enjoying being the deliverer of passive aggression instead of the recipient.

The weather had cooperated for the birthday party. A Canadian high had swept the heat and humidity south. Around six, dinner was served. An hour later the temperature had dropped enough that many of the ladies in attendance had put on light sweaters. Others, who had no interest in the car distribution, had taken the slight chill in the air as their cue to head home.

As the sun went down, we had thinned down to the hard core of friends and family when Edna used a spoon to tap the edge of her glass to get the attention of the gathering. "Everyone!" Mom said loudly, "I would like to make a few announcements."

Charles made eye contact with Paige. She then pulled out her phone and began recording Edna's speech.

"To avoid any potential conflict over my estate." Edna's eyes drifted in the direction of Robert, who squirmed slightly. "I have decided to go ahead and transfer my thirty percent stake in O'Connor Industries to my grandchildren, Robert O'Connor, Jr., Charles Clark and Angela Clark, and," Edna raised her glass in the direction of Gabrielle and pointed to her mid-section. "And a player to be named later." This brought a ripple of applause and laughter from the crowd. "Each will receive 7.5 percent of the voting stock, effective immediately."

Angela and Charles nodded their approval.

"Game on," I heard Charles mutter softly to his sister. Angela shushed him.

"Next," Edna said, "As most of you know, it was Charlie's wish, and was included in his will, that when the twins reached eighteen years of age, his classic cars would also transfer to Charles, Angela and Robert, Jr. That day has arrived." Edna held her glass high. "Happy birthday!"

"Happy birthday!" the crowd answered.

Mom took a sip of her drink, made a sour face at its lack of alcohol content, and put it down.

"Gabrielle," Edna said apologetically. "Charlie had not anticipated any additional grandchildren, so I'm afraid we must stick to the terms of my late husband's will."

Gabrielle waved Edna off and patted her stomach. "The seven and a half percent of the company stock is more than generous."

"Classy broad," Tillie muttered.

"Which brings us to the business at hand," Edna said. "Charlie had nine classic cars, so each of the three grandchildren specifically named in Charlie's will shall receive three of them. The question

201

is how to fairly divide them. I have decided that each of my grandchildren will draw a number out of the hat that will determine the order in which they will get to pick. To be fair, the order of selection will be 1-2-3. Then we will reverse the order with 3-2-1 picking next..."

"Grammy," Angela said softly.

"Yes, dear," Edna answered.

"Charles and I have a suggestion for the order of selection."

"Let me guess," Cousin Bobby said with a snort. "Ladies first?"

"Actually, Bobby," Angela answered softly. "Charles and I both agree that the selection should be made by age with the oldest grandchild going first."

"That means your cousin Bobby will get first pick," Edna said as a wry smile broke across her face. She had no idea what was going on, but the twins clearly had one of their schemes fully in motion, and she couldn't wait to see where this was headed.

"We know," Angela said sweetly.

Edna raised an eyebrow at her granddaughter. "Are you sure?"

"Absolutely," Angela answered.

"Charles?" Edna asked.

"I think this is the way Grandpa would have wanted it," Charles answered.

"I think you are absolutely correct," Edna answered before turning to the gathered group. "The selection order in the first round will be Bobby first, Angela second and Charles third. Agreed?"

The three cousins nodded.

"In the second round," Edna continued, "the order of selection will be reversed. Charles, Angela and then Bobby. In the third round, Bobby will go first again, followed by Angela and finally Charles." Edna eyed her three grandchildren. "Any objections?"

I leaned into Aunt Tillie and whispered, "What are they up to?"

Aunt Tillie put her hand on my arm and shook her head. "Just watch."

"Very well," Mom said as she fought to keep the smile off her face. "For the record," She said as she glanced at Paige, who was still videoing the proceedings, "I would like to hear each one of you say you agree to these terms. Bobby?"

"Sure, why not," he said as he suppressed a yawn.

"Please say you agree out loud, Bobby," Edna said calmly.

Bobby threw up his hands in mock surrender. "I agree, okay?"

"Thank you," Mom said as she turned to Angela.

"I agree," she said without any prompting.

A half-beat later, Charles said, "I agree."

Edna looked around the gathering. "With you all as witnesses, my grandchildren have agreed to the terms of the distribution. Bobby, make your pick."

"Sorry, cousin." An evil smirk covered Bobby's face as he patted Charles on the shoulder. "Nothing personal, but business is business." Bobby cleared his throat then said loudly. "I'll take the GTO."

A gasp went up from the crowd. Bobby thought it was because everyone knew Charles had spent years working on his GTO, and for him to take it with his first pick was a low blow. Bobby's eyes turned to Charles and a stunned silence settled over him when he saw his cousin's reaction. Instead of being angry at such an outright betrayal, Charles was doing a happy dance. He grabbed Angela and lifted her off the ground.

"I can't believe he fell for it," Charles said as he spun his sister around.

Lindsey, who was standing next to me, was beaming with pride. He clapped his hands and muttered, "Well played."

I was still confused by what was unfolding and leaned into my ex-husband. "What's going on?" I asked.

"Our kids have just started something that, because of their age, if they pull it off, they'll be teaching in business colleges in a few years." Lindsey walked over and shook Charles's hand and then gave Angela a peck on the cheek.

I turned to Bernie and asked. "Any idea what just happened?"

"Not a clue."

Aunt Tillie broke from the crowd, ran up to the twins and muscled Lindsey aside. "Pure evil!" she shouted as she slapped Charles on the shoulder. "Letting Bobby draw first, knowing he would take the GTO, was such a Charlie O'Connor move. Your grandfather would be so proud of you two."

Bobby was as thunderstruck as he was clueless. "What's going on?" he demanded.

Tillie turned to Bobby. "Angela and Charles now have the next four picks and they will take the Corvette, ZL1, GT40 and the 'Cuda."

"Why would they want broken cars?" Bobby demanded.

"Broken!" Tillie roared. "They are four of the rarest and best examples of muscle cars in the world. If the twins decide to auction them, buyers will be phoning in bids from six continents." Tillie chuckled. "The GTO is worth around a hundred grand. The four cars the twins just picked are easily worth well north of ten million dollars!"

A gasp went up from the crowd.

"What!?" Lilith shrieked.

Charlie pulled a letter out of his pocket and handed it to Bobby. It was similar to one he had seen in the workshop.

"Sorry, cousin." Charles said, as it was his turn to pat Bobby on the shoulder. "Nothing personal, but business is business."

With trembling hands, Bobby, with his mother looking over his shoulder, started to read the letter.

> Dear Mr. Charles Clark:
>
> Thank you for the opportunity to view your grandfather's car collection. As one of the largest classic car auction houses in the country, we would be very interested in either placing your vehicles in our next major event or purchasing some of them outright.
>
> Considering the rarity of four of these vehicles, we are unable to make a cash offer but we would like to do a "Charlie O'Connor Auction" at your earliest convenience. Below are the estimated auction values of each vehicle. These are best guess estimates based on recent sales and

current market conditions. This should not be construed as a guaranteed price.

Chevy 1957 Belair	$40,000 - $60,000
Chevy 1967 Corvette L88	$2,500,000 - $4,000,000. With only 20 of these cars manufactured this is considered one of the rarest and hardest to find Muscle Cars ever built and seldom comes on the market. We sold a comparable one at auction three years ago for $3.2 million.
Chevy 1969 Camaro SS	$50,000 - $60,000
Chevy 1969 Camaro ZL1	$500,000 to $700,000. Top condition models with matching serial numbers such as your example have been selling for around $600,000.
Ford 1955 Thunderbird	$30,000 - $40,000
Ford 1965 Mustang	$20,000 - $30,000
Ford 1967 GT40 Mark 4	$4,500,000 - $6,000,000. This model has been increasing in value recently with examples in this condition bringing around $5 million.

| Pontiac 1971 GTO Judge | $125,000 - $150,000 |
| Plymouth 1971 Cuda | $2,750,000 - $3,500,000. With the combination of the big Hemi and being a convertible, this is an extremely desirable vehicle and is considered the last of the true Muscle Cars. |

Please feel free to contact me at the number below if you have any questions or wish to discuss this further.

Sincerely,

Matthew Border, VP Sales
You're Not Getting Older, You're Getting Better Classic
Car Auctions

Bobby crumpled up the letter and threw it at Charles. "You bastard." Bobby started to charge at his cousin, but Angela stuck out her foot and tripped him. He landed unceremoniously, flat on his face, in the grass.

"How dare you?" Lilith O'Connor snarled as she helped her son to his feet.

Bobby turned to Edna. "Grandmother, they cheated me out of my rightful inheritance!" Bobby said, fighting back tears.

Before this could devolve any further, everyone was silenced by the sound of a piercing whistle. All heads turned and saw Tillie, pinkie fingers between her lips and fire in her eyes. "Immediate family! In the house. *Now!*"

Angela held her ground. "We would also like Aunt Beth to join us."

"I agree," Edna seconded.

Once inside, she pointed to Bobby. "You first."

"They deceived me about the value of the cars."

Edna glanced at Charles, who shrugged and said, "We told him multiple times he should get his own independent appraisal...."

"That's a lie!" Lilith O'Connor protested.

Charles snorted then motioned for Paige, who already had the video queued up. She pushed the play button on her phone and held it up for Edna to view. It clearly showed Bobby and Lilith in the garage.

"Any questions? You want to go over any of the vehicles?"

"I don't think so."

"You really should get your own independent appraisal. These cars are quite valuable."

"Naw, I'm good."

"Okay. We'll see you tomorrow."

CHAPTER THIRTY-EIGHT

EDNA'S NOSE FLARED as she turned her scowl to her former daughter-in-law. "You just lied to me, straight to my face."

Lilith O'Connor said, "I'm sure that Bobby…"

"Shut up, Lilith, and let the boy speak for himself," Edna snapped as she turned back to Bobby. "Why didn't you get an appraisal?"

Bobby, with tears rolling down his cheeks, wouldn't make eye contact with anyone. "I didn't think I needed it."

"Why not?" Edna demanded.

"I saw the letter Charles left out for me to find."

"What letter?"

Charles handed his grandmother the offer letter from the auction house for cash purchase of five of the cars. The room was completely silent as she read it. Edna sighed and handed the letter back to Charles.

"The offer letter clearly states they will not make cash offers to any vehicle with a value of over $250,000," Angela said softly.

"I can see that," Edna answered as she turned her attention back to Bobby. "How exactly did you come to see this letter?" She asked.

"Charles left it in plain sight."

"Plain sight?" Edna asked as she glanced up at Charles again.

"It was hardly in plain sight," Charles said calmly. "It was in an envelope on the workbench." Before Lilith could protest, Charles held up a warning finger. "Before you lie to Grammy again, remember we have video cameras all over the garage."

Paige waved her cellphone in Lilith's direction.

"You little bastard," Lilith hissed. "How'd you know I'd look at it?" she demanded.

"Because you've always been a sneaky little money-grubbing bitch," Tillie muttered, loud enough that it got a chuckle from those near her.

Lilith O'Connor heard it as well but ignored Tillie and continued. "He intentionally put handwritten notes on the letter to make me think the cars were broken and worthless."

"Is this true, Charles?" Edna asked.

"The auction house had asked for any details to include in the flyer and verify the provenance for the auction. Those were notes about the condition problems of the cars when Grandpa bought them. Most of the problems listed were repaired years ago."

"How do you know that?" Bobby demanded.

"Because, unlike you, I spent hours with our grandfather and loved listening to him talk about his cars."

"This will not stand. I'll sue," Lilith barked.

"And you'll get laughed out of court," Elizabeth Woodrow, Esq., said before apologizing with her eyes to Edna for intruding in family business.

"Please," my mom said as she motioned for Beth to continue. "Enlighten my former daughter-in-law."

Elizabeth cleared her throat and glanced around the room. "Charles and Angela have video evidence of them advising Bobby to get his own appraisal multiple times. They have video evidence of Bobby and Lilith stealing proprietary and confidential information, which they misconstrued and attempted to use to their advantage by using his first pick to get what they thought was the most valuable car. They also have video evidence of Bobby agreeing to the terms of the lottery which just occurred a few minutes ago in front of dozens of witnesses." Beth cleared her throat again. "If it ever got in front of a judge, at best you would be looking at a summary dismissal. Plus, the judge would also order you to pay any legal fees Charles and Angela incurred and court costs for filing such a frivolous lawsuit." Elizabeth's eyes locked on Bobby, then added. "At worst, if the judge happened to be in a bad mood, he might also impose civil damages on Bobby and sanction the lawyer who had wasted the court's time."

Edna sighed and turned her attention back to Bobby. "Well, what have you got to say for yourself?"

Bobby O'Connor glanced first at his mother, who was livid, then at his father, who was, as usual, profoundly disappointed. Neither one moved nor offered any advice.

Finally, Gabrielle had had enough. "Oh, for God's sake!" she snapped. "Man up, Bobby. This is your family. Admit you were an idiot who," Gabrielle pointed in the direction of Lilith, "thanks to your vile mother, you allowed yourself to be bamboozled. Apologize and see if you can fix this."

Aunt Tillie nodded her approval. "At least one person on that branch of the family tree has some sense."

Lilith O'Connor started to speak in her own defense but, when she saw everyone in the room glaring at her, thought better of it and held her peace.

Bobby drew in a breath, looked down and took a moment to center himself. When he looked up, he was a different man. The tears were gone and a calmness had settled over him.

"Grandmother," he began. "It is not fair that Charles and Angela cut me out."

A heavy silence settled over the room as all eyes shifted to my twins.

"We agree," Angela said in a rare strong, firm voice.

"You do?" Robert, Sr. said with a baffled expression on his face.

"Yes," Angela said softly. "Like Aunt Gabrielle said, we're all family here, and we want to be fair to everyone."

"I believe an apology is still in order," Edna said softly as her eyes locked on her eldest grandson.

A heavy silence fell over the solarium as everyone's attention turned to Bobby. He squared his shoulders and cleared his throat. "I was lazy and stupid and didn't do my due diligence on the cars. Worse, I tried to intentionally take my cousin's prized possession, his GTO, away from him." With clear eyes and his head held high, Bobby turned to Charles. "I am so sorry."

All eyes silently pivoted to Charles, who hesitated briefly before a broad smile broke across his face and he took two strides and gave Bobby a bone-crushing man hug. After a round of applause, it was Angela's turn to give her cousin a hug.

Angela released Bobby then motioned that he should join Charles and her on the patio. Lilith O'Connor started to accompany her son, but Angela shook her head and pointed a finger at her former aunt. "Just Bobby."

"Who do you think you are?" Lilith protested.

"We're the ones about to make your son rich enough he never has to take another ounce of your nonsense again for the rest of his life," Angela's eyes moved to Bobby and they were cold as ice. "If your mother walks out that door with you, then our current deal stands and you get screwed sideways."

Charles nodded and pointed at his sister. "What she said."

Aunt Tillie gave me a hip bump then leaned in close. "The force is strong in those two. Reminds me of somebody I used to know."

Edna looked at her eldest grandson. "It's time you make a choice, Bobby," she said with a hard expression on her face. "It appears your cousins are willing to offer you a lifeline. But, as far as I'm concerned, if the twins want the deal to stand because you can't say no to your mother, I have no problem with them getting the cars they selected and you getting the GTO."

Bobby inhaled and slowly released the breath before turning to his mother. "You stay here, Mom," he said firmly then added. "I think you've done enough damage for one day."

In a huff, Lilith O'Connor picked up her purse and stormed out of the room.

Before she got very far, Aunt Tillie let out whoop then shouted, "Ding dong, the bitch is dead!"

Lilith hesitated for a moment, but she knew she was beaten and, without even a backward glance, continued in the direction of the front door.

Angela leaned in close enough to Bobby where only he could hear her. He nodded and the trio of Angela, Bobby and Charles headed outside and out of earshot.

The rest of the family watched through the windows as Angela, as usual, was doing most of the talking. For once, Bobby didn't have much to say. After a few minutes, Bobby nodded and Angela tapped on the glass, pointed to Beth and motioned for her to join them. Beth made her way outside and listened intently to Angela. Elizabeth Woodrow, Esq., pulled out her phone, and like Paige previously, first recorded Angela speaking, then Bobby and finally Charles.

Angela extended her hand to her cousin, who didn't think that was nearly enough. He grabbed his petite cousin around the waist, lifted her off her feet and spun her around.

The three cousins and Beth Woodrow walked back into the house. All eyes were on Angela.

"We've come to an agreement," Angela said in her usual soft-spoken manner. "Charles will keep his GTO, Bobby will get the Camaro SS and I'm keeping the T-Bird. We will place the other six cars up for auction and divide the proceeds equally between all of Charlie O'Connor's grandchildren." Angela smiled and her eyes locked on Gabrielle. "Including those yet unborn."

"Wow!" Aunt Tillie said. "Wow! That is amazingly generous."

"We're family," Angela said as she turned to her beaming grandmother, who nodded her approval.

After hugs and congratulations, Angela and Charles found a quiet corner near Aunt Tillie and me.

Aunt Tillie put her arms around the twins' shoulders. "If you're doing what I think you're trying to do," she said with a grin on her face, "good luck, but remember, never let the colonel count your chickens."

"So far, so good," Charles said softly to his aunt.

"Yeah," Angela answered. "Now comes the tricky part."

CHAPTER THIRTY-NINE

"THAT WAS REALLY nice what you did for Gabrielle's baby," I said to my twins. "What's the tricky part?"

Charles laughed. "You heard that?"

"Yeah."

Angela glanced at her brother, who nodded. "We're going to need your proxy for your shares of O'Connor Industries."

"May I ask why?"

Before Angela could answer, we all turned when we heard the soft whir of Edna's motorized scooter approaching.

"So, did you get it?" Edna asked Angela.

"Get what?" I asked.

"I've watched this pair in action since they were toddlers and I know all of their moves," my mom said with a grin as she turned her attention away from me and back to her granddaughter. "You put together a perfect trap for your cousin Bobby."

"Trap?" asked Angela innocently. "What trap?"

"You just happened to have someone make a video of you telling Bobby he needed to get his own appraisal. You just happened to leave the second letter where Lilith could find it. Then, surprise, surprise, leaving her alone with it."

Angela looked at Charles, and they both shrugged but offered no denial.

Edna shook her head. "You let Bobby out of the box, so you had to be after something bigger. Much bigger than your grandfather's cars…" Mom stopped mid-sentence and her head whipped back and forth between Charles and Angela. "Oh, my God!" Edna exclaimed. "I don't believe you two!"

Angela broke into a rare fit of the giggles and gave her grandmother a hug. Straightening up, she continued to laugh and had to wipe tears from her eyes.

"What is going on here?" I demanded.

"I'm just guessing, but the twins now have Bobby's proxy for his voting shares," Edna answered.

Angela nodded.

"What?" I demanded. "You went through all of that for a fraction of the voting stock that won't make any difference as long as Robert controls sixty percent...." Then it hit me like a lightning bolt.

"Jeez Louise!" I said as my head jerked around to locate Lindsey. He was on the other side of the room in deep conversation with Beth. Now I understood why my twins were having all of the meetings with their father, the master-of-the-universe dealmaker.

My two children, on their eighteenth birthdays, were planning on launching a hostile takeover of the family business.

"Did Bobby pick a side?" Edna asked.

"Team Charles and Angela," Charles answered softly.

"How did you convince him?" Edna asked.

"We made him an offer he couldn't refuse," Angela answered.

"Which was?" I asked.

"Have a shot at getting stinking rich or continue living under Lilith's thumb and in the shadow of his father," Charles said.

Edna nodded her approval. "The next part will be tougher."

Angela glanced at Charles. "We know."

"Do you two think you're ready?"

"Daddy thinks we're well positioned, but we'll find out soon enough," Angela said as Charles nodded his agreement.

Edna's eyes lost focus and she rubbed her chin. "Are you sure Bobby won't blab to his mother, or worse, his father?"

Angela shook her head. "No way. We have him on video confirming if he violated the non-disclosure, our deal is off and he could kiss the money goodbye."

"Non-disclosure?" Edna chuckled. "So Beth Woodrow is onboard?"

"She is having Bobby sign our agreement as we speak."

"You already had the agreement drafted? How long have you two been working on this?"

Angela nodded. "About two weeks."

Edna burst out laughing. "You are a pip, Angela." Edna's face turned serious. "Are you going to be as fair to Robert as you were to Bobby?"

"Absolutely," Angela answered.

"And I have your word on that?

"He's family, Grammy," Angela answered.

"That's my girl." Edna gave Angela's hand a squeeze.

"That was also very nice what you did for Robert's and Gabrielle's baby," Edna added.

"Grandpa would have wanted all of his grandkids to each get equal shares," Angela said with a shrug.

"Yeah," Edna said softly. "About that. We need to talk."

"What do you mean?" Angela asked.

"I assume you're planning on using the cash from the sale of the cars to finance your project."

"Yes," Charles said suspiciously, not liking where this conversation appeared headed.

"If you really mean you want all of Charlie's grandkids to get an equal share of the cars, your combined portion of the inheritance from the sale is about to drop from a half to a third." Edna's eyes twinkled. "You have two cousins you don't know about."

CHAPTER FORTY

"WHAT!" I SHOUTED so loudly even the people outside the room could hear me. "Are you kidding me!?"

"Go round up Bobby and your aunts and uncle," Edna said to the twins with a sigh. "They all should hear this from me. As the twins turned to leave, Mom added, "Ask your Aunt Beth and her husband to join us as well."

Beth I understood. She had pretty much been the O'Connor family consigliere for two decades, but why include Derek in this conversation?

Tillie was the first to arrive. "What's going on?" she asked me.

"Apparently Mom has some big news to share about relatives I didn't even know existed."

"Oh, hot damn," Tillie said as she looked at her nearly empty glass. "I need a refill before this gets going. Bring you anything?"

"Lynchburg lemonade and don't spare the Lynchburg," I answered.

Tillie winked and pointed a finger in my direction. "You got it."

Bernie gave me a sideways look combined with a silly grin.

"What?" I demanded.

"I was just thinking it was a nice night for a swim."

I shook my head, slugged him in the shoulder and glanced around. Robert and Gabrielle stood as far away from the twins and me as possible while still being in the same room. Aunt Jolene, with Paige at her side, was looking a bit befuddled after a long and tiring day. Paige found her a chair then scampered away to get her a glass of water. Lindsey was grinning like a Cheshire cat as Charles approached him but quickly turned serious as soon as my son started talking to him.

Angela had to race Bobby to his car and stop him from leaving. They arrived back in the kitchen at about the same time Tillie returned with my drink. I took a tentative sip and my eyes flew open. Hoping it was just topped off and not that strong top to bottom, I gave it a stir with my finger. It didn't help.

Bernie gave Tillie a thumbs-up, and I would have slugged him again but I was afraid I might spill my drink.

Beth wandered over with Derek and stood next to me. She was a bit confused as to why she had been invited to an obviously family-only gathering. She glanced in my direction for some insight.

Before I could say anything, my mom cleared her throat and immediately turned her attention to my brother. "Robert," Edna said. "I know you've had questions about all of the money your father gave away. It was all post-tax joint income from Charlie and me and had absolutely nothing to do with O'Connor Industries."

Robert, who had already heard the same information relayed by Gabrielle, still did not appear to be buying it. "What was the money for?" he asked softly.

"Child support," Edna answered, flatly.

Edna gave her bombshell a few moments to sink in, then continued to talk directly to my brother. "After you were born, your father had an affair with an unmarried woman that resulted in a child being born out of wedlock."

Edna paused again, then turned her attention to the entire room. "I was deeply hurt by what Charlie had done while I was struggling with my pregnancy and the first year with Robert. Times were different then and single motherhood was severely frowned upon. I did not want this child raised with the stigma of being the bastard offspring of a rich and powerful man." Edna paused again and took a sip of her drink. "We concocted an elaborate cover story that only three other people in the world besides me knew was false. Charlie, Bertram Ruggles," Edna's eyes locked on my lifelong best friend. "And Beth Woodrow's mother."

CHAPTER FORTY-ONE

D EER IN THE headlights didn't do justice to the expression on Beth's face. In less than thirty seconds, she had seen the entire façade of her life collapse under the weight of a secret revealed about a decision made before she had even taken her first breath. She had always thought her father had died before she was born; instead he had, unknown to her, been there her entire life.

That was why Charlie had given her mother the house next door. That was why Charlie always liked having her around. But on the flip side, that was why Edna never liked Beth. She resented her because she was a constant reminder of the time Daddy had strayed.

It was also why we were also so often mistaken for sisters.

We are sisters.

Yikes!

Thankfully, Derek was at her side to steady Beth or she might have collapsed in a heap on the floor.

"Whoa, Nellie!" Aunt Tillie exclaimed as she slapped Edna on the back of her head. "So this is the big dark secret you and my worthless brother have kept from me for over half a century." She slapped Edna again.

Edna shook a warning finger in Tillie's direction. "Don't make me get out of this thing and kick your more-than-generous butt."

Tillie waved Edna off and grabbed Beth in a huge hug. "I always thought the O'Connor grit had just rubbed off on you, girl." Tillie released her hug but held the limp Beth at arm's length and eyed her from head to toe. "Seeing how much you look like Allie and act like Charlie, I can't believe I never put it together." She hugged her again. "Welcome, officially, to the family."

I glanced in the direction of my brother, and he was just as stunned as I was.

I felt sorry for Beth. She must have felt like her life was somewhere between a Greek tragedy and an Elizabethan love story.

Beth, quivering and with tears in her eyes, gasped. "I have to call David and Michael."

Derek Woodrow, as usual, was already one step ahead of his wife. He handed Beth his cellphone. "I've got David on the line." Beth rubbed her hand gently on Derek's cheek and muttered a nearly silent thank you as she accepted the phone and walked to a quiet corner of the kitchen.

Tillie, obviously having the time of her life, cupped her hands around her mouth and shouted in Beth's direction. "Don't forget to mention to my new nephew that after the car auction he and his brother are both going to be millionaires!"

Without turning around, Beth flipped Tillie off before sticking her extended finger in her opposite ear from the one with the cellphone so she could hear her son better.

"All in favor of granting full membership rights of the Sisterhood to Elizabeth O'Connor Woodrow, please raise your right hand." Gabrielle's, Tillie's, Jolene's and my hands went up instantly. We all turned to Edna, who sighed, rolled her eyes, and then slowly made it unanimous.

Robert glared at Gabrielle; he hooked his arm under hers and they headed to the door. Apparently, with his history with Beth, her sudden promotion to full family member status was going to take him some time to process.

My newly discovered sister finished her call and, much to my surprise and disappointment, instead of heading in my direction grabbed Charles, Angela, Bobby and Lindsey and they moved their meeting outside. Through the glass, we could all see them deep in discussion.

I leaned into Bernie. "What do you think is going on?"

"I'm just guessing here," he said. "I imagine they were planning on using all of the revenue from the sale of the cars to finance their efforts, and reading their body language they didn't have much margin for error. They had already factored in Gabrielle's baby but David and Michael getting equal shares has thrown all of their numbers off."

"When did you get so smart?" I asked.

For once Bernie didn't have a snappy reply, and if I didn't know better I would have sworn my compliment made him blush a little.

The meeting broke up and Lindsey and Bobby both headed to their cars without bothering to come back inside. Charles and Angela spent a few minutes with their Aunt Beth before trotting off toward the doublewide, I assumed to run some numbers.

Beth took a moment to gather herself before she tapped on the glass and pointed in my direction.

I pointed to Derek to see if she wanted him to join us, but she shook her head. I handed Bernie my drink and said, "Don't spill any of that on your clothes. I'm pretty sure it will take the color out."

He accepted the glass, then leaned and whispered. "I'll be here if you need me."

I kissed him on the cheek. "Of course you will."

Before I got to the door, Tillie handed me a bottle of scotch and two heavy-cut crystal high ball glasses. "I'm going to give you a five-minute head start, then I plan to get sloppy drunk and rowdy with my new niece."

"Like you need an excuse," I answered as I accepted the glasses and whiskey.

The patio was nearly deserted with only the caterers and the band still milling around. I wondered how many people who had already left would be kicking themselves in the morning when the news of Beth being Charlie O'Connor's love child started making the rounds.

Beth saw me coming and moved over to a table near the swimming pool but took a chair with her back to the house. I fell heavily into the seat next to her and poured her three fingers of scotch and a similar amount for me. Completely out of character, she finished the drink in two gulps and put her empty glass in front of me for a refill.

"You may want to pace yourself," I said as I poured her two more fingers. "Aunt Tillie plans to get you rip-roaring drunk."

"I'm in," Beth said with tears in her eyes as she shook her head. "Can you believe how dense we both have been?"

"Embarrassing," I answered.

We sat in silence for a few moments before I finally said, "You know this doesn't change a thing between us."

"I know," Beth answered. "Will you come see me on visiting days?"

"What?" I asked.

"I'm planning on committing a double homicide." Beth took another generous gulp of her drink. "First I'm going to strangle Bertram Ruggles, then shoot my mom."

"If my mother wasn't already dying, I'd be in the cell next to you."

We both broke into a fit of the giggles. "What a family," I finally said as I regained control. "Did you get ahold of Michael yet?"

"With the time difference he was sleeping, but I sent him a text."

"What about David?"

"He's on his way over," Beth answered.

On cue, a car pulled in and David bounced out and sprinted in the direction of his mother. He took one look at Beth and whistled.

Beth held her glass up in her son's direction before taking another long pull.

"Okay, so it's going to be like that," David said.

I guess our five minutes were up. Out of nowhere, both Derek and Bernie joined us at the table. They shared concerned expressions but, wisely, did not offer any temperance suggestions. I saw Tillie over by the band with a large wad of bills in her hand, and they immediately began plugging their equipment back in.

Tillie wandered over and put an arm around Beth and my shoulders. "Ladies. It is time to get this party started."

Then it hit me. My head spun around until I located my mom. She was parked in a dark corner of the patio where she could see all of the activity but probably be unnoticed. She was staring straight at Beth and me.

I knew she didn't want to take this secret to her grave. I had to wonder, had she just checked off the last item on her bucket list? Tears filled my eyes as I raised my glass in her direction.

CHAPTER FORTY-TWO

OR THE FIRST time in my life, I could completely relate to a goldfish. Sitting in the glass bowl the bank calls a conference room, I could see the reception desk and the elevators, but the sound of all of the activity swirling just a few feet away was muffled.

My stomach was churning, and my twins, Charles and Angela, sitting next to each other on the other side of the table from me were pensive. My nephew, Bobby, was doing the breathing exercises Jolene had taught him as he tried to relax and center himself. Elizabeth O'Connor Woodrow, Esq., and the three young lawyers accompanying her, including her eldest son, David, were huddled in a corner making sure they had all their ducks in row.

At the moment, my ex-husband was in the opposite corner with two extremely young and extremely attractive female staffers. Old habits die hard. Lindsey was the only one in the conference room who was completely relaxed and brimming with self-confidence. And, why not? The amount of money we were going to be discussing with the bank today was a rounding error in his world.

Lindsey, seeing my concern, sat down in the chair next to me. "Relax, this will be fun."

"For you, maybe," I answered.

"Ah," Lindsey said to the room as he pointed in the direction of the bank of elevators. "Let the games begin." Lindsey nodded in the direction of a well-groomed young man in his early thirties who had just stepped off of the elevator. "That is Vice President Michael Tucker." Lindsey held up a finger. "Wait for it."

Tucker walked with a swagger, said something to the cute receptionist behind the desk, then pulled up short when he saw the crowd in the conference room. The smile vanished from his face and was replaced with a hint of panic.

Lindsey laughed. "Our young Mr. Tucker, as Tillie might say, *looks like he had some extra fruit in his looms.*"

Charles and Angela, who, as usual, were way ahead of me, chuckled.

"You called that one, Daddy," Angela said with a giggle.

"What's going on?" I asked.

"While having the title of vice president, Tucker is one of the junior associates in the loan department and only a small step up from a teller," Lindsey said with a mischievous grin. "His boss had sent him downstairs to politely blow the twins off. But," Lindsey continued as he nodded at Elizabeth O'Connor Woodrow, Esq., "seeing a named partner of the largest law firm in the area and the head of mergers and acquisitions of a company with assets that rival the banks, was not what he was expecting."

Tucker instinctively adjusted his tie and squared his shoulders before walking back over to the reception desk and, without asking, spun the phone around and dialed an internal number.

"In less than two minutes," Lindsey said, "the elevator doors are going to open again and either the CEO of the bank or the head of the loan department will be stepping off." Lindsey had a twinkle in his eye. "We're hoping for the head of the loan department."

"Why?" I asked.

"This deal is small enough, so he would have sign-off authority without needing board approval. The CEO would just slow things down. Plus," Lindsey added, "he's an asshole."

Tucker headed to the bank of elevators and waited. At almost exactly the two-minute mark, a small gray-haired man stepped off the elevator and pulled Michael Tucker aside.

"Excellent!" Lindsey said. "That's Winston Simpson, the head of the corporate loan division. That will make things easier since he's a decision-maker."

"What are they doing?" I asked.

"It is unlikely our request for a meeting ever rose high enough to get to Simpson's desk," Lindsey answered. "Tucker is bringing him up to speed."

We all watched as Tucker handed Simpson a document, which he quickly skimmed. Simpson asked a few questions.

"Tucker just told Simpson that Robert O'Connor's and the O'Connor Industries' loans have moved to being in default and we're here with an offer to buy the loans."

When the pair of bankers entered the conference room, the three lawyers with Beth and the two assistants with Lindsey immediately moved behind their bosses.

Lindsey took charge. "Nice of you to join us, Winston," Lindsey said. "Elizabeth you already know."

Elizabeth O'Connor Woodrow, Esq., nodded.

Lindsey then turned to me. "This is my ex-wife, Allison Clark." Lindsey continued around the table. "These are my children, Charles and Angela, and my nephew Robert O'Connor, Jr." He didn't bother to introduce the support team.

A light clicked on in Simpson's eyes. He now understood why someone on the level of Lindsey Clark was involved.

Family.

"What do you have in mind, Lindsey?"

"We're going to make you the deal of a lifetime, Winston," Lindsey answered.

I had never been in the same room when my ex was negotiating anything other than sex before, but he was obviously in his element. He was smooth and confident. Even Beth was more than willing to let him do all of the talking.

"How so?" Winston Simpson answered.

"Robert O'Connor owes your bank a great deal of money with little or no chance of ever repaying it."

"Robert O'Connor..." Simpson started to say, but Lindsey cut him off.

"Is not Charlie O'Connor. He lacks the vision of his father and it is only a matter of time before he runs the company into the ground."

Lindsey, with a twinkle in his eyes, chuckled, "Leaving you holding a rather large, empty sack. We're here to throw you a lifeline."

As I watched Lindsey jousting with a Senior Vice President of the twenty-seventh-largest bank in the country, I started to remember what I used to love about him. The confidence, the swagger. I sighed. How different my life would have been if he had only been able to keep his zipper closed.

As I looked around the table, while my stomach was churning and my heart was in my throat, everyone else was outwardly calm. Beth had her Elizabeth face on and the twins were more than happy to let their father take the starring role. Charles, particularly, was sitting absolutely still. He was almost like a small critter hoping to be overlooked by a passing predator by not moving and giving his position away.

"Lifeline?" Winston Simpson asked.

"Yes," Lindsey said. "We're here to make you a one-time offer to take all of these loans off your hands."

Now it was Simpson's turn to chuckle. "And acquire sixty percent of the stock in the company for pennies on the dollar."

Lindsey shrugged. "There is that, of course. But you'll never find a buyer with a bigger vested interest than the people at this table." Lindsey motioned to me, the twins, and Bobby. "The company is entirely privately held and the other forty percent of the stock that Robert – and by extension you – don't own is sitting at this table."

It not being his first rodeo, even with an internationally famous acquisition specialist and the biggest gunslinger lawyer in town on the other side of the table, Simpson did not show any reaction. Tucker, on the other hand, was trying his best to keep his poker face, but the sweat on his upper lip was an easy tell.

Lindsey gave his words a few seconds to sink in, then continued. "This could be a win for everyone."

"How is that?" Simpson asked.

"You get stinker loans off your books, O'Connor Industries doesn't move into Chapter Eleven, and Robert O'Connor doesn't have to declare personal bankruptcy. The O'Connor family retains control of the family business, but with better management." Lindsey smiled. "Like I said, all sides win."

"What's your offer?" Simpson asked.

Elizabeth glanced at one of her lawyers and a document appeared out of nowhere and landed in front of Winston Simpson. Simpson glanced at it, showed it to Tucker, and then smiled sweetly. "You'll have to do better than that, Lindsey."

"Come on, Winston. This is nickel-and-dime stuff and not worth the aggravation for a bank your size." Another document magically appeared. "Here's the current book value of O'Connor Industries."

One of Lindsey's assistants handed both Simpson and Tucker a file folder.

"Look at the executive summary on the first page," Lindsey said. "It is what you might get on a good day, after a ton of man hours, if you tried to sell off the company assets to recoup your losses."

"And," Elizabeth O'Connor Woodrow, Esq., said, "that's before I start tying you up in knots in court for the next decade or so."

I wondered if this "good cop, bad cop" thing Lindsey and Beth were using had been prearranged.

Simpson shook his head as he continued reading the documents. "I have a fiduciary duty to my bank."

"You certainly do," Lindsey answered with a laugh. "You also have the opportunity to get yourself a ton of goodwill here with people your bank would love to do more business with."

Even I knew what Lindsey meant, and so did Winston Simpson. The company Lindsey worked for was a major international player, and, he used to tell me, for local political reasons, the local banks always got a taste of the business. But, they only got the table scraps left over after Wall Street and the New York banks had picked the carcass mostly clean. This was a thinly veiled offer of "you scratch my back and I'll scratch yours. Do right by my kids and I'll do right by you."

Winston's head shot up and his eyes locked on Lindsey, but to his credit, he didn't take the bait. Tucker looked like he was an inch away from needing smelling salts.

"This offer will have to come up, substantially." He pushed the documents away. "Unless you have a better offer, I think we're done here," he said, but stayed in his chair.

Lindsey looked at the twins. "Sorry kids, but we tried," he said as he got up and reached for his briefcase. "Let's move on to plan B."

"Plan B?" Winston Simpson asked.

"We let O'Connor Industries go under, take the money we were going to give you today and rebrand under a new name." Lindsey started to his feet. "Are you playing in the pro-am next Wednesday, Winston?" Lindsey asked with a tone that indicted the meeting was over and he was moving on.

Simpson stayed seated but reached for the documents and pulled them back and read them again. He sighed. "Are you saying this is a cash offer? I thought we would be renegotiating the loan."

All eyes in the room followed Lindsey's as he looked at his son, who had barely moved for the entire meeting. Charles made eye contact with Beth and his head went up and down maybe a quarter-inch. Without looking behind her, she held out her hand, a certified check almost magically appeared, and she placed it on the table in front of her. As was her wont, she confirmed the amount and signatures.

Sitting next to Beth I could clearly see the check. It was from the account of Charles and Angela, LLC and was signed by both of my children. I was stunned when I saw the total.

It was substantially more than what the twins had netted from the sale of my dad's cars.

Then it hit me as I smiled first at Bobby then at David. Charles and Angela had convinced them to throw their share of the sale into the pot as well.

Beth slid the check across the table in the direction of Winston Simpson.

"Cash," Charles said softly. "One-time offer that expires in thirty seconds."

Winston Simpson nodded in Charles' direction as he, along with everyone else, felt the power shift from Lindsey to the real decision-maker on the other side of the table.

Simpson studied the check for a moment then, instead of passing it back, he slid it over to Michael Tucker.

Lindsey gave my knee a squeeze.

"Mr. Clark," Simpson said as he rose to his feet and extended his hand to Charles Clark and not Lindsey Clark. "We have a deal."

CHAPTER FORTY-THREE

I CAN'T REMEMBER ever being more uncomfortable or nervous in my entire life.

Sitting next to Beth in the second seat of the Escalade with tinted windows I had ridden in a month before, I nodded in the direction of the oversized driver I had previously met named Roman. Next to him in the front passenger seat was an equally impressive specimen named Viktor.

"Is this really necessary?" I asked.

"Yes," Elizabeth O'Connor Woodrow, Esq., answered in a flat monotone. "Sometimes these things go badly and there is no reason to take any unnecessary chances."

I leaned in closer. "Are they armed?"

"Do you really want me to answer that?" Elizabeth asked.

I thought about it for a moment, then shook my head.

The big car rolled into the parking lot of O'Connor Industries and Beth shook her head. "What a dump."

"My daddy." I caught myself and started over. "Our daddy wasn't a big one for flashy offices."

"Ya think?" Beth said as she waited for Viktor to open her door.

The world headquarters of O'Connor Industries, in a previous life, had been a privately owned home improvement center that couldn't compete with the national chains and had gone belly up decades earlier. It was located on a stretch of highway made moot by the completion of a nearby interstate in the 1970s. It was perfect for Charlie's needs, and he had scooped it up at a sheriff's auction for a song. Despite being a fraction of the size of a Lowe's or Home Depot, it had ample storage for building materials and equipment to maintain the company's multiple real estate holdings. It even had a covered lumber yard in the rear to store extra home construction products that he would buy cheap in down markets and hold onto until sales perked back up, to increase his profit margins.

The main building was 20,000 square feet in nothing much more than a metal shell. Daddy had subdivided about 5,000 square feet into office space. The place wasn't going to win any Architectural Digest awards, but it was incredibly functional and had been fully paid for and rent-free since before the Berlin Wall had fallen.

Waiting for us on the curb was Charles, looking uncomfortable in a suit, and Angela, looking twice her age in a dark business skirt and matching blazer. Standing next to them was my ex-husband, Lindsey.

As we pulled in and parked, a second Escalade pulled in next to us and two clones of Roman and Viktor opened the rear passenger doors. Beth's son, my recently minted nephew, David, exited the SUV out of one door as Gabrielle exited out of the other. Following close behind was Cousin Bobby, who looked like this was the last place on Earth he wanted to be.

"It looks like the gang is all here," Elizabeth said softly as she nodded toward the main entrance.

Roman and Viktor took point as we entered the building and the two other bodyguards took up the rear.

The door with "Robert O'Connor, CEO" printed on it was closed. Beth nodded at Roman, who opened the door and entered without knocking.

"Who are you?" Robert's startled secretary demanded.

Roman visually cleared the room before motioning us inside. Next, he opened the door to my brother's office. Again, without knocking. Apparently, Robert had heard the commotion outside his door and was about halfway out of his seat as we all entered.

"What is the meaning of this?" Robert demanded.

"Please keep your hands where we can see them," Roman said politely but with a decided edge to his voice.

"Robert James O'Connor," Elizabeth said flatly. "By a unanimous vote of the Board of Directors and the major shareholders of O'Connor Industries, your position with the corporation is terminated, effective immediately."

"How dare you," Robert barked. "I own sixty percent of this company."

"Not anymore," Elizabeth answered with a calmness I found more than a little unnerving. "You defaulted on your personal loans and loans to O'Connor Industries. As of noon today the bank has sold your collateral, including all of your shares of O'Connor Industries, to Charles and Angela, LLC."

Robert's eyes locked on Charles and he looked like he was about to explode. "Why, you little…" Robert stopped mid-sentence when he saw both his wife and son in the rear of the room. All of the color dropped from his cheeks and he fell heavily back into his chair. "I can't believe it," Robert muttered as his eyes locked on his wife. "You're both in on this too?"

Gabrielle weaved her way to the front of the desk. "Robert," she pleaded. "You need to listen to what they have to say."

"Why?" Robert answered, his voice dripping with bitterness and betrayal.

Elizabeth slid a stack of documents across the desk and in front of Robert.

"What's this?" Robert demanded.

"If you sign these documents," Elizabeth said calmly, "the lien will be removed from your personal residence, and all notes in which you were a signatory held by Charles and Angela LLC will be considered paid in full."

"Robert," Gabrielle pleaded with tears in her eyes. "We're debt-free. We can start over."

Robert began going through the stack of documents, and as he turned each new page, his mouth fell further and further open.

Robert's eyes scanned the room. "What's the catch?" he asked.

Beth slid another piece of paper across the desk. Robert read it, shook his head in amazement, then read it again. "Are you serious?" Robert finally asked.

Elizabeth's eyes moved to Charles.

"The offer is good for exactly the next thirty seconds," Charles said softly, "and is contingent on you not challenging any of our actions in court."

Robert scanned the document again. "Why are you doing this?'

This time Angela answered. "You are family, Uncle Robert," she said softly. "You've given your entire adult life to this company and took an amazing ration of abuse from Charlie O'Connor. It is the least we can do."

Elizabeth held out one of her firm's heavy gold pens.

"Gabby?" Robert said as he glanced up at his wife. "Is this what you want?"

Gabrielle, with tears streaming down her cheeks said, "It's what we both want, Robert." She wiped tears from both cheeks. "It's a dream come true."

"Well, I'll be damned," he said as he accepted the pen from Elizabeth and signed the agreement.

Before the ink was even dry, we all saw a change in my brother's attitude, demeanor and body language. He looked like the weight of the world had been lifted off his shoulders, and he also looked ten years younger.

"Is that it?" Robert asked.

"One more thing," Charles said with a laugh. "Get your butt out of my chair and take your beautiful wife home and get started on Gabrielle's business plan."

"We expect it on our desks within seventy-two hours," Angela added.

Robert quickly rose to his feet and turned his former chair around so it faced Charles.

Charles walked around the desk, sat down and made himself comfortable.

"Nice," Charles said.

"I don't see why you get to be CEO instead of me," Angela protested.

"What?" Charles answered with a snort. "Being president isn't good enough for you?" Charles started to his feet. "We can swap if you want."

"Sit. Down," Angela ordered as she eyed the room. "We'll need to take out that wall so we can both fit in here," she said.

My ex-husband, Lindsey, made a face. "So, who will be calling the shots around here? The CEO or the president?"

"Angela and I each have thirty-two and a half percent of the stock," Charles said. "So, if we're in agreement, the rest of the stockholders will have to live with our decisions."

"Brilliant!" Lindsey said with a proud smile.

"What?" I demanded.

"You still own your ten percent, right?"

"Right," I answered, still clueless as to where this was headed.

"Gabrielle's baby and Bobby each hold seven and a half percent, and each one of the Woodrow brothers hold five percent."

"They do? Since when?"

Angela laughed. "Since they put their share of the car auction money in the pot to help us buy the bank note."

"I still don't see any brilliance here," I protested.

"On the rare occasion when we disagree," Angela said. "One of us will need to get the support of at least three of the five major shareholders to get a majority share of the voting stock."

"Checks and balances, Mom," Charles said. "It will keep us from doing anything galactically stupid."

"Like I said," Lindsey added. "Brilliant."

"Hey, Uncle Robert," Angela said.

"Yeah?" Robert answered.

"How long do you need to clear your stuff out of here?"

"Can I have my old CFO office back?" Robert asked. "It has been empty since Charlie passed."

Charles and Angela exchanged concerned expressions.

"To prevent any blowback during this transition, we need you to be completely out of the building," Charles stated flatly in a tone that indicated that decision had been made and was not open for discussion.

"Understood, Boss," Robert answered.

Boss.

Then the twins glanced in the direction of their Cousin Bobby. "Plus, the CFO office might be a little crowded," Angela added.

Robert's eyes followed the twins'. "Good choice," my brother said as he nodded his approval in the direction of his son. "The company was at its best when we had the idea man behind the big desk and the detail guy down the hall poking him with a stick."

"Checks and balances," Angela said. "We also thought," she continued, "since the cars are no longer there, the perfect place to spin off your new division of O'Connor Industries would be Grandpa's garage at the Farm."

"With basically open floor space, Gabrielle can customize it any way she wants," Charles said.

"That would be perfect," Robert answered as he gave Gabrielle's hand a squeeze.

Charles pointed a warning finger in his uncle's direction. "If you haven't outgrown it in a year, we'll have to talk."

Lindsey sighed and shook his head. "Damnit," he muttered.

"What?" I asked with a chuckle.

"I had hoped to someday recruit the twins to come work with me."

"Okay," I said.

"Now it looks like they may be recruiting me to come work for them." Lindsey gave me a friendly squeeze and for the first time in years, I didn't flinch and felt no need to pull away. "I'll tell you what," Lindsey said as he kissed me on the forehead and we watched our twins moving around the room. "We at least did one thing right."

I had to agree.

CHAPTER FORTY-FOUR

ALL HEADS TURNED when we heard a soft tapping on the door.

"Come," Robert said, then apologized to Charles with his eyes, but my son waved it off.

Robert's secretary stuck her head in and had a concerned expression on her face. "Everybody was wondering if everything was okay."

Angela wheeled on the bodyguards that had accompanied them and pointed a finger in their direction. "You four stay in here and out of sight," she said before turning to her uncle. "They know you; they don't know us."

"We need you to make the transition seamless," Charles said. "If you don't mind, we would like you to introduce us to the staff."

Robert held up the agreement he had just signed. "After this, I'll do it naked if you want."

"That won't be necessary," Angela said, then nodded for everyone else to follow her.

Apparently the news of our dramatic entrance had spread like wildfire through the complex. Back on the warehouse floor around two dozen people, mostly male, were milling around with concerned expressions on their faces.

Angela leaned into Robert. "Introduce Robert, Jr., then me, then give the floor to Charles."

Robert nodded and took a step forward. "Everybody, listen up." He waited until he was sure he had everyone's attention. "Effective a few minutes ago I have been replaced as the CEO of O'Connor Industries."

This news caused a wave of whispers to ripple through the crowd. Robert motioned for silence.

"I've spent the past thirty-two years working at O'Connor Industries, and I'm here to tell you, today is the happiest day of my life. I am passing the reins of this great company into the hands where they belong." With tears of pride in his eyes, Robert motioned in his son's direction. "Please allow me to introduce the new CFO of O'Connor Industries. Bobby," Robert started and corrected himself, "Robert O'Connor, Junior."

Bobby waved, but didn't move from his spot.

Next, my brother motioned in his niece's direction. "The president, Angela O'Connor Clark." Robert put extra emphasis on the "O'Connor."

A ripple of polite applause filled the warehouse.

"Next," Robert said as he pulled Charles up next to him. "Let me introduce our new CEO and the man who was born to someday run this company. Charles O'Connor Clark."

Charles stepped forward and a heavy silence settled over the room. "My grandfather and namesake founded this company and he made it great by being smarter, quicker and tougher than the competition. He was able to do this because, as he liked to say, 'never be afraid to hire people better than yourself.' Looking around this room, I can see my uncle has had the same attitude."

Another ripple of applause as the room started to relax.

"Starting today, a new generation shaped and molded by my grandfather, Charlie O'Connor, will not only be restoring the old glory of O'Connor Industries, but we will be aggressively exploring new opportunities."

I felt a shiver go up my spine as I watched my son speaking. Like his grandfather, he had the power to hold an entire room in the palm of his hand and make everyone think he was talking only to them.

"We'll make mistakes." Charles's voice rose. "But we will never fear failure!"

Charles paused for effect and tried to make eye contact with every single person in front of him. His voice lowered. "None of our dreams and aspirations will be realized without the help of everyone in this room." His voice began to rise again. "While my cousin and sister and I carry the O'Connor name," Charles emphatically pointed at the people in front of him, "you are what will make this company exceptional. We cannot do it without the support of each and every one of you."

The room exploded.

"Questions?" Charles asked.

A man in the front row shouted, "I heard you sold Charlie's car collection."

"Most of it," Charles answered. "I kept the GTO my grandfather and I rebuilt together."

"Can I take her for a spin?" he asked with a chuckle.

Much to his surprise, Charles fished his keys out of his pocket and tossed them to the man. "It's out front. You better have her back in ten minutes."

"Be sure to clock out," Robert, Jr., shouted.

The room erupted in laughter.

"Boy," someone in the middle of the pack shouted. "That apple didn't fall far from the tree."

More laughter.

"On the subject of Charlie's cars: Just so you all know," Robert said after he waited for the crowd to settle down. "Your new management team used the proceeds of the sale of my dad's muscle cars to pay down the company debt. As of this morning we are on the best financial footing the company has been on in over a decade."

Another, louder ripple of applause.

"Will there be any layoffs?" a voice shouted from the rear of the warehouse.

"Exactly the opposite," Charles answered without even a moment's hesitation. "After we get our feet on the ground, you can expect to see a 'Now Hiring' sign in the window."

"No offense," another man said, "that was a really nice speech and all, but you look like a couple of kids."

Robert laughed. "Charles and Angela personally made over a quarter of a million dollars after taxes in the past year in a business venture they ran out of the doublewide parked at the Farm."

Everyone in the room was familiar with the Farm and the famous doublewide, so no further explanation was required.

Robert eyed the room and saw the shock and skepticism in the staff's eyes. "They did that while they were only seventeen and still in high school." Robert waited for that to sink in. "They would have made a whole hell of a lot more, but prom and homecoming took up a lot of their time."

A whoop went up from the crowd.

"You made all that money while still in high school?" one man shouted in disbelief.

Charles and Angela both shrugged.

"Of course they did!" Robert shouted. "Would you expect anything less from Charlie O'Connor's grandkids?"

The room erupted and the crowd surged forward to meet the new bosses.

Angela slugged her brother hard in the arm.

"What was that for?" Charles protested as he rubbed his arm.

"You could have used a little of that in your valedictory speech."

Charles laughed. "This was important, and I didn't care about that."

CHAPTER FORTY-FIVE

THAT SUMMER WAS the best three months of my life.
I worked with Mom in her garden every day the weather permitted. Actually, I did most of the work and Mom supervised. We laughed and made up for lost time.

A few nights a week, Robert and Gabrielle would swing by and team up with Jolene to make a world-class dinner. We started taking bets on what time the first argument between Gabrielle and Jolene would break out. Seeing the pair toe-to-toe shouting at each other in French always brought a tear to Tillie's eye.

We finally got to meet Gabrielle's parents at one of our dinners. Gabrielle's mother was around my age, but she could easily pass for Gabrielle's slightly older sister. Seeing her, it was instantly obvious from whom Gabby had gotten her good looks, and more importantly, her spine. She had a trick I really wanted her to teach me. With a single glance and without uttering a word, she could totally stop Gabrielle dead in her tracks. There were days I really wished I could work that magic on Angela.

Her father was unremarkable. Medium height, medium weight and with a rather silly comb over. He didn't say much and he perpetually had a wine glass in his hand. He had the look of a man who, between his wife and daughter, had years ago come to grips with the fact he would have little or no input into family conversations. He seemed fine with it. After all, he had a beautiful wife who obviously adored him and doted on him, and was also a gourmet chef.

Jolene was in heaven the entire evening. Partly because she didn't utter a single word of English the entire night, but mostly because when the cooking argument broke out, Gabrielle's mom took my aunt's side.

For the first time in our lives, my brother and I were actually getting along. One night we were in the great room and Bernie cracked a joke that made Robert laugh so hard he spilled his wine. As he brushed the chardonnay off his shirt, I caught Mom watching us from across the room with a satisfied smile on her face. I hope that was the face I would always remember when I thought of my mother.

The night Lindsey came over for dinner, I had to warn Bernie that if he grabbed my ass one more time I was going to send him home without any supper and develop a headache for the next few weeks. That worked and his hands never drifted south of the border again, but it didn't wipe the smug grin off of his face.

I didn't see much of the twins that summer. They were busy rebuilding O'Connor Industries. But to their credit, they both made time for their grandmother and, hardly surprising, always managed to show up before dinner was served.

A few weeks after the birthday party, Paige, who couldn't have been any closer to Jolene without being a conjoined twin, vanished. When I asked what happened, I was stunned. Jolene had paid for her to visit a few of her friends. In India and Tibet. When she came home in early August, she was somehow different but somehow the same. She now reminded me of the Aunt Jolene I remembered as a kid. While they still argued, often passionately, it appeared Dr. Jolene A. Marshall had found her personal mini-me.

Beth and Derek were regulars at our little gatherings and, since she had always been such a big part of my life, nothing really changed much between us. Edna fully accepted Beth into the family, and twice Beth showed up and helped us in the garden.

One thing Edna refused to do was make peace with Beth's mother.

With each day Mom seemed to be getting a bit weaker. She was going to bed earlier and sleeping later. For the first time I could remember, she began taking naps. I really started to worry when she cut back on her drinking.

Toward the end of summer, on a sweltering day, while weeding a bed of perennials, she stumbled and I caught her and gasped. She felt hollow and fragile.

Seeing the look on my face, she said brightly, "I think we need to have a Labor Day blowout."

"Are you sure you're up for it?"

"Invite everybody who works at O'Connor Industries or has ever worked there." Edna was on a roll. "Invite everyone and anyone the family knows and all of the neighbors."

Tears filled my eyes. "I know what you're doing," I said as I gave her a hug.

Edna patted me on the back. "I know you do." She held me at arm's length. "We had our time together and we've said all of our goodbyes." Suddenly she smiled and laughed. "And I want to go out in a blaze of glory."

Somehow, Edna willed herself to stay alive until the Thursday night before Labor Day. That night, after a spectacular dinner, surrounded by friends and family, she peacefully passed on. As she had planned, the Labor Day party was a wake for a remarkable woman who lived a long and full life.

Over two thousand people showed up for the remembrance, and there was more laughter than tears. It seemed that everyone had an Edna and Charlie story they wanted to share.

Robert and I were unable to bring ourselves to make the final toast, so it fell to Charles.

Flutes of champagne were distributed, and Charles tapped the microphone the band had used to get everybody's attention.

"Tonight we're here to celebrate a woman who was a loving wife, devoted mother," Charles raised his glass to Angela and Robert, Jr., "and loving grandmother." Charles turned back to the overflow crowd and made an odd face. "To say Edna O'Connor was a handful would be a mild understatement."

"You got that right!" shouted a voice in the crowd that drew a few chuckles and brought a huge smile to Charles's face.

"She always said she was going to wear out before she would rust out." Charles held his glass high. "To a life well lived!"

"To a life well lived," answered the crowd.

EPILOGUE

IT HAD BEEN four years since Edna had passed. When she died, I couldn't bring myself to sell the Farm, so I had moved in instead. Better memories. Better karma. Neither one of the twins wanted the house they grew up in, so I sold it to Robert, Jr., at one heck of a "friends and family" discount. His new wife gutted the dated interior and made it a showplace.

Last winter, Aunt Jolene got the flu that turned into pneumonia. She hung around for a week before going gently in her sleep.

Tillie was still as ornery as ever, but these days she needed a cane to walk around. Like my mom, Tillie had no appetite for assisted living. After Jolene passed, she moved in with me at the Farm and we hired a part-time caretaker. So far it has worked out well for both of us.

Bernie Williamson kept asking me to marry him and after a year, when I was sure the time was right, I finally gave in. Like Aunt Tillie would say, *persistence beats stupidity*. We got married at a cheesy chapel in Vegas, with both of us dressed like Elvis. Bernie wanted to put our wedding picture on the mantel, but I vetoed it.

The only problem with our marriage has been that Bernie can make me laugh so hard sometimes I would pee my pants.

Charles and Angela never made it to college. It turns out they are just as nimble and able to seize opportunities as their grandfather. With the surprisingly insightful help of Robert, Jr., who had hit his full stride and really found himself as the CFO of O'Connor Industries, the trio had completely turned the company around and diversified the business model.

My ex-husband, Lindsey, whom I now get along with better than when we were married, was working on an IPO to take the business public. Lindsey told me, if they pull it off, my ten percent of O'Connor Industries stock will make me an embarrassingly wealthy woman.

My brother, Robert, was also a different man. He now heads his own division of O'Connor Industries called "Gabrielle's." In payback for a lifetime of service to the company, Charles and Angela have given him total control and nearly unlimited financial support. Not that he has needed it. Gabrielle's is a food-takeout concept that provides home delivery of hot prepared gourmet meals, or meals ready to pop in the oven. They also offer a service where they will deliver the ingredients and you can prepare the meal yourself. The videos they created of Gabrielle explaining how to properly handle and prepare the delivered food were such an internet hit, she now has her own show on the Food Network. If you didn't want to bother preparing the meal, they would have one of the old tennis shoe team go to your house and prepare the meal for you.

As for my "sister" Beth: Both Ruggles and Knapp had gone on to that great appeals court in the sky, and her law firm was now Woodrow and Woodrow LLP with my nephew David's name on the door next to hers. Michael, with his thick wallet from his share of his grandfather's vintage car collection and the dividends he receives from his stock in O'Connor Industries, never really came home from his walkabout. Like his father, Derek, Michael had a gift with words and has written several popular travel books.

Speaking of Derek. He's still working on the great American novel.

A few years back, Lilith got her hooks into a rich guy she met on a cruise and now splits her time between Manhattan and London. Robert, Jr., still stays in touch with her, but no one else in the family has seen her for years.

In the past four years I've read and reread all of Jolene's self-help books and, with the help of Paige Thompson, who is now the head of the Dr. Jolene A. Marshall Foundation, I've managed to absorb some of her wisdom, but it is still a work in progress. It has made my life so much more livable; it is hard to put into words.

I no longer have the paralyzing primal fear and now rely much more on my intellect instead of my instinct. Paige says I'm now comfortably at Location Three on the "Persistent Non-Symbolic Experience" scale which, in layman's terms, means I don't let anyone manipulate me and just release the BS that flows in my direction. As Aunt Tillie would put it, *You wouldn't let an asshole in your house, why would you let them in your head?*

It is a lovely place to be.

Today was like old times at the Farm. There was a white tent, an open bar and rows of white chairs set up on the patio.

Paige Thompson had insisted she would get her college diploma before she would even discuss marriage. Last week she walked down the aisle in her cap and gown. This week she would be walking down the aisle at the Farm in a flowing white dress on her father's arm. Charles had once said, "Paige is the finest woman I've ever met." So he had been willing to wait. Of course, renting her a penthouse apartment just off-campus and spending most weekends together had kept the blush on the rose.

Charles had topped out at six-foot-three and filled out nicely since high school. While he still couldn't care less about his appearance, Paige made him dress for success and made him keep his hair cut and combed.

I really love my soon-to-be daughter-in-law. With her quirks, she was just as off-center as Charles but, like yin and yang, somehow they come together to form a perfect circle.

Hardly surprising: Angela, dressed in a Roaring Twenties tuxedo, was her brother's best man. Despite her stunning good looks and robust bank account, and with potential suitors lined up around the block, for now, my daughter didn't seem to have much interest in a serious relationship. She did what she called "recreational dating," which I really didn't want her to explain. I wasn't worried. Yet. She's only twenty-two, so the alarm bells weren't even close to going off on her biological clock. But, I've gotten the distinct impression she is hoping Paige will start dropping grandchildren and take the pressure off her.

We had all started to settle into our chairs for the ceremony when we heard a child howling behind us. Turning we saw the beautiful three-and-a-half-year-old flower girl, in a long pink dress and with an abundance of finger curls, hitting the ring bearer. Apparently, Paige's six-year-old nephew had accidentally bumped into her and caused her to spill some of her flower petals. Being twice the little girl's size, he found the assault to be more amusing than threatening. This infuriated the little girl even more.

Gabrielle, who was sitting in the front row next to me, growled and handed an adorable toddler wearing a bowtie and a carnation on his lapel to my brother. Next, Gabrielle dashed down the aisle and confronted the shrieking little girl. Gabrielle wagged a warning finger in the little girl's face.

"Behave yourself, Edna Jolene O'Connor!"

Fat chance.

OTHER BOOKS BY THE AUTHORS

By Rod Pennington and Dr. Jeffery A. Martin

What Ever Happened to Mr. MAJIC?

The Fourth Awakening Series

The Fourth Awakening
The Gathering Darkness
The Fourth Awakening Chronicles I
The Fourth Awakening Chronicles II
The Fourth Awakening Chronicles III
The Fourth Awakening Chronicles IV

By Rod Pennington

Indweller

The "Family" Series
Family Reunion
Family Business
Family Secrets
Family Honor
Family Debt

By Dr. Jeffery A. Martin
The God Formula
The Complete Guide to Reiki
The Complete Guide to Reiki, Vol. II
The Finders

Made in the USA
Las Vegas, NV
10 March 2023

68819285R00144